Core of Fear

A Paranormal LitRPG Dungeon Core

Written By: Jonathan Brooks

Cover Design: Yvonne Less, Art 4 Artists

Edited By: Celestian Rince

Dedication

To my wife, Melody, who first got me addicted to watching all those "ghost-hunting" shows and encouraged my love of supernatural-based horror movies.

Thanks to all my beta-readers who helped shape this into a better book!

Grant Harrell

Sean Hall

Aaron Wiley

William Harse

Douglas Geyer

Jake Battison

Maryam Winters

Tara Mulkey

Table of Contents

Prologue

The windows at the front of the house had been sealed shut with age, not having been opened in years. Decades even. Rusted shut and neglected by lazy homeowners, they were nevertheless the perfect deterrent for would-be thieves. The front door had multiple deadbolts, latches, and locks – and, from what he could see, a reinforced frame. The door was new – made of a sturdy, thick wood as well – so he assumed they had a problem with people barging in uninvited.

It wasn't necessarily a bad neighborhood, but things like that could happen anywhere.

After easily hopping over the waist-high fence that would barely prevent a toddler from accessing the backyard, he cautiously slunk around the side of the two-story Colonial Revival, its symmetrical façade wrapped around to the back side of the large house. It led to a massive patio and yard that, at least from what he could see in the dark, was well-kept and appeared to get a lot of use – completely at odds with the neglectful look at the front of the residence.

No, there was no point trying to force his way through the front, especially when there was easy access to a relatively new window in the back. He wasn't sure when it was installed; it didn't really matter though, because it was recent enough that he didn't see any signs of rust or weathering. Unlike the front and upper story double-hung windows that opened vertically, the rear bottom-floor windows were slider windows – which opened horizontally along a sliding track.

Perfect.

The new window he found was locked, but that didn't deter him. As he put his face up against the window, the bright hallway light crept underneath the closed door, revealing the shadowed details of the room inside. Although only a small amount of the room was illuminated, the tell-tale signs of waiting electronics were evident as tiny LED lights twinkled throughout the room. A router sitting next to a monitor and PC tower blinked its indicators lazily, painting the room in enough light to see that the window he was currently peeping through led to some sort of home-office.

Feeling around with his gloved fingers, he pulled a small pen-light from his front-breast pocket, clicking it softly to turn it on. The noise it made was so faint that he could barely hear it, though he didn't really worry about it alerting anyone. What he was going to do next would be much louder.

With the focused beam shining inside the window, he concentrated on the inside track. He wanted to make sure that it wasn't blocked...and he saw that it was good. If they had put in a wooden dowel preventing anyone from opening the sliding window, his efforts to open it would make A LOT more noise.

He placed the miniature flashlight between his teeth while he worked. After taking out a pair of suction cup lifters from an inside pocket – the kind that is usually used to move large panes of glass – he placed them against the inner sliding window and brought the handles together, creating a tight seal as the air was pumped out. The kind he used only supported up to 90 lbs., but that was more than enough for what he was using them for.

Most people thought that once you locked your windows, no one could open them without breaking the glass; however, if you had the correct knowledge concerning their manufacturing and installation, you would know that they had an inherent flaw. Because they were supported along the top rail so that they would be able to slide along the bottom, there was always a little give in them – otherwise they would be so tight that you wouldn't be able to move them. New windows like the one he was currently working on, were even more vulnerable because the new wood around the frame had yet to condense the aluminum window casing. Installers usually left a little room for settlement, otherwise over the years it would warp the frame, making it impossible to shift.

Of course, he hadn't done any window installations himself, but it was amazing what you could learn on You Tube if you applied yourself.

He shook the window up and down, attempting to make as little noise as possible as the entire pane shifted minutely. He took his time; he was in no hurry, and the faster he went, the more the possibility of making a mistake grew in proportion. After five minutes of measured friction, the lock keeping the window closed began to shift. At first, it was just a little bit as it was knocked out of its fully-locked position; soon enough, though, it was moving more and more as he shifted the pane.

No more than five minutes after it started to move, the lock was fully open; he spread the handles on the suction cup closest to the middle and transferred it to the outside edge where the other one was located. He brought out a small 3-oz bottle of lubricant, using it liberally to grease both tracks, ensuring that any squeakiness was eliminated. Lifting and sliding the window slowly, he was able to provide his access point without making more than a muffled thump that was swallowed up by the normal nature sounds that enveloped the sleepy home.

He removed the suction cups and placed them back in his inner pocket, before carefully lifting himself up and over the window frame. He touched down on the short carpet with a barely noticeable footfall and listened intently, trying to see if he had alerted anyone in the house. He let out a breath he had been holding to listen better, knowing that he had entered undetected as he didn't hear anything from the residents inside.

He didn't do a lot of research on his targets; he neither cared about their personal lives nor cared who they actually were.

The only thing he investigated was if they had a security system or pets.

Either of those would...complicate matters.

Seeing evidence of neither of those things as he opened the door leading to the hallway, he concluded that his original assessment of the house had been correct. There was nothing that was going to disturb him from his enterprise tonight.

The carpet in the home-office led to a hardwood floor along the hallway, which he padded down with soft feet. The room he had entered the house from was at the western end of the house, which meant that he had a bit he had to traverse before he found what he was looking for. Along the hallway, there was only a small doorway across from the office; the door was cracked, and he looked in – a small half-bath. Not hearing anyone within, he continued down the wood-paneled passageway toward the center of the house.

Twenty feet more and he encountered the kitchen off to the south side of the house, followed by the main living room. As opposed to the rundown-looking frontal exterior, the two rooms appeared to have been remodeled recently and were decorated in modern styles; the kitchen had dark granite countertops, white shaker-style cabinets, stainless steel appliances, and tiled floors, while the living room was minimally finished with comfortable-looking modern furniture and funky lamps. No TV or coffee/side tables; it didn't look lived in – it looked like it was only for show.

He searched the eastern side of the house located past the kitchen and didn't find what he was looking for – just another spare room and a door leading to the garage addition he had seen from the outside. Knowing that he wasn't going to find anything down there, he headed back to the living room and made his way to the curving staircase leading to the second floor.

Apparently, the remodel done on the rest of the house did not extend to the stairs. As he gingerly placed his foot on the first step, it began to creak horrendously; pulling his leg back swiftly, he looked for a way to make it up the stairs without waking up the entire household. He could see the wear on the wooden steps toward the middle; either they couldn't afford to replace and reinforce the staircase, or they liked the original look of it. All that mattered, however, was that it was going to be hell getting up without bringing down the house.

In the end, the only thing he could do was walk as close to the wall edge as he could; the wooden steps were supported by a framework that was strongest next to the curving, picture-laden wall. He took his time and – even though it took over five minutes to get up the stairs – he didn't make more than a few soft creaks that blended easily into the normal house-settling noises that homes this old usually exhibited.

He did accidentally brush up against one of the framed family pictures hung up against the wall – only with his quick reflexes honed by his intense concentration was he able to grab it before it hit the ground. He placed it back on the wall, where he looked at the first of many family photographs.

It wasn't as well-lit where he was, but he could make out an older couple surrounded by many children, most of them looking to be older themselves as the photos progressed up the stairs. He looked back down and saw the oldest photographs; they had made a timeline from the earliest nearest the bottom and the newest toward the top. As he passed by the last of them, the latest pictures didn't show children at all; instead, the previous kids were all grown-up and shown as middle-aged adults.

Ignoring all that, he got back to the matter at hand. From the top of the stairs he had two options: left or right. Neither direction looked any different from the other; they both contained four shut doors – two on either side of the hallway. Directly in front, he saw a full bathroom with its door swung wide open, indicating that that direction was useless to him.

He picked the right, as it was closest to where the stairs ended. Silently tiptoeing across the carpeted upper hallway, he held his breath as he opened up the first door on his left side, expecting the door to creak as badly as the stairs. Fortunately, they had updated it enough that it smoothly glided open with but a whisper of sound.

The room was lit up from the outside by the half-moon hanging low in the clear, Colorado summer sky. Cluttered shapes were sprawled across the room in a bare semblance of order – a junk room. It may have at one time been used for a spare bedroom, but now it was only being used for storing everything they didn't want cluttering up every other room.

The next three rooms on that side of the upper story were empty, though it was obvious that they actually *were* spare bedrooms. They were plain and as minimalist as the living room downstairs: full-size bed, a single nightstand, and a single sleek table lamp sitting on top of said nightstand. When he was sure what he was looking for wasn't in there, he closed the doors silently and made his way back down the hallway.

A sudden squeak of the floorboard under the carpet made him freeze in anticipation; it was loud enough in the thunderous silence that he wouldn't be surprised if it woke up everybody from a deep sleep. When nothing happened after he had been standing like a statue for almost ten minutes, he relaxed his tense muscles and ventured back down the hallway – making sure to avoid the spot that nearly gave him away. Staying near the edges just like the staircase, he approached the first door leading to the front side of the house and opened it on silent hinges.

Inside, he saw what must've been the master bedroom. Two large double-hung windows highlighted the king-size bed, two identical wooden nightstands, two identical table lamps, and two identical digital clocks that read 1:42. Oh, and the two figures deeply-sleeping underneath some flannel sheets. He noted as he closed the door that despite the symmetry inside the room, one clock was running at least a few seconds faster than the other.

He checked the other doors and found three more guest bedroom; unlike the other side of the house, however, these ones had queen-sized beds and were all dually occupied. After closing their doors without alerting a single person, he walked silently back down the hallway toward the master bedroom

He slipped inside just as quietly he had traversed the rest of the house (other than a few extraneous creaks) and looked around. There was a closet full to bursting with a crazy assortment of women's clothes on the right-hand wall, with a matching closet on the opposite side of the room that had more-orderly men's clothing. He disregarded them and approached the side of the bed where he could see an older man sleeping.

Though he wasn't necessarily old, he appeared to be in at least his fifties – same as the woman he could see on the opposite side of the bed. He distantly recognized their faces as belonging to the eldest couple in the pictures along the stairway. Remembering the faint glimpses he had of the people sleeping in the other rooms, they appeared to all be siblings of one sort or another and their partners.

Hmm...their parents must've died and left it to their eldest. Must be why this guy here is sleeping in the "big" bed.

He watched them sleeping on their backs for a few minutes, slowing his own breathing until it matched theirs. When he was ready, he reached behind him to a special sheath he had strapped to his back and pulled out a long-bladed bowie knife.

The metal shone in the moonlight streaming from the window as he bent over and placed it underneath the sleeping man's chin.

With a quick thrust, he shoved it inside the man's jaw, piercing through the layers of skin, fat, and cartilage until it reached the brain – which snuffed the life from him almost instantly. The man was dead so quickly that he didn't even make a sound, just a quick twitch as his body responded to spastic signals that were coming from the damaged brain.

He withdrew the knife with a slurping sound, the blood from the man seeping out and covering that side of the bed in a rapidly expanding pool. He swiftly walked over to the other side of the bed and did the same to the slowly waking woman with practiced efficiency. She had been disturbed by her husband's movement and was fighting her own need for sleep to see what was going on; he silenced her curiosity with a foot of sharpened steel.

He withdrew the knife from underneath her jaw and let himself *feel*. Sensations of what he imagined were ones of euphoria flooded his body, making him nearly cry out with the intensity of it. Fortunately, this wasn't the first time he had felt that way; he was able to contain his excitement and pleasure until his body finished riding the wave of ecstasy. All too soon it was over, the joy of the kill draining him as quickly as it came until he was left without feelings or emotions.

Just like every other minute of the day.

Knowing he still had a few more opportunities to experience the rapturous effects he received from killing another person, Clive Logan slipped out the doorway of the master bedroom, leaving it just as silently as he arrived. His bowie knife bared to the world, dripping blood from his previous victims, he slowly entered the room next door, remnants of the bliss still in his system causing him to smile in anticipation.

At least a little.

Chapter 1

Clive stared at the ceiling, all thoughts leaving him as the guards uncuffed him in the preparation room with guns drawn; he didn't resist as they secured his wrists and ankles to the gurney. *At least they lined the restraints with something soft – they wouldn't want to hurt me or anything.*

The stained and sometimes warped ceiling tiles of the outside hallway flew past him as he was wheeled hurriedly into the execution chamber. He was aware of them doing something against the skin on both his arms, but he didn't feel any pain.

He never felt anything.

Unless he was killing someone.

But that had been a long time ago. He was arrested in Kentucky after a nation-wide manhunt after a nanny-cam caught him killing the residents of a house in Georgia. Of course, he had already done the deed, so to speak, so it didn't affect what he had done to that "poor, defenseless, innocent couple." Or that's what the prosecution called them. *They should be happy I didn't kill the children.* He was a killer...but at least he drew the line somewhere.

To be truthful, he did kill a young teenage boy – but he didn't receive any sort of satisfaction from it. From then on, he left them all alone; they would grow up soon enough to be fed to one of his knives.

Out of the corner of his eye he could see two tubes strapped to either arm, pumping what looked like water into his body. *Must be the saline solution they told me about.* He was shaken out of his introspection as he heard a curtain being drawn; he couldn't see anything – his head was still pointing towards the ceiling.

Despite what was probably ultra-thick glass, he could hear a rumbling coming from what he knew was a one-way mirror. Behind that mirror, he figured the families of everyone he had killed were in there to watch him be executed; though, how they expected to put the families of over 362 people in what was likely to be a small room he didn't know. He figured they would be recording it so those that wouldn't fit would be able to see his death.

It was a shame that he wasn't arrested in Utah before they switched to lethal injection – that way he'd be able to choose to be killed by firing squad. Alas, he was extradited to Colorado because almost a third of his killings had been there; lethal injection was the only method they used there. Though he had heard that some of the guards wanted to personally strangle him because they knew someone who knew someone that had died by his hands.

Well, bowie knife – it was the most efficient way he could kill someone who was sleeping without causing a ruckus.

The prison warden was there; he only knew his identity from the one time he was forced to meet with him, three years ago when he was first sentenced. From that time on, he had been in solitary; they didn't trust him not to try to kill other inmates. *I guess I do have a bit of a reputation.*

"Do you have any final words before your sentence is carried out?" the warden asked, the inflection in his voice hinting that he hoped not.

Clive just stared straight ahead without responding, having nothing to say to anyone. His parents had passed away when he was in middle school and he didn't have any friends; any extended family he had didn't want anything to do with him now – not that they had before everything came out about him. As to the families behind the one-way mirror…he didn't care about them. His victims were only a means to an end.

When he didn't respond right away, the warden rightly took that as meaning he wasn't going to say anything and stepped back, out of the way of the witnesses in the adjoining room. Clive could still hear murmuring coming from behind the mirror, with a few undecipherable shouts coming every once in a while, while the execution chamber was silent as a tomb – other than the ticking clock on the wall behind him.

He knew his was to occur at precisely 12:01 am; they wanted to off him as soon as possible on his execution day. As the time ticked down, he couldn't help but think that everything in his life would've been so much different if he had just been able to—

His thoughts floated away as he saw the warden signal with his hand as the time had come. He had been informed by the guards as to what would happen to him in great detail, their dislike of him letting them take great pleasure in telling him how he was going to die.

He knew that Sodium Pentothal would be up first, designed to put him into a deep sleep as a general anesthesia (though with the amount they were going to use it would probably kill him before anything else). Next, they would flush the lines with more saline solution before pumping a paralyzing agent, Pavulon, into him – stopping his lungs and diaphragm. With a last flush of saline solution, they would pump him full of Potassium Chloride, stopping his heart.

He had been expecting to feel sleepy first, but that wasn't what happened. Either they had mixed up the order, or they deliberately didn't give him any anesthetic; the first thing he knew, he had trouble breathing. He couldn't catch his breath and just pumping his lungs enough was getting more difficult by the second. Eventually, he couldn't breathe at all and he started to suffocate; fortunately, he didn't have the emotional capacity to panic. It didn't hurt – nothing hurt him. If he was able to feel pain, it probably would've been excruciating. As it was, he only detachedly experienced it as...something odd.

His vision started to fade from the lack of oxygen to his brain, and he felt his heart start to slow, its beating stopping within a few seconds. Again, there was no pain, just a general awareness that all wasn't working as it should be.

As his visual and auditory senses faded completely from the world, he tried to dredge up the feeling of anger toward the individuals who had skipped the Sodium Pentothal that he knew he should be experiencing. He thought that the taking of one more life would allow him to *feel* again – even if it was his own life.

He was wrong.

*   *   *

His consciousness was floating in a void, the vast expanse around him granting him the same feeling of nothingness he had felt all his life. Even from when he was very little, he couldn't ever remember feeling any type of emotion or physical feelings: happiness, sadness, anger, jealousy, confusion, satisfaction, fear, excitement, pleasure, pain, and everything in between. His parents and school had taught him what they were, but he had never experienced them.

He could get hurt; but he felt no pain. He could accomplish something great; but he felt no satisfaction for doing it well or correctly. He knew when he didn't understand something; but he was never confused – he knew exactly what he didn't know. He could pick something up with his hand; his sense of touch worked enough to function properly, but a boiling pot of water felt the same as a tepid one. He had hurt himself a lot when he was younger; fortunately, he had learned to live with the limitations his lack of feelings afforded him.

That was, until someone decided that they wanted to have sex with him.

Since he wasn't distracted by friends and doing things for pleasure, he had thrown himself into his schoolwork without anything better to do. Words on a page and numbers in equations were much easier to deal with than people; it wasn't that he was confused, but he didn't have the emotional depth to understand their reasons they acted the way they did. He wasn't a genius, but he **was** able to finish high school early and graduate from college, despite the fact that he had to spend most of middle school and high school in a foster home. With a full-ride to college on an academic scholarship, he acquired a degree in Computer Science.

He used it to acquire a job at a company that designed video games; his excellent coding prowess landed him a position as lead programmer. It was a small company, however, so he was the only one on the team – which was how he liked it. He had very little interaction with the rest of the people in the company and only communicated with them through different forms of digital messaging. At first, they were confused at his hesitance to interact face-to-face with them; however, after they saw what he could accomplish in barely any time, they didn't care as long as he got it done. He worked alone and didn't see any reason to change it.

And then he met Samantha. Clive had worked out of his spotless third-floor apartment on the southside of Denver, where he usually had everything delivered. He didn't get out much because his work was a priority; it was a waste of time if there was an alternative. Samantha was a delivery driver that dropped off his groceries once a week on Fridays; he didn't eat much so there was never a huge amount that she had to walk up three flights of stairs.

She acted strange around him – stranger than people usually were, at least. He eventually learned that she was attracted to him, but he didn't – and couldn't – return the sentiment. She convinced him to let her "stay over" for the night, which he thought was fine; if she needed somewhere to sleep, he wasn't using the couch in the small living room he possessed. Actually, he hadn't ever used it – he didn't watch TV and it wasn't in him to just sit and be lazy.

As one might guess, she didn't want to sleep – she wanted **him**. Without going into too much detail, he decided to treat the whole experience as a learning experience; once he finally understood what she wanted, he went with it. Unfortunately, his lack of attraction, arousal, and physical response apparently made her mad. She started yelling at him incessantly and wouldn't leave (*it didn't matter to him that it was 2 am*) so he grabbed her by the throat, shaking her with the intention to shut her up.

He couldn't control his own strength, though, and ended up snapping her neck. As soon as that happened, he felt a rush of euphoric feelings circulate through his body, electrifying his nerve endings and sending him to ecstatic shock, knocking him out when his spasming body knocked his head against a shelf. He woke up later – hurt but feeling no pain – and found that the sensations had all but left. There were still traces of it that lingered for another day, but after that he was back to normal.

So that he could experience that joyous pleasure again, he started his rampage across the country, starting and racking up quite a few kills in Colorado before spreading to almost every state in the contiguous United States. He maintained his position as lead programmer in between killings and was able to stay on the move using mobile Wi-Fi hotspots to pay for his travels. It was the best two years of his life, with only a few times falling back into his emotional void in between kills.

Which was what this felt like – an emotional void. Though, now that he thought about it, it was a physical void as well. His body was nonexistent; he experienced everything as if his mind had been freed of its corporeal shell and was free to do what he wanted. Looking around, however, he saw nothing for him to do. He began to feel something that he had never felt before – boredom.

There was no way to tell time in that place, so he wasn't sure how long he sat there bored. All he knew was that he didn't like it; which was another novel feeling – not liking something. He couldn't care about anything when he was alive, there were only things that were or were not. All black or white: no grey area. Now, however, although the experience of being able to feel something was new, he couldn't help thinking he was missing out on so much more.

Which, of course, was when he was instantly transported straight to Hell.

Chapter 2

Pain. Glorious, wonderful, unending pain is what he felt for hours, days, years; it all blended into a miasma of pleasurable existence that he couldn't tell how long he was feeling it. He was **feeling it**! Although he couldn't see anything other than a block of fiery red wherever he looked, he didn't care – he had seen things before. But experiencing what felt like his skin being ripped off his body, his under-musculature being burnt to ash, and his bones being crushed beneath some giant demonic burning foot was new.

And awesome.

He couldn't believe how great it felt to be tortured endlessly without letup. *This is what I was missing all that time? How I survived 27 years without experiencing this is a wonder in and of itself. I wasn't really living before – now, this is living!*

Unfortunately, the pain of being flayed alive, burnt in the fires of hell, and having his bones ground into dust was getting old. It was the same thing over and over; the only thing that occasionally changed was the speed at which each stage happened. Even that started to get boring and predictable. He wanted to ask for more variety, but the only thing that would come out of his figurative mouth when he tried to do it was a scream. Which sounded strange to him, as he hadn't screamed the entire time he had been tortured; if anything, he would've been laughing in sheer joy if he could.

Resigned to be bored for the rest of eternity, he ignored everything around him until even the wonderful pain that he was experiencing was dull. Before he knew it, he was able to completely block it out and retreated to his own little world of non-feeling and non-emotions. At least it was a change.

He experimented with switching back-and-forth from experiencing nothing...and then unimaginable pain...then nothing...then excruciating bodily devastation...then nothing. Even that got old. If he could've died from boredom in Hell, he would've perished long ago.

So, it came as a surprise when the pain he was reluctantly inserting into his daily routine to stave off a little bit of the boredom was suddenly and completely shut off without his volition.

"Hey, what gives? I was enjoying that!"

"I know, that's why I stopped it," a voice interrupted his complaint. "This is Hell, Clive, not a day spa. You're supposed to be burning in the fires of hell for all eternity for your sins – which, congratulations, you have a lot of – not enjoying every minute of it."

He couldn't see who was speaking to him, as he was back in the formless expanse that he had first experienced when he had died. "It wasn't *all* enjoyable...it was quite boring after a while."

"See, that's what I'm talking about – anyone else that had experienced what you did would've lost their sanity and screamed incoherently for eternity, but you...got bored. I know that you felt the pain, but you *enjoyed* it more than anything," the voice said.

As what was now obviously a female spoke, a figure started to materialize in front of his...perspective? He didn't necessarily have eyes, so even if he tried to look away, she was right there in the forefront of his vision.

Framing a face that was pale as the moon, she had long night-black hair that cascaded to a non-existent floor, where it pooled around her feet. Surrounding her body, a wispy black dress that barely covered her curves meandered across her breasts and midsection, leaving very little to the imagination. With her symmetrical face, blood-red lips, and the all-black pulsing orbs she had as eyes, she looked like an exotic "sexy" vampire he had seen in some of the games he had helped to program.

He supposed she was attractive, but in that place his feelings were even more muted; he couldn't tell if he enjoyed looking at her or not. Not that it mattered – since he didn't have a body – but he thought that it would've been...enjoyable to see if he could get aroused.

"And that's another thing; the sight of me would've overwhelmed any other man – and many women – with desire, whereas the only thing I can sense from you is curiosity. Your soul is a strange one."

He didn't know how to respond to that, so he waited. He figured she had brought him there for a reason.

"Look, here's the deal. Souls come down to Hell and are tortured for eternity, feeding me power from their unending torment; but it only works if it causes their incorporeal form actual pain. Although you could feel the pain I was inflicting upon your soul, you weren't affected by it. I received nothing from you; in fact, I spent more power trying to crack your psyche than I'd used on the previous 10,000 souls that waltzed their way down here. Do you get what I'm trying to say?"

"...You want me to pretend to not enjoy it?" he asked, curious for the first time in his life. Or afterlife.

"Fuck! You're an idiot." She looked thoroughly distressed at his response. "That won't work – only genuine fear of the pain I can inflict upon your soul will work. And I don't think you'll ever get there even if I did it for the next thousand years. No, I have something else in mind for you: you're going to help me recoup the power I wasted on you *and* help me get even more."

This curiosity thing is awesome! Clive was really interested in learning more, even if he had no idea what she was talking about. "I would...like...to help. How do I do that?"

She looked a little more pleased at his quick acceptance. "Ok, here's the thing. I'm going to offer you a one-time deal, so you only have this one chance to accept. It won't work if I have to force you, so you have to...volunteer for this." *That sounds intriguing.* "But if you refuse, I will leave you here where I don't have to deal with your crazy-ass soul. You'll be stuck in limbo for eternity with no physical stimuli, no 'emotional exploration', and nobody to talk to. For eternity," she repeated, as if driving that point home.

The now-insatiable curiosity was starting to affect his judgement and sending his thoughts flying in different directions. He understood that what he decided would affect him for the rest of his eternal afterlife, but all that came out of him was, "Who are you?"

Taken aback at his abrupt change in thought processes, she blurted out, "I'm the damned Goddess of the Underworld, you stupid...motherfu...never in my...how...y'know, I just can't deal with this." And with that, he literally brought the leader of Hell to tears. For a very brief moment.

She recovered quickly, however; being immortal, she had seen enough over the eons that a little something like an un-torturable soul didn't put her down for long. The tears that she shed evaporated with small flashes of flame, and her demeanor calmed enough that she was able to address Clive (who was watching everything with fascination – another new feeling!) with a steady countenance.

"Anyway, let me explain what I am offering you. I have the ability to place your soul in a 'Spirit Core' and send you back to Earth, where you can use a special spiritual energy to affect the

31

world around you. I'll explain more if you decide to volunteer for this…special project."

"How come I've never heard of a 'Spirit Core' before this? And why would you send me? Do you have many of these Cores?" The questions kept coming, but she cut him off.

"Shut up! Fine – I'll explain a little more if that will help you decide. I actually don't have *any* Spirit Cores on Earth at the moment, nor have I ever been able to *successfully* transport one. Before you ask," she cut him off when he started talking, "the process is…intense. I've tried countless times, but always ended in failure.

"You see," she appeared worried that whatever she was going to say would turn him off from volunteering, "when I convert a soul into a Spirit Core, the transformation is literally the most painful experience imaginable; and then a million times more intense than that. Every soul – including not a few of my own personal demon servants – has fractured from the overwhelming torture, leaving them insane and useless for the job I created them for. Unfortunately, their eternal souls had to be destroyed…permanently…lest they call attention to my meddling of mortal affairs."

She looked at him intently before saying, "You, on the other hand, are different. Not only do I believe you will succeed where the others have become hopeless broken husks, I think you'll actually enjoy the experience."

He was silent for a moment as he digested the information she had provided. He didn't have to think long, though – a new experience was better than the vast expanse of nothingness around him. "Sounds awesome! Where do I sign up?"

She smiled for the first time since she had appeared. "It's easy. All you have to do is pledge your eternal soul to my service, and we'll be good to go."

"Ok," he said, before he did as she instructed.

And then there was the most magnificent, superb, fantastic, outstanding, terrific, unimaginable pain he could ever experience. It felt like every atom of his being was being ripped apart from him one by one, sliced in half, burned to ash by the sun, digested inside the stomach of a giant demon, regurgitated while covered with caustic acid, run over by a planet, and crushed into nothingness by an entity the size of a galaxy.

And he never wanted it to end.

Chapter 3

But it had to end sometime. One moment he was luxuriating in the feeling of absolute pain and destruction, and the next everything he could feel was shut off like a light switch. Not only gone was the pain, but his feelings of curiosity, boredom, and even hints of arousal that came from looking at the Goddess of the Underworld. He felt as empty and unfeeling as he did when he was alive.

If it were possible, Clive would have been royally pissed off.

As it was though, he was following a more practical approach. He couldn't see anything, though he didn't know if it was because he was blind or if he didn't have eyes – or even if he had a body. He tried to sense **anything** with his ears, nose, or whatever he had for eyes; after a few moments of absolutely nothing, he gave up.

Well, this wasn't exactly what I was expecting. This is actually worse than that featureless expanse – at least there I could feel something. Did it not work?

Since he couldn't dredge up any feelings of curiosity, he left it there and...floated...in a sea of nothingness. He wasn't bored, he wasn't annoyed, he wasn't angry: he just...was.

An indeterminate amount of time later, he heard her voice for the first time since he had agreed to pledge his eternal soul to her service.

"Clive? Are you there?"

He couldn't figure out how to speak, so he didn't try to respond. Fortunately, his reception of her words was enough to establish a connection. "Finally...I thought I lost you there for a moment. Hold on; this is the first time this has actually succeeded and I'm still trying to figure out how to get you working properly."

He waited...and waited...and waited. There was one thing that he still had a lot of from his previous life: patience.

And that patience was rewarded as he felt an abrupt lurch and shift in his awareness. Flowing streams of unintelligible symbols flew across his still-black vision in a rapid succession, their varied hues adding some color to his previously colorless world. He couldn't tell if they were just meaningless strings of nonsense or if they were supposed to represent words or meanings, but something about them triggered a memory of his former mortal existence.

He was booting up.

Eventually, the "start-up" sequence finished as the symbols disappeared, and he was back to where he started; the big difference was there was a blinking white "cursor" at the top-left corner of his viewpoint. *She must have adapted the old MS-DOS programming for this.*

"I'd like to think that Gates stole it from me, not the other way around," she interjected after obviously hearing his thoughts, "and yes, now that your core is initialized, you can just *think* what you want to communicate to me."

What is going on?

"I had a Hell of a time getting you up and running, but now you're good to go. Everything is now on your end – I have no control from here; the whole 'don't interfere with the mortal world' pact with Heaven is limiting my actions."

He had no idea what she was talking about, but he figured it didn't really matter. *What do I do?* he asked, after staring at the prompt still blinking lazily at him.

"Oh...uh, sorry...it's been so long since I designed this that I forgot what you needed to do for a moment. Everything you will need to do is controlled by your thoughts, so start with thinking *spiritcore.exe* and that should start you up."

Clive immediately thought the command and saw *spiritcore.exe* type itself out near the flashing cursor. When it didn't do anything after that, he saw the problem: he needed to hit *enter*. As soon as he did that, the words disappeared and the black gradually lightened until it was a dark grey color – but that was it.

He thought something might be wrong until his awareness started to gain focus on something. Indistinct shapes sharpened gradually as if he was waking up, his vision blurry with sleep, until he was looking at a bedroom. His viewpoint, however, was in the upper corner of the room, as if he was a voyeuristic camera placed to watch the action inside discreetly. It was daytime, though, so there was no one currently sleeping in the king-sized bed.

Where am I? What am I doing here?

"You're in an old, small house in South Carolina, about 50 miles west of Charleston. However, where you are isn't as important as what you're going to be doing here," she told him, before her tone changed to one of instruction. "Now listen carefully, because I can't afford the power to stay here long with you. The energy that was needed to get you here has drained me so much that once I leave, you're on your own unless something really important comes up. I've left helpful notes in your system that should help with any general information you may need to know, so you should be covered unless you are in danger of being exorcised – but we'll get to that later if we have time."

He supposed that he should have worried about whatever "exorcised" meant, but as he still didn't have any of his feelings back, he ignored it since it didn't seem important.

"Now – what are you and what are you doing here? Your soul has now been painfully transformed into a Spirit Core, a sneaky little creation of my own design that subverts the rules established between Heaven and Hell at the beginning of time. I can't directly affect or influence the mortal world, and neither can my damned sister."

Who's your sis—

"We don't have time for that right now, let me finish this so I can get back and recharge. Since you are essentially a separate entity from my own power, you are able to operate in the mortal world without breaking the pact. However, whatever you do has an immense impact on me and my power.

"As a Spirit Core, you can use Spiritual Energy, or Force, to subtly and not-so-subtly affect the mortal world. You can grow in power as you do so, allowing you to accomplish more and more as you strengthen your Core – to the point where you can manipulate physical objects. A high enough Spirit Level will even allow you to temporarily hitch a ride with a human, experiencing the feelings and emotions that they experience."

Perfect. That's what I want. How do I—

"Save your questions for later, we don't have a lot of time," she interrupted him, and he noticed that her voice was a little fainter than it had been. "Now, as to what you need to do: capture innocent souls. From what I know about your past life, you shouldn't have any moral quandaries about this. Torturing an innocent soul in Hell is like...eating a perfectly cooked filet mignon covered in bacon, sitting on top of a massive bowl of the tastiest, creamiest ice cream you can imagine – and it also gives me a huge power boost. In comparison, sinners like you are like eating a stale piece of bread: it fills me up when I need it, but I'd rather be eating something else.

"Now – and this is important – to capture them, you have to kill them inside your area of influence, which at this point is limited in scope. This small house is the limit of what you can effectively control, though with time you can move to a different, larger location if you so desire."

Seems easy enough.

Her voice was even fainter than before, and he had to really concentrate to hear it. "It's not as easy as you might think. Follow the system guides and learn how to successfully operate your new Spirit Core. Do well enough and you will be rewarded for your service."

Silence followed that statement, and he thought that was all she was going to tell him because her voice was a bare whisper by the end. He didn't know exactly what he was supposed to do now; before he could do anything, however, her voice came back with a sudden burst of volume. "AND DON'T CALL ATTENTION TO YOURSELF!" The silence was even greater now, and he assumed she was gone for good.

Well, let's see what I've got here.

$$*\qquad*\qquad*$$

Welcome to Spirit Core v.1.0

Now initializing Guide-assisted Intuitive User Interface...

....

Guide-assisted Intuitive User Interface initialized...

Now transferring control of Spirit Core to the soul previously

known as Clive Logan...

It only took him a few moments of thinking about his Spirit Core for the boot-up sequence overlay to appear in front of his face. It wasn't as shocking as he supposed it would be for other people, since it was familiar territory for him: computers, programming, and coding had been his life (other than his near-nightly killing sprees) for the last few years. Oh, and he couldn't feel any sense of surprise in the first place.

The words faded from his vision as soon as the sequence was complete, and he somehow "sensed" that he was in control. He couldn't explain the sensation; it felt like the first time he had gotten behind the wheel of a car, that now that he could drive, he had many more options available to him. Overhearing some classmates in school, they had mentioned that **they** had felt powerful, like they could go anywhere and do anything they desired. Clive never understood it – to him, driving was a means to an end.

He **still** had no real idea of how he was supposed to kill innocents, if there even were any around. Nothing had changed in the bedroom the entire time he had been talking to the Goddess of the Underworld, nor had the passing of time really been on the forefront of his mind. Now that everything was as "ready" as he supposed it was going to be, he figured he should be going about it.

Decision made, he looked all around himself and tried to figure out what he was supposed to do. The bedroom he looked down on was sparsely furnished, though it had a plethora of abstract artwork hung up around the room. He never understood art; it was supposed to evoke feelings when you looked at it, but – again – no feelings meant no understanding of it.

There was a tall light-colored wooden dresser on the far side of the room opposite of the king-sized bed, and the mirrored closet doors looked right out of the 70's or 80's. Two nightstands were located on either side of the bedframe and the leather-padded headboard, each with their own bronze-based, shaded lamps. A digital clock sat on each of the stands, different in design if not function, and a face-down book with a fuzzy bookmark was settled next to the lamp on the one farthest from the door. The other one held a picture standing prominently where it was easy to see even if someone was lying down.

Recognizing a source of information, Clive strove to see the picture better, but his location was such that he couldn't see more than the side of it. Suddenly, his viewpoint started moving toward it, as he thought about somehow getting close enough to make out more details.

Congratulations!

You have discovered the ability to move within your Area of Influence!

- With this, you can instantly transport from one space to another, or smoothly float your way to wherever you want
  - You cannot leave your Area of Influence unless you are moved to an entirely different location
- Walls, floors, and other inanimate objects are no hindrance to you as you can freely pass through them with impunity
  - Warning!!!
    - Though invisible to the naked mortal eye, passing through mortals – humans or otherwise – will alert them to your presence

Is this a video game of some sort? He recognized some of the verbiage and the design of the notifications; he certainly had coded enough of it to tell. However, as he had never actually *played* any of the games he helped to program, he didn't know what was going on.

While not a video game in the simplest of terms, the Guide-assisted Intuitive User Interface resembles one for ease of use. To make the transition from soul to Spirit Core easier to

understand, the basic framework of your new existence is streamlined into one complete package!

The words from this and the last notifications only stayed up for a moment before fading, though it wasn't really necessary because he was able to absorb the knowledge it was imparting instantly. In fact, he thought that the notification was unnecessary; it didn't do any more than block his view.

He ignored the excited-appearing notifications and moved his...Spirit Core...closer to the picture on the nightstand. Standing atop a rough stone platform overlooking a view of the ocean, a relatively young couple was posing for the picture in what Clive recognized as wedding attire. Along the bottom of the frame, the words "Happily Ever After – May 12th, 2012" were cleanly burnt into the natural wooden frame.

There wasn't any more information that could be gleaned from floating around the room, so he decided to investigate the rest of the house.

And look for the ones he needed to kill.

Chapter 4

Based on the various clocks he saw around the small house, Clive spent more than four hours floating around, looking at everything in an attempt to glean more information about its residents. He didn't learn much more about them, other than their names:

Mark and Andrea Stone.

Oh, and that they had an unusual assortment of sex toys in their bedroom closet.

It was a...strange experience, essentially phasing through solid objects. His first attempt to pass through something was when he had to get out of the bedroom he started in because the door was closed; he didn't seem to have any hands, so opening it up appeared to be out of the question.

There was no resistance as he slowly moved through it, his vision swallowed up by the wooden shell of the lightweight bedroom door. He paused while halfway through; instead of complete darkness inside the hollow interior of the door, he found that he could see everything as if it had been lit up from hidden sources. Not that there was much to see – it was the inside of a door, after all.

I guess this means I can see in the dark now.

Your Spirit Core can observe everything in or out of the visible light spectrum. The darkness is your friend and your friend is the darkness!

Despite the overly cheerful response to his inquiry, Clive dismissed the notification with the knowledge that nothing was barred from his sight. He was neither pleased nor disturbed by this revelation; it was just another aspect of his new existence.

He moved from the bedroom door to find himself in a small upstairs hallway, with a staircase he could see on his right-hand…right-core?…side leading down. Directly to his left he could see an open doorway that led to a small full-bathroom: a single vanity with a large square mirror secured to the wall, an unremarkable toilet with a remarkably bright-pink carpeted cover, and a basic shower/tub combo in the corner. Everything inside the room was neatly organized and virtually spotless; either they had just cleaned it or they somehow managed to keep it clean despite daily use.

Further down the hallway and across from the stairway landing, another closed door greeted him as he hovered across the second floor. He quickly flitted inside – noticing in passing that this door was solid wood instead of hollow – and quickly became accustomed to his new ability to pass through doors and walls without harm.

Nothing of note was inside – a spare bedroom/office, about two-thirds of the size of the master bedroom. There was a small twin bed up against the far wall, with a perfectly made-up, flowery-designed coverlet and numerous extraneous pillows. It appeared to not have been disturbed for a long time; he figured they didn't get a lot of guests that stayed the night.

The other half of the small room had a long wooden desk setup with multiple cubbies and two filing cabinets underneath the flat surface. Along with the rest of the house he had seen so far, everything was perfectly organized: files were filed, and the desk was free of clutter.

Although the lack of light didn't hinder his efforts to see inside the filing cabinets, the fact that the hanging file folders were stuffed to capacity did. He was only able to visually make out a few of the front papers, which looked a lot like tax forms, bills, and other important papers like the deed to the house and car titles. From the names he saw, he concluded that the man in the picture he saw earlier was Mark Stone, with his wife Andrea by his side.

There wasn't much else to provide him information inside that room, so he left it as soon as he had seen what he was able to inside the filing cabinets. *If I had hands, this would be much easier.*

Physical Manipulation of objects is not currently available.

Clive had no idea what that was supposed to mean, so he ignored it in favor of departing the room and exploring the first floor. He realized that he could simply pass through the floor to get there, but the normal habits of a mortal human were still ingrained inside him: he took the stairs.

Worn but clean carpet covered the steps, which led to a living room that was just as clean as the rest of the house, though it did appear to get much more use than everywhere else. The cushions on the oversized-for-the-room couch had seen a lot of use, there were scratches and rings on the wooden coffee table, and the giant flat-screen 65" LED TV was featured prominently along the wall next to the entrance. On the wall below the TV, various video components sat on a shelf and had their cords hidden inside the wall, before emerging behind the TV.

Since the couch took up most of the room, there wasn't much space left over for an eating area, which was located near the front door. A small, square, wooden table with four chairs sat there with place settings and an elaborate faux-floral centerpiece; this was the first thing he had seen that showed signs of neglect or disuse. Dust settled lightly over everything on the table, including the place settings, hinting that the entire "dining room" was more for show than anything.

The only interior walls on the first floor hid the kitchen but allowed access from two directions: from a small hallway located next to the stairs and from the dining room. The small hallway was lined with more abstract art and a few more pictures of the couple in various exotic locales; there weren't that many, however, so either they didn't get to travel much or couldn't afford to take many vacations.

The kitchen was a basic affair, though it looked like it had been updated at some point over the last decade. Ceramic-tiled floor encompassed the biggest of the changes, which contrasted with the carpet everywhere else in the house, as well as modern wood, glass, and metal-accented cabinets and drawers. The appliances were newer, but not stainless steel like he had seen in a lot of the remodeled kitchens he had visited in the past. And, now that he thought about it, he had seen *a lot*; his nightly forays into strangers' houses gave him a unique perspective.

The fridge and cabinets held an assortment of foods, running the gamut from extremely healthy to downright pure junk food. On prominent display in the fridge, for instance, were a variety of fresh vegetables and homemade leftover salads stored in specially designed food storage containers; however, looking further, he found a stash of crème-filled sandwich cookies and frosted snack cakes hidden behind some expired canned foods and other ingredients on the top shelf of one of the cabinets. Someone obviously had a sweet tooth.

From the hallway leading to the kitchen, a back door led out to a respectable fenced-in yard, with overgrown grass and a tiny shed in the corner. Clive tried to go out back to check it out some more, but his progress was stopped as soon as he attempted to pass through the door.

Error!

You are not able to leave your Area of Influence at this time.

With that, he was effectively shut off from the rest of the world. He hadn't tried leaving from any other parts of the house, but he suspected that it would be the same the entire way around. It was effectively his prison; though, to be fair, he had a lot more freedom now than he had inside the prison cell he had lived out the last few years of his life. Plus, the error said something about "at this time", which meant that there was a possibility that he would be able to venture out from the relatively tiny residence.

Maybe when I kill these people, it will allow me to leave.

No guide-assisted notification popped into his head after that thought, so he assumed he was correct: Clive needed to kill Mark and Andrea Stone so that he could move on from his temporary prison.

With his departure from the house stymied at the moment, he found another door across from the kitchen and next to the back door, located directly underneath the staircase leading to the second floor. It was closed; by now, however, the presence of a closed or locked door didn't make him hesitate in the slightest.

Passing through the solid, thick, and heavy wooden door, he found stairs leading down to an unfinished basement. Exposed floor joists, electrical wiring, and plumbing were evident along the ceiling, while the walls and floor were made entirely of concrete. He noticed evidence of patching along the walls, suggesting that there may have been some minor foundation issues at some point in the home's history; researching the best ways to enter and navigate through strange houses had led to some diverse information regarding construction and house layout/designs.

In one corner of the room, a water heater was connected to a variety of pipes running in and out of the cylinder-shaped appliance; in the opposite corner, a relatively new washer/dryer pair was surrounded by dirty laundry in laundry baskets, as well as a variety of detergents and fabric softeners.

Along the rest of the room he found the reason the house upstairs appeared so clean and uncluttered: it was all down in the basement. Every inch of the walls was covered in sturdy metal shelving, as well as another bank of shelves leading straight down the center. And every shelf was full of something.

Old records, sports equipment, board games, used kitchen appliances, toys from (presumably) their childhoods, extra linens in vacuum-sealed bags, some binders that contained old baseball cards, outdated electronics, holiday decorations, and even some matching bowling balls were neatly arranged by type along the shelves. To Clive, it looked like a garage sale waiting to happen.

He spent the most time looking through everything down there, though in the end, he only learned that the junk in storage was as clean and anally organized as the rest of the house. The dust over everything, even, wasn't worse than the dust on the dining room table; they appeared to clean down there intermittently, which was a big difference from most basements he'd seen.

With the absence of anything worthwhile in the basement, Clive took to exploring every inch of every cabinet, drawer, nook, cranny, and closet he could find – which wasn't much. Which is how he went about finding the abnormally large box of sex toys in the closet; not only was it unexpected from the way everything in the house was cleaned and organized, but it implied that there was more to the couple whose house he'd invaded.

If he was in the least curious, he would've done more to investigate – as it was, however, he still didn't have any feelings of curiosity. His exploring wasn't done out of any need to know everything; it had been done out of having nothing better to do. If he thought watching the time tick away would've been more productive, he would've stayed inside the master bedroom and stared at one of the digital clocks.

He had an ultimate goal now; based upon what the Goddess had told him, there was the possibility that he would be rewarded with experiencing emotions and feelings from some people he could hitch a ride with. That was why he had explored the house: he was gathering information to make killing them easier. Nothing else mattered to him in his little world.

With everything explored, with at least a cursory inspection, he went back to the master bedroom and waited for something to happen. With a patience only someone who couldn't become bored would show, he stared at the digital clocks on either side of the king-size bed.

And watched time tick away.

Chapter 5

Alert!

(1) Mortal approaching your Area of Influence!

Location: Front External Door

Automatically transfer to alert location? Yes/No

Right as the clocks rolled over to 5:19pm (which, after watching them for hours, was about two seconds apart), he received an alert. Which was a unique experience, since he didn't know that he could receive alerts, but it was helpful to know when someone was nearby. He thought **Yes** to the question it was asking and immediately found himself looking at the living room from nearby the stairs.

There was no transition; he was just suddenly there. It was a little disorienting at first, going from one viewpoint to the next, but he likened it to a CCTV system he had seen before in a store that switched between different cameras every few seconds. After knowing how it was accomplished, he quickly transferred his Spirit Core back-and-forth between the master bedroom and the living room a few times to get used to the experience.

All of that took less than two seconds, which was why he was prepared to see the front door open and the woman from the pictures – Andrea – make her way inside and drop her keys on a small table next to the door. She kicked it closed, because her hands were full of her purse and a few plastic bags full of groceries, which she immediately brought to the kitchen. Clive easily floated along behind her, careful not to touch her yet, though he noticed that she didn't seem to detect his presence at all. The guide was right – he was essentially invisible.

He watched as she unloaded some fresh vegetables and a half-gallon of milk from the bags, which she immediately shoved in the fridge. When that was done, she grabbed a small folding stepstool that was propped up against the fridge and plopped it down in front of one of the cabinets. Pulling another box of snack-cakes from one of the bags, she brought it up to the top of the cabinet with rarely used ingredients and exchanged it for the nearly-empty box already there.

After ensuring that no one (other than Clive, of course) could easily see her hidden stash, she stepped down and practically devoured the two-pack of sweet, frosting-enrobed chocolate cakes. When she was done, she threw the protective plastic bag that previously held the snack-cake in the small, half-full trash can underneath the sink, pushing the wrapper toward the bottom so that it wouldn't be obvious with a casual glance.

I would've taken Mark as the one hiding the junk food.

Clive hadn't made his move to kill her yet because he was trying to figure out how and when. On his killing spree back when he was alive, he chose to approach his targets when they were the most vulnerable – and preferably asleep. Fighting with them was too messy, and the few times he had accidentally woken up his victims before ending their lives were not experiences that he wanted to repeat. While he wasn't in any danger himself, it was much more difficult to kill an awake victim that wouldn't let you just shove a knife into their brain. Disposing of his blood-covered clothing afterward was an unnecessary hassle to his mind.

But now he didn't have to worry about bloodying his clothes, or risking injury to himself; at the same time, unfortunately, he didn't have his bowie knife. She was alone right now in the house (his guide-assistant would've told him otherwise, he was sure), so he didn't need to worry about her calling for help, though he wasn't sure how much help someone would be against an invisible attacker. Nevertheless, he hesitated because he wasn't exactly sure how he was supposed to be able to kill her.

A few methods came to mind: strangulation, bludgeoning, and (because he could move in between objects) entering inside her body and destroying some vital organs such as her heart or her brain. Somehow. He still hadn't been able to affect anything physically, nor had he really taken the time to try yet.

No time like the present.

When she was putting the rest of the room-temperature groceries away, Clive glided forward until he was centered right in front of her neck and attempted to strangle her. He didn't have any arms or hands, but he didn't let that stop him.

Error!
You can only perform actions or attacks between the hours of 8:00pm and 4:00am.

What? No matter what he tried, he kept getting the same error message. He was careful to avoid actually touching the woman because he was still cognizant of the warning that he had received earlier about mortals being able to detect him if he passed through them. There was a close call when she turned around abruptly to grab her phone from her purse on the counter, but he was literally able to move as fast as he could think it.

Since he still had a couple of hours to wait, apparently, he settled for watching her finish putting things away before heading to the upstairs bathroom. He had no shame or embarrassment from watching her loudly void her bowels inside the toilet in an explosion of various noises; they weren't emotions he had ever experienced before, and still hadn't.

She looked at something on her phone while all the porcelain destruction was going on, but she soon finished her business and made her way back downstairs, just in time for another alert.

Alert!

(1) Additional mortal approaching your Area of Influence!

Location: Front External Door

Automatically transfer to alert location? Yes/No

He said **No** because he was already there, watching the lock on the door turn ineffectually. The woman had forgotten to lock the door after she got home, having just kicked it closed due to her full arms, so after a moment of apparent confusion, the man Clive had seen from the pictures walked in with a strange expression on his face.

"Honey, I told you to lock the door when you're home alone. This isn't a *bad* neighborhood, but it's better to be safe than sorry. You'd never know it if someone got in the house when you weren't looking, attacking when I wasn't here to defend you."

"I can take care of myself, Mark, I've been taking self-defense classes on the weekend, you know."

"That won't matter if they have a knife or, even worse, a gun," he retorted angrily, before softening his voice. "Just...try to remember next time, okay? For me? Please?"

"Ok, I'll try to remember from now on," she responded, before giving him a quick hug followed by a lengthy kiss. "Welcome home, love."

"Mmm, thank you, baby. It's good to be home...is that chocolate I taste on my lips?"

Without missing a beat, Andrea made up an obvious excuse (at least to Clive, who had seen her destroy the chocolate snack-cakes not even twenty minutes earlier), "Must be some of that flavored coffee I had at work. I needed a pick-me-up toward the end of the day."

He smiled at her. "I know what you mean, I needed three cups today just to get through that boring meeting."

"Oh, hey – I went grocery shopping after work and picked up some more of that kale you really liked. I was thinking of including it in tonight's dinner – quinoa with grilled chicken sound good to you?"

"Oh, sure...sounds wonderful."

Clive ignored the rest of the conversation, as it didn't seem important. Now that he was able to see both of them, they appeared to have filled-out a little since they had taken their wedding picture. He supposed that was why they were attempting to eat healthier; though with the way the woman was sabotaging her own diet, it wasn't going to make much difference in the long run. Also, they would be dead soon, so it *really* didn't matter now.

The next few hours passed in a blur, as Clive watched them cook, eat on the couch while watching TV, and then only moving from that spot to bring their dirty dishes to the kitchen sink. The only thing that happened that was mildly interesting was when the man snuck into the junk food cabinet to get some cookies while his wife was upstairs changing into what she called "comfy clothes". He ate them quickly with practiced speed and swished around some water afterwards, cleaning out any lingering chocolate cookie particles, though Clive didn't think it did anything with the smell on his breath.

The woman either didn't smell it or chose to ignore it.

By the time 8pm ticked by on the clocks, they were curled up together on the couch under some blankets, watching what he decided was supposed to be a scary horror movie. The dramatic music and sudden stops in background noise was enough to tell him that it was supposed to be suspenseful, but all Clive could think of was how inept the killer with the chainsaw was. He observed multiple times where he essentially just let his victims escape without harm, all the while advertising his presence with the unwieldy, gas-powered outdoor cutting implement.

If he had snuck up on them with a knife, for example, he could've killed them within the first five minutes.

Physical weapons are not available for use by a Spirit Core.

Thanks, but that doesn't help me. He ignored any response that came from the system guide and watched the time tick over to 8pm. Immediately, he sensed a difference in the environment. Although it didn't impede his vision, a shadow seemed to fall over everything.

You are now free to perform any available actions or attacks. Caution: any lingering attacks will dissipate at the end of the attack period.

He didn't need any other invitation. Clive moved toward the man, knowing that he would be the biggest threat. Once he was dead, it would be much easier to handle the woman.

Words and numbers floated around the man lying on the couch, made visible as he concentrated on him. They didn't make any sense, nor did they matter to Clive, as he decided to try strangling him as he had attempted to do to the woman earlier. Floating closer to the half-dozing husband, he envisioned his hands grasping the thick neck and squeezing—

Error!

FEAR Level of target and Spiritual Level of Spirit Core is below the requirement for:

Physical Manipulation – Strangulation

Clive pulled back, wanting to get out of range of any sudden movements of either of the movie-watchers while he tried to discover what had just happened. Nothing his guide-assistant had just told him meant anything to him. All he knew was that his attack on the man was entirely ineffective.

What does all that mean?

FEAR: *Focused Extrasensory Assault Reception*

FEAR Level: *How likely the target will be susceptible to a focused extrasensory spiritual assault. The more FEAR they possess, the more likely they will <u>believe</u> and be more receptive to FEAR-based attacks.*

Spiritual Level: *The higher the Spiritual Level of the Spirit Core, the more options are available for FEAR-based attacks.*

Uh...ok.

Chapter 6

Now that his attempts to kill either the man or woman had been blocked by his own lack of knowledge, he was in no hurry to mess things up. The entire process of killing innocents wasn't as cut-and-dry as the Goddess of the Underworld had made it seem when she was telling him about the Spirit Core. He had to wade through some new, strange information now to make sure he didn't jeopardize his chance to feel something.

Clive looked closer at the man, concentrating on him again until he saw the same words and numbers that he had seen prior to trying to choke him out. They swirled around him in sporadic circles; it was only by "locking" his focus onto the man that he was able to see it clearly as it stabilized enough to read.

Mark Stone

FEAR Level: 1

Resistance to FEAR attacks: 15

Weaknesses: Unknown

Perception: 2/10

Fatigue: 60%

None of that made any sense, so he transferred his focus to the woman curled up in his arms.

Andrea Stone

FEAR Level: 4

Resistance to FEAR attacks: 5

Weaknesses: Unknown

Perception: 6/10

Fatigue: 40%

He definitely saw a difference in the two, but they were only small differences – so small that he wasn't sure what to make of it. That, and he still didn't understand what was going on. He was about to think about each of the elements to see if the guide-assist could tell him more about the different terms, when he noticed that the FEAR level was fluctuating on the woman, but not the man.

He floated backwards to see what could be causing it, trying to get a bigger picture of everything. The only difference he could see was that the woman was actively watching the movie, whereas the man seemed to be dozing off. Whenever the music would become dramatic (or stop altogether), there would be a rise in her FEAR level; at one point, it had spiked to 10 before gradually reducing back down to a steady 4 or 5. It took him a minute or two before he realized what was happening.

She was afraid.

Never having experienced fear before, he didn't know what it felt like and couldn't identify with the things that were said to cause it. He knew about the emotion from the books he had read, but he had trouble understanding why anyone would be afraid of the most common fears: public speaking, heights, bugs, drowning, needles, being enclosed in small spaces, flying, strangers...darkness...and ghosts. Something was starting to click in his mind as he considered what he had seen so far.

He was only able to "attack" them during the night.

His targets had number values attached to them that were related to their level of fear.

He was a Spirit Core; another name for "spirit" was...ghost.

*I'm supposed to **scare** them to death.*

Correct!

Using your Spiritual Force, you need to heighten the FEAR Level of your targets using your lower-grade FEAR attacks that you currently have access to. Once their FEAR Level is great enough (and your Spiritual Level is high enough), you will have access to FEAR-based attacks that can kill your targets, thereby capturing their innocent souls.

There are two ways that you can kill your victims:

- **By raising their FEAR Level high enough, you can cause their heart to fail due to toxic levels of adrenaline**
- **As a secondary effect of one of your FEAR-based attacks**

Well, that certainly explains a bit…but then again, not nearly enough. Based upon what he was told, *he* wasn't going to physically harm them; however, by using his new abilities as a Spirit Core, he could essentially kill them with their own fear or as a result of their fear. By ramping their FEAR Level up…somehow…they would get so scared that they would keel over and die. He thought it was a little far-fetched – who would believe that being scared would kill them?

Apparently, this system did, because he couldn't see any other way to do it if he didn't have a physical form. He tried again and again to somehow physically contact the two people on the couch, even with a small poke – but was stopped every single time with the same error he originally received. Giving up on that avenue of attack, he concentrated on the numbers floating around them and "asked" in his mind what they meant.

Resistance to FEAR attacks: Natural skepticism towards FEAR-based attacks. A higher resistance requires stronger attacks to overcome this skepticism; resistance is subtracted by current

FEAR Level when determining effectiveness of FEAR-based abilities.

Weaknesses: If any specific FEAR-based attacks are known to have a greater impact on the target, they will be listed here.

Perception: The awareness that the target has of their surroundings; affects how likely they'll be influenced by a FEAR attack. The higher perception the target has, the more susceptible they will be. Factors that affect Perception: FEAR Level and Fatigue.

Fatigue: Targets with a higher Fatigue are less likely to be susceptible to attacks.

Ok, that makes some sense; if they are tired, like the man here on the couch, they will have less Perception because he is half-asleep. Likewise, since the woman is watching the movie, she is actively listening and more perceptive to any outside influences. He wasn't sure what he could do against the natural resistances they seemed to have, other than powering through them; although, he noticed that it was going to be much easier to effectively attack the woman because of her lower resistance.

As for how he could attack them, he still wasn't entirely sure what he was supposed to do. Physical attacks were obviously out of the question based upon his own experimentation, but what did that leave?

Current FEAR-based Attacks Available at Spiritual Level 1:
- **1. Localized Cold Spot**
- **1. Errant Breeze**
- **1. Piloerection Reflex**
- **1. Depressive Miasma**
- **1. Spectral Cobwebs**

Fortunately, his guide-assist was there to help him out with a very compact list of strange "attacks". *These are what I'm supposed to use to kill them? How is a gust of wind supposed to do that?*

1. Errant Breeze (EB):

Description: *Generates a brief room-temperature breeze in an otherwise calm environment*

Magnitude: *Variable – strength and size are dependent upon SF used*

Duration: *Variable – duration is dependent upon SF used, lasting from 1 to 3 seconds*

SF Cost: *Variable – depending upon strength/size/duration desired, starting from 20 up to 100*

Target FEAR Requirement: *Level 3*

Max Generated FEAR: *10*

Unmodified Reward Upon Successful Attack: *20 SF*

More questions. He wasn't sure what all of that meant, but now that he saw something that he could do, he decided to try it out to see if would work. He observed the woman for a few minutes, timing his actions with a rise in her FEAR Level and an apparently dramatic scene in the movie. When her FEAR topped off at 8, he concentrated on generating the strongest Errant Breeze he could, blowing it straight into her face.

Andrea couldn't believe her husband fell asleep AGAIN; it was starting to become commonplace for him to sleep through all the movies she liked to watch. Of course, if it had been one of those "superhero" movies he loved to watch, he would've been all over the couch – keeping **her** *awake. Despite all their years together, it was rare that they could both finish a movie without one or the other falling asleep – or both.*

She didn't let it bother her too much however; whenever she would jump at the scenes where the chainsaw-wielding maniac came out of nowhere, he would wake up a little. She got a little satisfaction each time this happened: sleep through **my** *movie, will you? Besides, later before bed, she would make sure he was awake for a little fun – it had been way too long. Days even.*

A chainsaw shoved its way through a wall, inches in front of Chasity's face. She had been hiding quietly in a closet, but the killer somehow sensed she was there; instead of opening the door (which Andrea had been expecting), the chainsaw psycho had gone outside the room and attacked the closet from the hallway, startling both her and the scantily clad teen on the movie. As she screamed, giving herself away, Andrea felt a little spike of fear herself as she watched her run out of the closet and through the doorway leading to the hallway, where she was instantly chased by the maniac.

He had her cornered in an adjacent room, raising his chainsaw above his head for the final blow...when Andrea felt a small draught of wind gently caress her face, causing the stray hairs that had been creeping down from her ponytail to tickle her left ear. It was so unexpected that she panicked, screaming so loud that she hurt her own ears. She threw the blanket off and ran to the kitchen, ignoring the confused questions of her sleepy husband as he tried to ask what was wrong.

A rush of fear entered his Core, exploding through his mind in a magnificent spike of emotions. It was wonderful; although it was nowhere near the ecstasy he used to experience when he killed someone, it was unexpected and welcome for what it was.

Emotional Feedback is currently set to ON, would you like to change this? OFF is recommended. Yes/No

NO! In fact, turn it up!

Feedback levels cannot be adjusted. Warning: higher-level FEAR-based attacks will increase the Emotional Feedback. Knowing this, do you still wish to have Emotional Feedback set to ON? Yes/No

Yes! Leave it on!

Emotional Feedback: ON
You are free to change these settings at any time, if you decide otherwise.

All too soon, the feeling of fear left his Core, the wave of emotions draining away like a receding tide. It didn't happen all at once, but it was quick enough that Clive knew it was inevitable that he would be empty and unfeeling again only minutes after his attack.

Chapter 7

When he felt all traces of the emotion leave him, there wasn't a want or need in him for more of the fear he created in the woman. He didn't have those feelings; it felt more akin to learning how to recognize his normal bodily functions back when he had a body.

Hunger and thirst – along with the need to use the restroom – were all things he had to physically think about. Since he couldn't *feel* the way others did, there were many times during preschool and even kindergarten where he soiled his pants, not recognizing the sensations that told him he needed to void himself. Eventually, he was able to distinguish the various pressures inside his digestive system that indicated what was needed; he developed his own rigid system he had adhered to even through adulthood to ensure a steady stream of nutrients and waste removal.

Although he could smell and taste food, he experienced no pleasure or disgust at what he was eating, essentially meaning that he could eat anything that would satisfy his body's needs. He had to make doubly sure when selecting what he ate: spoiled or expired foods wouldn't "taste" any different to him. Because he only ate what was needed to ensure he had enough energy, his figure was kept lean and free of most excess fat. He ate to live – not lived to eat.

Clive didn't have those same pressure-focused sensations in his current form. Nevertheless, the Spirit Core he inhabited experienced something similar: a slight pressure on his mind that told him that it wanted more of the emotions he just experienced. With this in "mind", he turned his focus back to the scene unfolding in the kitchen.

The woman was hysterical, crying into her husband's arms as she tried to explain what had happened. He noticed that their statuses had changed while he was "away" experiencing the fear that he had caused in the woman (though he still didn't understand why the Errant Breeze he created was so effective). The biggest changes were in the woman, but the man had become less-fatigued and more Perceptive as a result.

Mark Stone

FEAR Level: 2

Resistance to FEAR attacks: 15

Weaknesses: Unknown

Perception: 7/10

Fatigue: 20%

Andrea Stone

FEAR Level: 18

Resistance to FEAR attacks: 5

Weaknesses: Unknown

Perception: 8/10

Fatigue: 10%

Her FEAR Level had shot up 10 points to 18, though as Clive watched her husband calm her down, it slowly dropped until it hovered around 11. Her Fatigue also started to rise as her Perception dropped, which he ignored as he started to attack her again with his Errant Breeze.

*Andrea didn't know exactly what happened, but she **knew** she experienced the brush of wind against her face, despite Mark telling her it was her imagination. However, it felt good being in his arms and his gentle caresses against her back were calming her down. She was positive she felt something, but it was entirely possible that it was her mind playing tricks on her after a long day at work – like Mark was trying to convince her of. And watching the slasher flick at the same time probably didn't help.*

She felt her heart rate slow from the frantic race it had been running, at times feeling as if it wanted to bust out of her chest and run outside the house without her. She was still freaked out, but she was getting tired and decided to head to bed early. She had enough scary movies for the night; all she wanted now was a good night's rest and to put the incident behind her. I'm sure I'll laugh at myself tomorrow.

She opened her mouth to say the same thing to Mark, when she felt another breeze rush past her face, followed by another, and then another. She stood stock-still, the fear so great in her that she stopped breathing and couldn't say or do anything. Mark tensed up around her as he felt the wind as well, and she felt strangely grateful that he was experiencing it as well.

After almost a minute of constant breezes that stopped and started, however, the fright started to abate as the weirdness of it became apparent. "D-did...you feel that?" she asked, when the paralyzing fear finally loosened up enough for her to communicate.

"Yes, I felt it. We probably have a hole somewhere in the siding leading to the outside. That heavy storm we had last week must've knocked something loose. I'll have someone take a look at it tomorrow. Shhh, it's okay – nothing to worry about," he softly responded, running his hands down her back in comforting circles. "Now, let's shut everything down and get ready for bed...it's been a long day."

As much as she had earlier wanted to participate in some other...activities...before going to sleep, she was too frazzled to even think about it now. She could tell Mark felt the same way, though he wasn't as scared – startled, I was just startled – *by the small gust of wind.*

When she was lying in bed trying to fall asleep a little later, she started laughing at herself, to think I got all scared shitless over a little breeze! What's next, I'm going to start jumping at ghosts? *The thought of her own baseless fears was almost comforting, as she was finally able to calm down enough to pass out, exhausted by the day's events.*

But a little kernel of fear still existed, questioning the reasonable explanation her husband offered. "What if it wasn't a hole in the wall?"

The flood of emotion was overwhelming, the pleasure of *feeling* something was almost more than he could handle with the sudden onslaught. Fortunately, he had previous experience with concentrating on his surroundings after being inundated with pleasure; his nightly escapades killing unsuspecting people had allowed him to partition a part of his mind. It would focus on his surroundings, ensuring he didn't get snuck-up on while the rest of him fully experienced the ocean of emotions he experienced.

Therefore, while he relished the heightening fear the woman exhibited and soaked it in (with some coming from the man as well, though in much, much smaller quantities), he kept the Errant Breeze going, one after another. He felt the fear building and building until it plateaued in what he thought was an almost orgasmic sensation...before abruptly plummeting to a low simmer.

He didn't know what had happened. He was using the Errant Breeze and, at least based on the requirements for it, was well within the parameters it had stated. Her FEAR Level was much higher than was needed, her Resistance hadn't changed, and her Perception was higher than ever. Her Fatigue was now a bit higher, but at the time it should've been just right for his attacks.

The partitioned part of his mind had absently noted – while he was reveling in emotional bliss – that her FEAR Level had actually topped out at 30 before rapidly de-escalating. From his calculations, the number of Errant Breezes he'd used should've had her to at least FEAR Level 58, so something else must've been at work. *I was following the instructions, so what went wrong?*

Note: Repeated uses of a singular FEAR-based attack can have diminishing returns, as well as a detrimental effect on FEAR Levels if used too often in a short period of time.

Clive wasn't sure why this would be, but as he heard the husband come up with a logical explanation he began to understand. It was what *he* would've thought of; jumping straight to the conclusion that something other than a stray breeze from the outside wouldn't have even crossed his mind when he was still alive.

But by repeatedly making the breeze blow in their faces, it forced them to abandon their fear and look for a reasonable, rational, logical explanation for the phenomenon they were experiencing. When the part of their brains that strove to explain something logically latched onto the strangeness of an almost constant gust of wind, it halted the rise of their FEAR Level and even reduced it. In fact, now that he looked at the woman, her FEAR had dropped back to 8 and hovered around there, fluctuating slightly up or down as she went about the business of getting ready for bed.

As a net result, his repeated actions had caused the previously high FEAR Level to drop, becoming ultimately worse than after the first use of his attack. Although it showed a positive gain in her base FEAR Level, he wasn't sure if it would stay that way. As for the man, he was ultimately unchanged except for a small bump in his FEAR.

Clive was used to a cut-and-dry result from calculating numbers and formulas; the conditional nature of emotional fear was incomprehensible to him. He had no personal experience to draw from. Despite asking for help from his guide-assist, there was nothing to explain exactly *why* people reacted to fear the way they did. He assumed that the system was made for those who knew the reasons why a breeze in the face was frightening – he was not one of those people.

There was no help for it: he was going to have to do everything by trial-and-error. This first night was obviously an error. But he would learn from it.

When the married couple settled down to sleep, Clive attempted to blow another breeze in her face to see what kind of result it would have on her. He thought that it might make a difference being in a different location and further apart in terms of time.

Error!
Insufficient SF for this FEAR-based attack.

What is this "SF" I keep seeing?

Spiritual Force (SF): The energy the Spirit Core uses to perform FEAR-based attacks. Spiritual Force is earned from successful attacks and is rewarded at the next attack period. In addition, Spiritual Force is regenerated each day for use during the next attack period, the specific amount dependent upon Spiritual Level.

For more information on current SF, please check your Spirit Core Status.

Well, why don't I do that then.

Spirit Core Status – Transformed Soul of Clive Logan

Spiritual Level: 1

Lifetime FEAR Generated: 0/100

Spiritual Force (Current): 0/500

Spiritual Force (Nightly Recharge): 100

(FEAR and rewarded SF are calculated at the end of the current attack period)

Well, that it explains it – I used all of the Spiritual Force I had. With no other actions he could take, he spent the rest of the night hovering over the king-sized bed, watching the numbers fluctuate on the man and woman beneath him. He noticed that a few spikes of FEAR Levels occurred during the night – in both of them – for a few moments, before settling down to a low baseline. He assumed this was due to their dreams, though he couldn't say for sure; he had never dreamed, or, if he did, he didn't remember them. As the night went on, he saw their Fatigue drop as they got some sleep, while their Perception wagged between 0 and 1; all of which made sense.

At least something does.

Chapter 8

The nightly attack period ended precisely at 4am without much fanfare, except for the elimination of any visible numbers floating around his two targets who were still sleeping. Nothing much had changed over the night and watching the fluctuating numbers kept him occupied, at least enough that he chose not to busy himself with anything else.

At 4:01am, he received an update on that night's activities.

Congratulations on completing your first Attack Period!

Results

SF Used: 500/500

FEAR Generated (Andrea): 10(EB) + 8(EB) + 6(EB) + 4(EB) + 2(EB) = 30

FEAR Generated (Mark): 3(EB) + 2(EB) + 1(EB) + 1(EB) = 7

Total FEAR Generated: 37

Lifetime FEAR: 37/100

SF Earned (Andrea): 100(EB) + 80(EB) + 60(EB) + 40(EB) + 20(EB) = 300

SF Earned (Mark): 30(EB) + 20(EB) + 10(EB) + 10(EB) = 70

Total SF Earned for next attack period: 370

If he was reading it right, Clive could see the diminishing returns of using the same attack repeatedly. Instead of 50 FEAR points that he should've generated from his actions, he had only earned 30 – a 40% reduction. Even though his attacks were successfully completed, they were modified by those same diminishing returns – but at least they gave a minimum amount.

It made more sense now that he could see it in numerical form; the abstract personal results didn't compute to his analytical mind. In addition, he was also able to see what a higher Resistance to FEAR attacks had on his assault: Mark was conscious of the attack, but it barely returned much in the FEAR and SF reward department. He supposed that some people didn't get frightened as easily.

It wasn't a total failure, however; he did learn that he had initially succeeded with his first attack. Added to that, he earned enough SF for the next night for nearly a repeat performance, though he was hoping he would have a better result if he changed things up. It wouldn't be as much as he started with, but with the nightly recharge it would be close.

He noticed that he didn't "scare" the man as much as the woman; he figured it was a result of the Resistance factor. It was interesting to note that it hadn't been completely negated, however. It boded well for the future when he needed to somehow overcome the husband's natural skepticism.

He watched them continue to sleep until their alarms went off at 6am, where they were slow to wake up. The woman got up first, commandeering the bathroom, whereas the man dragged himself out of bed and headed downstairs. Clive followed him since the woman was busy taking a hot shower, the steam she generated fogging up the mirror inside the closed bathroom.

The husband was wearing nothing but a pair of boxers, but that didn't seem to bother him as he started brewing a pot of coffee and heating up a skillet. Taking some eggs out of the fridge, he quickly cracked them and blended it in a small bowl with some skim milk, salt, and pepper. When the skillet was hot enough, he poured the mixture inside, almost splashing it on himself as his still-blurry eyes fought his attempts at making a healthy breakfast.

Healthy, at least, until he raided the junk food cabinet for some more cookies while his wife was still upstairs.

By the time she was out of the shower and made her way to the kitchen – dried off, with a robe wrapped around her and a towel in her hair, he had finished his cooking. Without a word, he pushed a plate full of eggs, a sliced grapefruit, and a cup of low-fat Greek yogurt over to her. She took it and dug in, any attempts at decorum completely disregarded.

"Did you sleep well?"

"Ugh...off and on all night. I couldn't help thinking about last night. I know you're probably right about some sort of hole in the wall, but you have to admit it was a little creepy," she responded after she had devoured her meal.

"It was weird, I'll give you that; I'll look into getting someone to check the outside of the house to look for any cracks or openings. I think I can take a long lunch today so that I can make some calls."

"Mmph...good idea – I wouldn't trust you to hold a hammer, let alone try to DIY up a fix," she smiled at him, obviously ribbing him on some long-standing argument.

"Hey, I'll have you know that I've improved since that..." Clive stopped listening to their back-and-forth about failed household projects, watching them instead get ready to leave for the day. They were surprisingly quick about it, the woman only taking a couple minutes to put on a minimum of makeup before dressing up in some casual-looking business attire. As for the husband, he was wearing a dark-blue three-piece business suit, complete with a white button-up shirt and tie.

He left before the wife, so it gave her plenty of time to sneak a cookie before she left. When she reached inside, she looked perplexed at the package; noticing the reduced number of cookies from what she expected inside, her expression grew thoughtful. Clive had no clue why she had a look of intense thought at the discovery – his research into different emotions would've thought she would be angry at the theft and subsequent deception. He chalked it up as another thing that didn't make sense to him over the last day.

When she eventually left, the house was quiet. Clive floated around, aimlessly looking into places that he had already searched the day before, looking for what, he didn't know. Eventually, he brought his Spirit Core back to the living room and floated there six feet off the floor, at about the same height he would've been if his former body had been there. It was the most...normal – if that word could be used for his current existence.

With nothing else productive to do, he started looking into the other FEAR-based attacks he could utilize. He had gotten a list of them before, but they didn't explain what they did; even after the explanation, they were still a mystery on why they would induce any type of emotional fear.

1. Localized Cold Spot (LCS):
Description: *Generates a perceived temperature drop in a specific area*
Magnitude: *Fills a sphere 500 cubic inches in volume (Approximately the size of a basketball)*
Duration: *5 minutes*
SF Cost: *50*
Target FEAR Requirement: *Level 1*
Max Generated FEAR: *5*
Unmodified Reward Upon Successful Attack: *50 SF*

1. Piloerection Reflex (PR):
Description: *Generates a large spiritual field that affects all targets within its vicinity; causes target's hair to stand on end*

Magnitude: *Fills a large rectangular box about 60 cubic feet in size (Approximately the size of a telephone booth)*

Duration: *2 minutes*

SF Cost: *100*

Target FEAR Requirement: *Level 5*

Max Generated FEAR: *10*

Unmodified Reward Upon Successful Attack: *100 SF*

1. Depressive Miasma (DM):

Description: *Generates a field of negative spiritual energy that induces a depressive state for those that stay within it; depressive states can increase the effectiveness of FEAR-based attacks*

Magnitude: *1 entire room inside your Area of Influence*

Duration: *Lasts for the remainder of the current attack period*

SF Cost: *200*

Target FEAR Requirement: *Level 7*

Max Generated FEAR: *0*

Unmodified Reward Upon Successful Attack: *0 SF*

1. Spectral Cobwebs (SC):

Description: *Creates an invisible, rectangular floating screen; a target passing through it is subjected to the feeling of cobwebs on their skin*

Magnitude: *4 square feet*

Duration: *Lasts for the remainder of the attack period or until contact is made, whichever comes first*

SF Cost: *250*

Target FEAR Requirement: *Level 9*

Max Generated FEAR: *25*

Unmodified Reward Upon Successful Attack: *250 SF*

He was currently sitting at 370 SF at the moment, with another 100 rolling into that when night-time fell. Some of the FEAR Level requirements were above the last baseline he saw for both of his targets, but he assumed he could use them if he was able to raise it first.

Thinking back to the previous night, for instance, he could've placed a Spectral Cobweb near the entrance to the kitchen, where the woman would've run into it as she fled from his initial attack. Her FEAR Level had been raised up to 18, which was plenty high enough for the requirement. *Too bad I didn't know about this last night.*

Now that he was armed with the knowledge he needed, he spent the rest of the day thinking about the different ways he could utilize his attacks. Unfortunately, he had no sense of appropriate timing; he was only lucky that there had been a movie playing last night that allowed him to see when the woman's FEAR was elevated. If there wasn't a movie tonight, however, he was unsure of when to do what.

He didn't let that deter his planning session, however.

Chapter 9

Alert!

(1) Mortal approaching your Area of Influence!

Location: Exterior

Automatically transfer to alert location? Yes/No

If his resident targets kept to their normal routine (which he was unsure of, since he had only been there one day), then whoever was outside wasn't either the husband or wife. It was too early in the day, and a quick glance at the wall clock in the living room told him it was only 1:16pm. Since he had finished planning his attacks out for the night (as much good as it would do if they changed up what they did from the night before), he selected **Yes** and was instantly transported to the upstairs master bedroom window.

Since he couldn't leave his Area of Influence (essentially, the house), the best he could do was peek outside through various windows. Clive adjusted his viewpoint down and saw a large, bearded man in dusty blue overalls; he was wearing a toolbelt which jingled a little with the various tools hanging off it as he walked along. He was slowly making his way around the outside of the house, pressing on the siding and inspecting everything with determination.

A small five-step ladder joined his perusal of the exterior, allowing him to investigate harder-to-reach areas. A few times he whipped a caulking gun off of his belt, filling in various cracks and holes he must've seen with some clear waterproof silicone.

An even larger ladder came out after the entire first floor had been looked over, sending the workman onto the roof. Clive couldn't see him up there, because there were no windows looking there, but he did discover a previously unknown (at least to him) location: the attic. It wasn't that big of a find, however; the only access to it appeared to not have been used in a long time, as the trap door leading to it had a thick layer of dust. As for what was up in the largely inaccessible trussed attic...insulation.

And a family of mice living in said insulation.

He inadvertently passed through one of them, not knowing it was there at first. His contact with a living being created a weird visible spark that made him freeze in place for a few minutes.

SF lost with contact with living being: -20

While he personally lost 20 SF points and couldn't move, the mouse didn't make it. The spiritual shock to its system apparently overloaded its vital organs, ending its life instantly. The familiar sensation he was accustomed to feeling from killing something wasn't there, though he hadn't suspected it would be. He had experimented with killing small animals after his first experience accidentally causing the death of Samantha, but he never felt anything from it. It was only when killing other people that he felt the euphoric rush.

He didn't think it would be prudent to try that with his human targets.

Physical contact with living beings can have adverse effects, including (but not limited to):

- Visibility

- Temporary loss of control

- Inadvertent discharge of spiritual energy, resulting in the loss of SF

- Vulnerability to some or all forms of Exorcism

I guess I made the right choice. He left the other mice alone, retreating back to the living room when he heard the overall-ed man finish his inspection.

"Hey, Mark......yep, I finished looking at the house and found a couple of spots which may have contributed to the breeze you felt......don't worry, I've already sealed them up, so you shouldn't have any more problems......oh, no trouble at all. And if you still feel any breezes, call me and I'll come out free of charge; I stand by my work and want to make sure it's all good......well, thanks – I'll be sure to let him know. Call me if you need me for anything else...bye."

Clive watched him put his cellphone away and stash all his tools back in his pickup truck, placing the ladders on two specially made racks sticking up from the side. He soon drove away, leaving Clive alone with his thoughts.

At least temporarily.

*　　*　　*

Alert!
(1) Mortal approaching your Area of Influence!
Location: Front External Door
Automatically transfer to alert location? Yes/No

He selected **No** because he was already there, where he had been waiting since the workman had left a few hours before. Same as yesterday, the wife was home first, though this time she was only carrying a single plastic bag along with her purse. Since she didn't have full hands, she remembered to lock the door after closing it; after dropping her keys on the nearby side-table she hurried to the kitchen, where she put down both the plastic bag and her purse.

Grabbing the stepstool, she placed it in front of the junk food cabinet before stepping up towards the treats hidden behind everything. She left all the snack-cakes alone, instead grabbing the half-empty package of cookies. Placing it on the counter, she removed them all and threw them directly in the trash; grabbing the plastic bag, she brought out another, smaller package of cookies that looked very similar to the original. Taking out enough to fill it back up halfway, she tossed the rest into the trash and covered everything up with a plastic bag.

Clive had never tried them, but he suspected that the husband wouldn't like Dr. Woofers "Crème-filled" Dog Biscuits.

The deed done, she placed it back on the shelf behind everything...but then she hesitated, staring at the full boxes of snack-cakes. A moment of contemplation later, she grabbed the three boxes of frosted, jelly-filled, and powder-sugared confections and angrily threw them in the trash. She smiled to herself before she looked wide-eyed at the cabinet again.

After emptying out the boxes and placing them empty back on the shelf next to the "cookies", she tied off the bag of trash and brought it out back, where Clive heard a *thump* and a lid shutting as she tossed her junk food in the curbside trash pickup bin. She came back inside and locked the door, before rushing upstairs to void her bowels again. He thought she must hold it all day – there was a lot more than he would expect from someone of her small stature.

When she was done, she came back downstairs, where she threw herself on the couch and brought out her phone. After less than five minutes, her husband came home, eliciting another prompt from Clive's guide-assist (which he again said **No** to), greeting her as warmly as yesterday – though without the reprimand to lock the door.

"Hey, what do you think of going out to dinner and a movie tonight? I hope you'll say yes, because I've already made reservations at Leonardo's, 6:00 sharp. It's Friday, so it's not a school night!"

"Absolutely, but...why? What did you do?"

He looked mock-guiltily at her before smiling. "Nothing, honey. I just wanted to take you out to try to get your mind off the...stuff from last night," he told her sincerely, grabbing her around the waist, pulling her close against his body, "and to apologize for not getting the house checked out after that storm. In my defense—" he held his hands up in a surrendering gesture— "everything looked fine, but now we've got confirmation – Bruce came by earlier and checked the house out from the outside and patched a few holes he found."

"Apology accepted – now let me go so I can get ready." So saying, she quickly ran upstairs, pulling off her clothing as she went. By the time she got to the master bedroom, she was down to her underclothes; flipping through various dresses in the closet, she pulled out a deep red-colored dress that she immediately slipped over her head.

She spent the rest of the time before they left putting on a lot more makeup than she used before going to work, while the man sat in his same suit from work, watching TV on the couch. 5:50pm rolled around and she was ready to go, rushing out the door while calling back to her husband, "C'mon – you took forever to get ready – let's go!" He hurried out the door chuckling to himself, locking it once he was out and Clive's plan for the night was thrown into disarray.

Who just decides to go out to dinner and a movie at the last minute?

Not him, that's who; he rarely, if ever went out if he could help it – there was no need if he was able to get everything he needed to survive delivered. Of course, after the whole Samantha dying situation, he spent a lot of time on the road, but even then, he only stopped temporarily to eat when necessity demanded it.

He had a whole plan for tonight; even if they didn't watch a movie, he was expecting them to keep the same sort of schedule they had last night. He was adaptable – but there was nothing he could adapt to if they weren't even there. *There's no help for it, unfortunately.*

So he positioned himself back near the front door, waiting for his targets to come home like a lonely puppy waiting for his owners to come home from work.

Except puppies didn't usually want to kill them.

Chapter 10

Clive never had a single drink in his life – he didn't see the point in it – but he was well aware the effects imbibing large amounts of alcohol could have on your body. In college he didn't partake in the parties that were thrown nearly every night; instead, he studied and watched the inebriated frat boys and sorority girls yelling and running down his dorm hallways. Which was strange because they had houses off-campus, yet they decided to disturb the peace in a place where they didn't necessarily belong.

Nevertheless, he instantly recognized the signs of drunk people when his targets came home: stumbling, laughing, slurring of speech, and a few hiccups thrown in here and there by the woman. Thinking it might actually be fortunate, as their inhibitions would be lower – therefore being easier to assault with his FEAR-based attacks – he focused on the numbers floating around them.

Mark Stone

FEAR Level: 1

Resistance to FEAR attacks: 15

Weaknesses: Unknown

Perception: 1/10

Fatigue: 40%

Andrea Stone

FEAR Level: 1

Resistance to FEAR attacks: 5

Weaknesses: Unknown

Perception: 1/10

Fatigue: 50%

But he was wrong.

Their perception was so low that they might not even be aware of what he might try against them, and their FEAR Level was next-to-nothing. The intoxication had wiped-out any gains he had made last night; now, he wasn't even sure if he could make any progress that night. Although it was late, almost midnight, he still had some time to try out some of his attacks – even if they weren't completely successful.

He followed them into the kitchen, where they popped open **another** bottle of something alcoholic, drinking what appeared to be some red wine slowly over the next 20 minutes. They talked about nothing in particular, laughed every couple of seconds, spilled the wine out of their glasses every once in a while, and generally acted like the smashed people they were.

With the low FEAR Levels they were currently at — which shifted from 1 to 2 for no reason that he could see — there was only one attack that he thought might have a chance to succeed: Localized Cold Spot. He thought about what he wanted and formed the small sphere around her head, enveloping it in chilled air.

It worked...though neither of them seemed to notice or care that she was producing clouds of condensed breath as she talked and laughed. And it also didn't do squat in the FEAR department; he didn't even feel any type of fear-based emotion. All his interference led to was them wanting to do something to warm themselves up.

Which is how Clive ended up hovering over their bed, watching them go at it with wild abandon. It was...educational to watch; the closest he actually came to sex during his "lifetime" had ended badly (at least for Samantha), so he had never seen the act in all its entirety before. It didn't last long, however, as the husband's Fatigue level had shot up toward the end, hitting 95% after...completion. Conversely, the woman's Fatigue actually dropped after the act; she had more energy and decided to "finish herself off" after her husband drunkenly passed out next to her.

He tried making two more cold spots during their activities, but they were entirely ineffective; in fact, they might've actually helped them not to overheat during their obviously strenuous sport. He saw no change in either of them all night, other than their Fatigue and Perception Levels. Contrary to the night before, when their Perception stayed right around 1 or so while they were asleep, both of their scores dropped to 0. Clive thought that it would probably take their house exploding to wake them up. Once they were asleep, he chose to save his SF for the attack period instead of fruitlessly wasting them.

He spent the rest of the night staring at them, strategizing on his possible actions during the next attack period. *If they do this every night, I'm not going to be able to kill them...ever.* If he could worry, he would've been tearing at his figurative hair; fortunately, that was part of the emotions he didn't have access to. Patience, on the other hand, he did have.

After an unsuccessful night, he studied the results of his second attack period when the guide-assist informed him of it.

Attack Period #2

Results

SF Used: 150/450

FEAR Generated (Andrea): 1(LCS) + 1(LCS) + 1(LCS) = 3

FEAR Generated (Mark): 1(LCS) + 1(LCS) = 2

Total FEAR Generated: 5

Lifetime FEAR: 42/100

SF Earned (Andrea): 10(LCS) + 10(LCS) + 10(LCS) = 30

SF Earned (Mark): 10(LCS) + 10(LCS) = 20

Total SF Earned for next attack period: 50

He did note that even though his attacks were wildly unsuccessful, he did generate a little FEAR – even if it was momentary. His last two cold spots had been positioned so that both of his targets passed through them, netting him additional FEAR and SF; he earned enough SF that, with the normal recharge rate, he would be back to where he started. It wasn't necessarily progress, but it wasn't a net loss.

They ended up sleeping late, waking up groaning and complaining about the pounding in their heads around noon later that day. This was his first opportunity to really see them during the day – and it wasn't much different than seeing them at night. They ate breakfast, drank some coffee, and left to go get the husband's car; apparently, they had taken a cab last night when they were both too drunk to drive.

All in all, the day for Clive was like the others he had experienced – the homeowners didn't come back until almost 6pm, laden down with shopping bags they had picked up while they were out. Some of it was groceries, while others appeared to be clothing; peeking inside the bags when they were set down, his assumptions were confirmed when he saw shoes, a dress, and some shirts.

After getting home, they cooked a quick dinner and lounged on the couch watching TV. Soon enough, they argued about what movie to watch and Clive started to really pay attention, hoping they would choose another fear-inducing horror movie.

"No, I'm not watching another slasher flick, just for you to fall asleep when something freaks me out again. Pick something else."

"How about that new Sergeant Massacre 5 movie – I heard he kills like...50 people with a pencil or something," the man suggested, his distracted tone of voice inexpertly hiding his enthusiasm for the action movie.

"Nah – that will put *me* to sleep. How about Violet Tenderness, I've been wanting to watch it because it's got some of my favorite actresses in it."

The man rolled his eyes. "If it would make you happy, we can watch – but I can't guarantee I'll stay awake."

With deliberate thought, the wife slowly offered another suggestion, as if she was dredging it up from the depths of her brain, "How about Grandparent Academy Unveiled 4: It Depends? The trailer looked hilarious and I'm sure you'll love the stunts those jackasses love to pull."

Pretending to think about it, the husband "reluctantly" agreed, "I guess that would work; and hey, we both might actually stay awake for this one." Putting his words into action, he selected it from the options on their TV; after they rented the movie, they expected to settle down for a comfortable night of funny-movie watching.

Not if Clive had anything to do with it.

* * *

Andrea laughed at the teenager dressed up in old-person makeup and clothes, literally snorting as she watched him pretend to fall down some stairs in front of a crowd of witnesses. When he landed with his crotch slamming against a cement post, she almost peed her pants. I should've gone before the movie, but I was too lazy to get up.

There was still at least half an hour before the movie was done, and she thought they might actually be able to get in another one tonight since it was only about 8:15. They didn't work in the morning; they could stay up as long as they wanted to.

"Hey, pause it for a couple of minutes – I gotta go use the bathroom. Be right back!" So saying, she threw the blanket off her and jumped up, vaulting herself over the back of the couch with an ungraceful hop, before racing upstairs. Sometimes she wished they had a bathroom downstairs, but that would require a whole lot more space than they had – or a bigger house. With the market what it was at the moment, however, that wasn't going to be anytime soon.

She reached the bathroom just in time; another few seconds and she would've made a mess. As she sat there, granting herself some much-needed relief, she noticed how quiet the house was. With the movie paused, the bathroom door closed, and with the *weather outside cool enough that they didn't need to run their two window AC units, the house was almost deathly silent. The only thing she heard was herself, and when she had finished her business, her breath sounded loud to her ears.*

Suddenly, she started to shiver as a wave of chilly air condensed around her face and neck, almost as if she opened the freezer and stuck her head in. She stared around in confusion, seeing the foggy clouds of her breath obscuring her vision as she searched the far wall, looking for an open window. Did the temperature drop outside when I didn't know it?

She started to panic when she remembered that their bathroom didn't have a window. Why, why, why did I come up here alone?

She was frozen to her porcelain throne, the temperature drop doing more than just keeping her stationary. What's the use? Nothing we do to make this house our own is working. We can't even keep air from getting in from the outside, and now there's areas where everything is freezing. We should just move...but, no, that's stupid, Andrea – plus, that would take a lot of work. I guess...we should just stay here and live with all this shit.

She didn't know where these thoughts were coming from; she wasn't normally so down on herself – and she loved this house. Granted, it wasn't her dream home, but it was better than being homeless...right? It had problems, just like every other house did...at least she thought they did.

The cold was fading, her breath returning to normal – although her negative thoughts still remained. Somehow breaking out of the lethargy plaguing her, she started to finish up so that she could get back to the movie. Hopefully that will break me out of this strange funk. I wonder how long I've been up here? In the middle of pulling up her comfy lounge pants, she froze again – though this time it wasn't because it was cold.

It started with her arms, a tingling sensation traveling from her wrist to her shoulder, causing her near-invisible arm hair to raise straight up in the air. She could feel it travel down her back, gliding down her legs until the small hair follicles that she hadn't shaved in a week stood at attention. As the rest of her body felt like she had stuck her finger in a light socket, it almost became painful as her scalp felt like someone was stabbing little pinpricks on her head, as the ponytail-constrained hair was prevented from sticking straight out.

Her chest began to hurt as she realized that she had stopped breathing, and with an effort of will she forced herself to take a breath. She inhaled a huge lungful of air and she wanted to scream; unfortunately, any hope of that was killed when she kept standing there, paralyzed with fear.

Which was broken a few seconds later as she heard a yell from downstairs, her husband's angry exclamation breaking whatever spell held her trapped in place. She grabbed the handle of the door, flung it open, and practically jumped down the last six steps leading to the living room, her fear lingering with her but abating as she had something else to focus on.

Chapter 11

Clive was relishing the rush of emotion that hit him, a tidal wave of fear that was as enjoyable as it was short-lived. When he was experiencing the woman's awesome fright, all he could think about was wanting more, the craving for delicious emotions drowning out anything else. The flood of emotion that crashed into him after he placed the cold spot on her face and chest was so great that it took more than a minute for him to pay attention enough to enact the next phase of his plan.

While there was no visible indication that his Depressive Miasma was working, the increase (and change) in the emotions he was feeling was like a jolt to his system. Doubling, or even tripling – possibly more, he was so lost in ecstatic emotions that he was unable to correctly determine the amount – the powerful combination of depression and fear, he was almost blinded by the sheer euphoric feelings he experienced.

Fortunately, he came to as his Localized Cold Spot was ending, also freeing up the woman from her shivering statue impression. He saw her visibly shake off her fright a little, standing up and getting ready to head back downstairs. But he wasn't done yet.

He thought the emotions coming from her couldn't get any stronger, but when he activated his Piloerection Reflex attack, it started to ramp up until it was almost painful – which was pleasurable in and of itself. This time, however, it didn't hit him all at once; the gradual increase of fear as he visibly watched the hair stand up on her arm, followed by the hair on the back of her neck, meant that he was able to maintain his concentration while still soaking in all of the pleasure.

Which noticeably lessened when he heard a shout from the husband downstairs, causing the paralyzed state of fear the wife was experiencing to shatter. He followed along, strangely feeling curiosity at what was going on as he rode the diminishing waves of emotions coming from the woman. He had to hurry as she ran, mentally transporting himself to the first floor as she skipped the bottom half of the staircase, landing unhurt in a crouch before racing toward the kitchen.

Her dog biscuit-cookies.

Clive had been preoccupied with the wife, so he had no idea what was happening downstairs. Apparently – from what he could make out from the scene – the husband got bored waiting for his wife to finish in the restroom and snuck into the kitchen to get a secret cookie treat. When he found out that they didn't quite taste the same – in fact, they probably tasted terrible – he yelled out in surprise and anger.

By the time his wife arrived, however, he was already starting to see the humor in the situation, having discovered that the rest of the snack-cake boxes were empty. She ran in, breathing heavily and looking around with wild eyes.

"What? What is it? What's wrong?"

Chuckling at her while shaking his head, he smiled as he said, "Nice job, you sneaky girl. How long have you known I've been sneaking your cookies? You got me good, I've got to give you that."

She walked up to him and smacked him on the arm, hard enough to leave a mark. "Bastard! I thought you were hurt or something – don't do that again!"

He rubbed his arm at the pain, with only a little bit of exaggeration (since her smack *did* look like it hurt). "Sorry, baby; you were gone so long that I thought I had some time to get something to eat. What took you so long, by the way."

Clive knew why, but for some reason incomprehensible to him, she didn't mention his attacks. "Uh...well, you know...something didn't agree with me from last night's dinner, I guess. Must've been the shrimp, or maybe that coupled with a *little* bit too much to drink."

"Oh, ok – are you feeling better now, at least?"

"...Yes?"

Although that part of her statement wasn't an obvious lie like her minor case of food poisoning, she was only partially correct.

Andrea Stone

FEAR Level: 34

Resistance to FEAR attacks: 5

Weaknesses: Depression

Perception: 8/10

Fatigue: 20%

When she first went upstairs, her FEAR Level had been at a steady 3; as she sat alone in the silent bathroom, however, it slowly climbed until it hit 7 – before dropping back down to 6 almost instantly. Clive hadn't waited to see if it would climb back up, so he took advantage of her heightened FEAR and struck. By the end of his assault, she had peaked at 66 – so her current 34 was...better, at least for her.

The jump in her FEAR Level was not what he was expecting, however. He wasn't going to complain, though; but he did intend to find out why it happened in the first place. As the emotions drained out of him even faster than the woman's FEAR, he took a closer look at the biggest change he had seen so far in the information floating around her.

Weakness: Depression
Normally, depressive states can double the effectiveness of most FEAR-based attacks, depending on current FEAR Levels and Resistance. Having a weakness in depression (usually as a result of already having depressive tendencies), however, can negate

resistances and <u>double</u> the previously doubled effectiveness of the depressive state.

Ah, that's what happened. Some quick math in his head confirmed that this was indeed what caused her FEAR Level to jump up so high. If her husband hadn't called out, Clive would've tried something else to push it even higher – though he didn't have many more SF to spend: just 100.

He decided to save it for now; since neither of them were in the bathroom, any attacks he used on them wouldn't be as effective, though he was tempted to throw another Errant Breeze at the still-frightened woman whenever she was alone again. Unfortunately, she clung to her husband for the rest of the night, as if afraid to be out of his sight.

The only time they were separated was later that night when they were getting ready for bed; even then, she stayed near the bathroom door while he was in there, chatting away while he did his business. The Depressive Miasma was still ongoing, but it did very little to the man; either his Resistance was too high, or he was in and out so fast it didn't have time to visibly work on him.

Clive expected to get another chance when she went in herself, but she told her husband that she was fine and that she didn't need to use it. He didn't say anything about it, apparently used to her little quirks, and they headed to bed.

By that time, the wife's Fatigue and Perception were at the point that anything he did either wouldn't be noticed, or just plain ignored. Her exhaustion was obviously a sign of what he did to her earlier, as the husband didn't show the same sort of increased Fatigue. He filed away that little tidbit of information; it might come in handy sometime.

The rest of the attack period passed in relative silence and uneventfulness. He was ready in case the woman woke up at any point with an Errant Breeze, but she stayed asleep all through the night – the same with the man. Her FEAR Level dropped drastically over the next few hours until it bottomed out at 10; there were a few spikes in it as he hovered over their prone forms, but he figured they were just a reaction to whatever she was dreaming at the time.

At 4am, the numbers floating around their bodies faded out and his attack period was over. He thought it was interesting how her FEAR Level hadn't dropped below 10; if it stayed that way through the day and continued through the beginning of his next attack period, it would make it much easier to affect her with his FEAR-based attacks.

Attack Period #3

Results

SF Used: 350/450

FEAR Generated (Andrea): 5(LCS)*4(DM) + 10(PR)*4(DM) = 60

FEAR Generated (Mark): 0

Total FEAR Generated: 60

Lifetime FEAR: 102/100

SF Earned (Andrea): 200(LCS) + 400(PR) = 600

SF Earned (Mark): 0

Total SF Earned for next attack period: 600

Congratulations!

Your Spiritual Level has increased to 2!

Max and Nightly SF Recharge has increased!

New FEAR-based attack available!

Clive wasn't exactly sure what all that meant, so he thought about his Spirit Core Status to see what had changed.

Spirit Core Status – Transformed Soul of Clive Logan

Spiritual Level: 2

Lifetime FEAR Generated: 102/225

Spiritual Force (Current): 600/1000

Spiritual Force (Nightly Recharge): 150

His status informed him that he now had a larger SF pool to work with, which meant he could string many more attacks together. It also meant that if he messed up during the night, it would take that much longer for it to fully recharge. He would have to play it smart to make sure he kept the momentum of this last, successful night.

And at some point, he was going to have to start wearing the husband down.

Chapter 12

It was Sunday, and Clive figured that they would sleep in as late as the day before. He knew that a lot of people worked Monday through Friday, having the weekends off; that was never him, because he used to work every day from home, not having any need for time off. So it was contrary to his expectations when he found out he was wrong. They didn't get up as early as they did when they had gone to work the first morning, but they were still up shortly after sunrise.

The husband got up first and hit the shower, quickly finishing in the bathroom before the wife had even gotten out of bed. Clive watched him dress in a clean white button-up shirt and tie, with a pressed pair of black slacks and shiny Oxford shoes – all while the woman finally got out of bed and dragged herself to the bathroom.

As soon as she closed the door behind her, she froze in place with a strange look on her face. She looked wildly around for a moment as if she was searching for something; when nothing jumped out at her, she visibly relaxed and shook her head vigorously, apparently trying to shake something off. Heaving a heavy sigh, she undressed out of her nightclothes and took a quick shower, retreating to the bedroom to get dressed.

While she put on in a floral-printed shift dress with a complementing pair of short pumps, the husband had been downstairs watching TV, doing his best but barely succeeding in avoiding creating wrinkles in his outfit.

"Let's go, honey! We'll be late for the service if you take too much longer! And I want to pick up a little something before we get there – I'm starving. Dog biscuits don't really fill me as much as they used to!" he yelled up the stairs, the smile on his face translating through his voice.

"Don't worry, we'll be fine. I just need to put on my face and I'll be ready to go." So saying, she went to the bathroom again – leaving the door open – and quickly and expertly applied her makeup in the small makeup mirror she had attached to the wall. Five minutes later, she was done, and they took off for whatever service they had to get to.

Silence reigned in the house, as Clive was once again left alone to his own devices for the day. He thought about how well the night before went with his progress toward building up his Spiritual Level; from what he was told – and somehow understood instinctively – he knew he needed to be much stronger to be able to kill them. With the attacks he currently possessed, there wasn't anything that could even harm them, let alone kill them.

With those attacks in mind, he remembered that he received another attack when he leveled up:

2. Peripheral Anxiety (PA):

Description: *Causes the target to experience seeing indecipherable objects out of the corner of their eyes, prompting a heightened sense of stress*

Magnitude: *Single target*

Duration: *Single use*

SF Cost: *300*

Target FEAR Requirement: *Level 15*

Max Generated FEAR: *30*

Unmodified Reward Upon Successful Attack: *300 SF*

The more powerful attack required a higher FEAR Level than the others (and had a higher SF cost), but the benefits of a successful attack would be impressive. If he was able to successfully combine it with a Depressive Miasma, he could potentially boost the woman's FEAR to over 100. With the increases in the requirements he had seen in the attacks so far, he figured that an attack that could harm or kill someone would carry a hefty price tag.

He attempted to make plans for when they got back, but other than some general ideas regarding combinations of attacks, he couldn't really do much. It all depended on what was happening at the time; he would have to adapt to changing circumstances. All he knew was that he had to start working on catching both of them in his attacks, thereby increasing their FEAR at the same time. And boosting his own level, as well.

Now that he could see the potential benefits and successfulness of his nightly assaults, Clive reasoned that it would only be a matter of time before he could experience the euphoric feelings their deaths would give him.

*   *   *

Andrea smiled at her husband, watching him carry the bulk of their purchases from the car to the front door. After church, they had spent the rest of the day doing one of her favorite things in the world: thrift shopping. There were a couple of large thrift shops nearby, but there was also an antique mall about a half-hour away that they rarely visited; however, every time she went, she inevitably found some sort of steal she couldn't pass up.

They didn't have a lot of expendable income, so the $100 they spent during their trip today blew most of what was left over from their date night on Friday, as well as paying for the handyman to fix cracks on the outside of the house. That was ok, though, since her shopping itch had been scratched for a while. They still had plenty in the budget for grocery shopping, so they weren't hurting too bad as far as normal expenses; it just meant that they had to watch what they bought otherwise.

She loved how much Mark enjoyed shopping with her too — at least, she thought he did. Either he was a better actor than she pegged him for, or he generally liked spending all day with her looking at old stuff; nonetheless, she appreciated how he didn't complain like most of the other husbands she saw standing around looking bored and wishing they were home watching the football game. Mark enjoyed watching sports but wasn't a fanatic about it: if an important game was on and they were home, he would watch. Otherwise, it was the same as any other program.

The...incident...last night had almost completely faded from her mind while they were out shopping. However, as they approached the front entrance of their house, everything came crashing back. She missed a step and nearly fell, but she caught herself on the side railing, before getting ahold of herself and shaking off the lingering effects of the memory.

"Are you ok, honey?"

"Yes, I'm fine – just forgot how to climb steps for a minute, apparently." She laughed off her misstep, attempting to dispel the gloomy thoughts that were assailing her as she brought out her keys and opened the front door.

A half-hour later, all of their purchases had been put away, including a few that needed to go into their basement storage area until she could get to them. She had plans on turning the old, broken, antique-but-gorgeous lamp she bought into a centerpiece with some DIY work. She had always loved crafting, but there never seemed to be any time for it. I'll get to it one day...along with all the rest of my projects.

Since it was after 7pm by the time they got home, they fixed themselves some quick microwavable meals from the freezer – healthy ones, at least. It was hard staying on track with their diets; though, with the elimination of her secret stash, she thought there might be some better visible results within the next couple of weeks. Mark always had an easier time than she did losing weight, but she was hopeful that by not cheating with her favorite snack-cakes that she might match him this time.

By the time 8pm rolled around, they were curled up as usual on the couch watching nothing in particular. They were both dressed in their comfy clothes, and Andrea had put her hair up in a bun on top of her head, tired of messing with the stray strands falling in her face all day. They were both tired after the long day of shopping and didn't feel like a movie, so they figured they would watch the news and hit the sack. She really needed to pee, but there was no way she was going upstairs by herself again if she could help it. I don't want to take the chance that something will happen like it did last night—

She was snuggled up against Mark, nestled underneath his arm with a blanket covering both of them; despite the warmth the *closeness of their bodies generated, she suddenly felt a blast of frigid air between their hips. It was so unexpected that she reached down with her hand to see if a piece of ice had fallen out of her glass of water, but it was dry – and freezing.*

Mark had noticed it as well and reached down between them, grasping her hands as she felt around the cold spot. "What the hell? Did you drop some ice down there?"

Andrea was all set to answer with a "no", confusion and not a little worry crowding her mind, when she felt a gentle brush of air against the back of her neck; it wasn't cold like the area beneath the blanket, but it nevertheless caused the hair along her neckline to shoot straight up in the air. She froze for a moment, too shocked at the suddenness of it to do anything, before she screamed at the top of her lungs.

Throwing off the blanket, she jumped up and rushed over to the opposite side of the room, wanting to get as far away from the couch as possible – but not being brave enough to want to lose sight of her husband. Speaking of Mark, he was startled at her reaction; he sat there for a moment in shock before hopping off the couch himself and grabbing her in a tight embrace, while she hysterically sobbed into his shoulder.

"Shhhh…it's ok, it's ok, everything is fine…now, what happened? You scared me half to death there, did you know that. I never knew you could scream that loud – even when we're, you know…." His attempt at humor fell on deaf ears, as she was just trying to concentrate on not screaming again.

In her head, she kept replaying the brush of air against her neck, trying to come up with a rational explanation – but finding nothing. The house should be sealed up tight as a drum against any drafts coming from out—

The hair on the back of her neck had been falling as Mark calmed her down, rubbing her back in soothing motions and kissing the top of her head; she felt her tears finally starting to dry up, when every hair on her body felt like they wanted to pluck themselves out of her skin and fly away. She was too scared to scream again, her breath and voice frozen in her lungs – but she was aware enough to feel her husband's body stiffen around her.

Oh my god, this is just like last night! He feels it too – it wasn't just my imagination! *After the incident in the bathroom, she had thought that it was her body and mind playing tricks on her, but now that Mark felt it too – she felt a little better somehow.*

They must have stood there for half a minute, stiff as statues as their skin seemed to want to crawl away from them; she felt her chest start to burn as the breath she was holding was stuck inside without hope of release. She was frantically trying to force herself to breathe – and then hopefully to move – when Mark screamed like he had just been knifed in the back.

*It made her jump, raising her own fright, and she started to breathe again as he released her in one quick move and ran toward the kitchen, his eyes wild. She turned to follow him – there's no way I'm staying here by myself – and took a few steps when she saw him apparently run through something, which elicited **another** scream (though this one was much higher-pitched). He appeared to be desperately trying to get something off his face, pulling invisible strands of...nothing...as he almost drunkenly stumbled the rest of the distance toward the kitchen.*

Not wanting to run into whatever he had, she took another route to the kitchen, only to see Mark visibly trying to get ahold of himself: holding his hand to his chest, taking deep breaths, and closing his eyes. She rushed up to him, something in her nature wanting to calm him down despite being freaked the fuck out herself.

She grabbed him by the waist, burying her face in his chest, startling him momentarily before he held her in return. The beating of his heart was so quick and powerful she could feel it through their intimate contact; but it couldn't compete with her own that felt like it would burst out of her ribcage any moment.

They stood there in each other's arms for more than an hour, not saying a word...and braced for any more occurrences of frightening activity.

Chapter 13

The stronger emotions of fear lingered with Clive for longer this time, and he reveled in the exquisite feelings he…earned…from his work. With every successful use of his FEAR-based attacks, the strength of the emotional feedback increased as his victim's FEAR Level was raised. *This was even better than last night; if I can keep this up, I'll be killing them in no time.*

He had waited until he had seen an unexpected spike in the wife's FEAR, activating Depressive Miasma (which covered the entire room, catching the husband as well) once it was high enough. Though it had started at the beginning of his attack period at a steady 5, something must have happened to shoot it up to 10; by the time he reacted with the depressive field, however, it had dropped back down to 8. Before it could drop any lower, he visualized a Localized Cold Spot underneath their blankets, targeting the woman but intersecting with the man as well.

The fear they elicited wasn't that strong at first (especially from the man, whose Resistance was so high), but it was enough to distract him temporarily with the awesome feelings he received. It was harder, and yet easier, to maintain his concentration; knowing what was coming made him compartmentalize his mind: one section was entirely focused on the next attack, while the other one was fully experiencing their emotional feedback. At times, over the next few minutes at least, the feelings he absorbed were so powerful it blocked out everything else. Fortunately, he was able to maintain enough attention to react to their actions.

Since it was the most accessible part of her skin exposed to the air around the wife (other than her face, which he had already tried before with less-than-great results), a small Errant Breeze to the back of her neck worked even better than he was planning. As an additional benefit, her reaction to his attack also caused a jolt of fear to course through the husband – and that was sweeter than all the rest for some reason. Since he hadn't planned on his fright, it was almost like a bonus. *What was that saying, "There's nothing better than free?"*

With a liberal use of his Piloerection Reflex that encompassed them both while they were embracing away from the couch, followed up with another Errant Breeze to the back of **his** neck, the waves of fear flowing from his victims threatened to drown him in euphoric ecstasy. He was barely able to coherently form enough thought to throw a Spectral Cobweb in the husband's way during his flight toward the kitchen. With that last attack, he lost himself swimming in the lake-full of emotions that drifted toward him in a seemingly unending assault.

Part of his mind had automatically kept an eye on them while he was experiencing their fear, so by the time their FEAR Levels had dropped back down to just slightly elevated – 30 down from 110 for the woman, and 40 down from 140 for the man – Clive was able to gather his wits enough to see where they ended up.

They were in the kitchen, standing there holding each other and not speaking. A glance at the digital clock on the microwave told him that they must've been standing there for nearly an hour based on the time, and the fact that his attacks all took place within about six minutes. He was completely tapped out of Spiritual Force, so there wasn't anything left for him to do other than watch and listen to what happened next.

Eventually, the wife unwrapped herself from around her husband and gave a big sigh, extricating herself from his own embrace and leaning against the counter in exhaustion. He followed suit and leaned against the counter as well, arms crossed, and sight focused distractedly on the floor.

Her voice was raw when she finally spoke, "Something...like that happened to me last night, in the bathroom upstairs. I was afraid to tell you because I thought it was my imagination."

Her husband continued to stare at the floor, giving no indication that he even heard her. It was only when he finally responded a couple of minutes later that it was obvious that he did, indeed, hear her, "Well, it wasn't your imagination – I felt it too. I don't know what's going on in this house, but I don't like it. I haven't been that frightened before, and I don't know how to explain it."

They were silent again for a few more minutes, before the man stood up straight and grabbed her hands gently, prompting her to look into his eyes for the first time since everything happened that night. "I know we're not the most devout of Catholics, but I think we need some...priestly help."

"There's no way I'm going into our church spouting tales of our house being haunted – some of the others still look at us with disgust for missing two Sundays in a row last year. Especially Beverly Johnson; I think I'm finally getting her to forgive me for not bringing anything to the bake sale a couple of months ago. I don't want to be the crazy neighbor – we have a hard-enough time getting by without everyone thinking we're nuts."

He had nothing to say to that, apparently, but Clive could see him considering what she said. Finally, after opening and closing his mouth a couple of times without anything coming out, he seemed to come to a solution. "Ok, then let's do what we can by ourselves. I don't know if you remember this or not, but it was ingrained in me by my mother just as much as Our Father. It's a prayer for the protection against evil – just repeat after me."

They recited the prayer multiple times while holding hands, staring at each other's eyes. The conviction in their voices strengthened each time they repeated it.

Living Lord,

I am yours.

I wear the helmet of salvation and hope.

I carry the shield of faith and—

Clive didn't listen to the rest of it, as his guide-assist had popped up.

Prayers, religious symbols, and any other spiritual/religious artifacts have no impact on the effectiveness of a Spirit Core. However, the belief of those using these various defenses will benefit from them in the form of a temporary reduction in FEAR Levels and an increased FEAR Resistance. Just like the belief in their own fear enhances the effectiveness in the attacks you perform, belief in their protection against those same fears can be just as powerful – up to a point.

Warning: the restriction regarding harm against the Spirit Core is eliminated if an ordained/proclaimed direct religious/spiritual representative is the one utilizing them.

When they were finished, he looked at the information still floating around them to see if what his guide told him was correct.

Mark Stone

FEAR Level: 40 - (32 Temporary Reduction) = 8

Resistance to FEAR attacks: 15 + (20 Temporary Boost) = 35

Weaknesses: Spiders

Perception: 6/10

Fatigue: 40%

Andrea Stone

FEAR Level: 30 - (24 Temporary Reduction) = 6

Resistance to FEAR attacks: 5 + (20 Temporary Boost) = 25

Weaknesses: Depression

Perception: 6/10

Fatigue: 60%

It was interesting to see that the reductions and boosts were only temporary, though he thought it might cause a problem in the future if they constantly prayed throughout the night. He figured it might hamper his future assaults; their increased resistances were a major obstacle that would be hard to overcome. *Well, I'll handle that if it comes to pass.*

Clive also saw that whatever "system" he was operating under had identified "Spiders" as a weakness for the husband, which helped to explain the high-pitched scream that came out of his mouth when he ran into his Spectral Cobwebs. Although it was more expensive than even the Depressive Miasma that the wife was weak to, it might be worth using again in the future.

The only thing that gave him pause was the warning about religious representatives. He assumed that this meant that if a priest (or any other equivalent clergy) came into the house and prayed or did...something...religious-like, it would negatively affect him somehow. He didn't really know too much about religion, as he never had any belief in anything (as having emotion is a foundation of belief). Therefore, he hadn't ever studied it other than in very general terms while in school. As his parents weren't religious in any way (as far as he remembered), he was never brought up with anything other than the knowledge of *what* it was; but he never understood the *why* of it – the basis of it was beyond his comprehension.

As a result, his incomprehension of religion led him to dismiss the threat of possible retaliation. He didn't understand it, so why factor it into his plans at all? If it came up at any point in the future, he would deal with it then.

After their prayers – and the obvious reduction in their FEAR Levels – the married couple was calmer and, as a result, exhausted. After quickly shutting off the TV (which had been on the entire time) in the living room, they headed upstairs with an unspoken agreement between them, which caused them to stick together for the rest of their night. Clive watched as they even went into the bathroom together to get ready for bed, all modesty in using the bathroom in front of their partner forgotten in their need for visual reassurance.

They lay in bed later, the wife laying her head on his chest as they settled in for sleep. "We'll get through this, honey. As long as we're together in our belief in God, nothing can harm us. Just remember that, my love."

She tilted her head up at him, smiling at his words for the first time that night. "I love you, too – thank you for helping me calm down earlier. And thank God for his safety and protection against whatever is happening here," she said, before crossing herself underneath the covers. The husband followed suit, before reciting another prayer; she followed along, a half-step behind as if she was trying to remember the words of the almost-forgotten verses.

They fell asleep a couple of minutes later, Clive watching as their floating numbers got another small boost from the prayer, although nothing as dramatic as the one before. He watched them for the rest of the night (or at least until 4am when the attack period finished) and saw that the temporary reduction/boosts were slowly creeping back to their former states.

It wasn't a dramatic change by the time the numbers went away, but it was a good sign that their defensive measures weren't permanent. If they did nothing else, they would be back to normal by the time the next attack period came.

Now he just needed to ensure they had no reason to invoke their protections.

Chapter 14

Attack Period #4

<u>Results</u>

SF Used: 700/700

FEAR Generated (Andrea): 5(LCS)*4(DM) + 4(EB)*4(DM) + 10(PR)*4(DM) + 26(CI) = 102

FEAR Generated (Mark): 1(LCS)*2(DM) + 12(CI) + 6(PR)*2(DM) + 6(EB)*2(DM) + 25(SC)*4(DM+Weakness) = 138

Total Bonus Correlated Incidentals: 26(Andrea) + 12(Mark) = 38

Total FEAR Generated: 278

Lifetime FEAR: 380/225

SF Earned (Andrea): 200(LCS) + 160(EB) + 400(PR) = 760

SF Earned (Mark): 20(LCS) + 120(PR) + 120(EB) + 1000(SC) = 1260

Total SF Earned for next attack period: 2020

Congratulations!

Your Spiritual Level has increased to 3!

Your Spiritual Level has increased to 4!

Max and Nightly SF Recharge has increased! (X2)

New FEAR-based attack available! (X2)

He saw something new on his results: Correlated Incidentals. It apparently counted twice in the FEAR he generated, but he had no idea what it was – which was important, because otherwise he wouldn't know how to replicate it.

Correlated Incidentals: The strong emotions generated in another person who witnesses an attack but is not the intended target/or are the unintended results related to an attack. Correlated Incidentals ignore resistances and are counted twice during the end of attack results, as they are made of purer, more-concentrated fear when compared to regular FEAR-based attacks. Does not count toward Spiritual Force gains.

That didn't explain much, but Clive reasoned that it was a result of his victims' reactions to seeing their partner get scared by his attacks. So, when the wife screamed after he blew some air on her neck, the husband must've been frightened at the same time. The same had to have happened in the reverse when the man screamed – twice. It appeared to be a way to boost FEAR Levels while getting around Resistances, which would most likely be important as his victims continued to fight back.

That was all well and good; however, he had no idea how to duplicate his successes with it. He thought he figured out *why* they occurred, but he didn't *understand* why they happened. *Why would seeing someone else afraid make you afraid yourself? Doesn't make any sense.* From what he could decipher,

Correlated Incidentals were more of an accident than anything else.

Since it was now Monday, his victims had to get up early to go to work. They both dragged themselves out of bed, dark circles under their eyes as if they hadn't slept well. He did watch them toss and turn all night, though he saw very little change in their numbers (for as long as they were present). His attacks must've affected them even more than what was obvious.

Nothing much occurred in the morning, other than them not speaking more than a few sentences to each other. He didn't think it was for any particular reason; they just appeared so tired that they didn't have the energy for a lengthy conversation. Coffee in the morning perked them up a bit, but by the time they left they still appeared to have woken up a couple minutes before.

With nothing else to do while they were gone again, he pulled up his new Core Status and the new attacks he received.

Spirit Core Status – Transformed Soul of Clive Logan
Spiritual Level: 4
Lifetime FEAR Generated: 380/550
Spiritual Force (Current): 2000/2000
Spiritual Force (Nightly Recharge): 250

3. Spectral Touch (SpTo):
Description: *Ignoring all clothing or other physical defenses, cause the target to feel an invisible touch on any chosen part of their body; does*

no physical harm, though a slight pressure can be felt by the target; can be moved to different parts of the body if there is sufficient duration available

Magnitude: *Single target, no larger than the size of an adult hand, though it can be reduced down in size depending upon need*

Duration: *Variable – 1 second to 1 minute, depending upon SF spent*

SF Cost: *Variable – 100 to 985, depending upon duration desired (100 for the first second, 15 for each additional second)*

Target FEAR Requirement: *Level 18*

Max Generated FEAR: *100*

Unmodified Reward Upon Successful Attack: *100 SF*

4. Auditory Hallucination – Footsteps (AHF):

Description: *Causes all targets within range to hear the sounds of heavy footsteps coming from a specified direction*

Magnitude: *1 entire room inside your Area of Influence*

Duration: *Variable – 1 to 12 footsteps, depending upon SF spent*

SF Cost: *Variable – 150 to 1250, depending upon footsteps desired (150 for the first footstep, 100 for each additional)*

Target FEAR Requirement: *Level 20*

Max Generated FEAR: *125*

Unmodified Reward Upon Successful Attack: *150 SF*

Clive noticed that his Spiritual Force was maxed out, and the excess he earned last night had disappeared. In addition, since he was already full, the recharge wouldn't do anything for him; he knew he had to watch that in the future, so that he wouldn't waste potential resources. All in all, though, he had achieved a lot: not only had he increased his Spiritual Level twice, he had gotten two new attacks that would add much-needed variety to his repertoire.

He still remembered the lesson he learned from the first night: diminishing returns from repeated uses of a single attack. Although he used a few different attacks last night, he figured that if he just did the same thing the next night, then he wouldn't get as positive of a result. A change of his strategies and mixing things up a little bit would be beneficial in the long run.

He spent the rest of the day looking over the house, devising different ways to take advantage of each room and trying to calculate how likely his attacks would be successful. He stopped after a few hours of this, as anything he planned for wouldn't necessarily work; depending upon what the husband and wife chose to do, things might not line up exactly the way he thought they should.

If he were organizing things to attack himself, for instance, he knew exactly where he would be and what he would do every night – and could plan accordingly. With his target's varied days and nights, however, he couldn't accurately predict what was going to happen. With that in mind, he switched to combining his attacks together in new and what he thought might be effective combinations. Of course, he had no idea how they would ultimately react to them: he was guessing most of the time.

Oh well, time to guess some more.

Chapter 15

Alert!

(1) Mortal approaching your Area of Influence!

Location: Front External Door

Automatically transfer to alert location? Yes/No

He absently selected **NO**, as he did every time that he saw the alert. It was becoming a regular occurrence, so much so that he barely even paid attention to it anymore. He supposed that was why the repetitive use of his attacks had diminishing returns; the more you saw something, the more...accustomed...you became to it. Anyway, it wasn't causing any harm to have the alerts, so he didn't think to do anything about it.

The wife was home first as usual, though this time she arrived with a large, old, beaten-up box. She brought it to the kitchen and left it there while she put the rest of her things down – though she didn't head upstairs to change like he would have expected she would've.

Since it was closed, he couldn't see what was in it from the outside; when he floated inside, he could see that it was full of aged wooden crucifixes that varied with the amount of carved detail on them. They came in multiple colors – though the most prevalent was white – and were accompanied by a few small medals attached to chains along the bottom of the box.

He pulled out just in time to see the woman come back and open the flaps, pulling out one after another and lining them up along the counter. He had seen one already in the house in their bedroom, but as it hadn't done anything before, he wasn't sure what she was doing with her new acquisitions.

Prayers, religious symbols, and any other spiritual/religious artifacts have no impact on the effectiveness of a Spirit Core. However, the belief of those using these various defenses...

He quickly dismissed the information his guide-assist provided him, since it was the same as it had told him before. He still wasn't sure what a little wooden carving could do to defend against his assault later that night.

She pulled out a small box of nails and a tack hammer from a drawer full of random supplies in the kitchen. Going around the inside of the house, she placed a crucifix on each wall, until every room – including the kitchen and bathroom – had one of the wooden religious implements visible. He flew up to and through each one, seeing if they would have any negative effect on him, but he experienced nothing out of the ordinary.

Oh well, if she wants to waste her time tacking these things up all over, it doesn't matter to me.

By the time her husband got home, the entire home was fully "protected". Well, all except the basement – which she made him do as soon as he was through the door. He took the cluster of crucifixes without complaint and headed down into the well-lit, organized basement and hammered some nails into a few cracks already present along the cement walls. That done, he joined his wife upstairs and they both got comfortable before making another healthy dinner of grilled chicken salad, full of leafy greens and light on the dressing.

Before they ate, they recited another prayer (which they hadn't done before, at least while he had been there). It seemed unfamiliar to them both – more the woman than the man – but they managed to finish it at the same time. Clive couldn't see what possible reason they could have to do it; it wasn't like they were currently being attacked by him.

"I like what you've done with the place. It feels more...secure. With our increased faith in God, his Will should destroy any malicious entities that are in this house. I wouldn't be surprised if we never experience anything ever again."

The wife looked a little less confident. "I hope so...we'll see."

"Don't be that way; believe that it will be true, and so it will be."

"You can preach all you want, but they say, 'the proof is in the pudding' – we'll see tonight."

The husband scoffed at her reticence. "You'll see –
everything will be fine."

He was right – in a way.

As soon as 8pm hit, they were already on the couch,
watching TV – though they were lying in a different spot (as if that
would make any difference in his attacks). Clive began
marshalling his plans for them tonight, when he was stopped after
he got a look at their floating numbers.

Mark Stone

FEAR Level: 30 - (29 Temporary Reduction) = 1

Resistance to FEAR attacks: 15 + (20 Temporary Boost) = 35

Weaknesses: Spiders

Perception: 4/10

Fatigue: 30%

Andrea Stone

FEAR Level: 20 - (18 Temporary Reduction) = 2

Resistance to FEAR attacks: 5 + (10 Temporary Boost) = 15

Weaknesses: Depression

Perception: 3/10

Fatigue: 40%

He wasn't sure why their reductions and boosts were
different, but he suspected it was because the woman didn't
seem as confident in her "belief" of their protective defenses.

Overall, it didn't matter why; what mattered was that their FEAR Levels were effectively too low and their Resistance too high to successfully attack them. There were things he could do, of course, at least based on the FEAR requirement; but he'd have to use them multiple times just to raise it enough for something to be effective.

Not the best use of his resources.

Instead of assaulting them right away, he watched their numbers and waited for an opportunity.

*   *   *

Maybe he's right – I haven't felt **anything** tonight, not even a random breath of air, *she thought.*

Andrea followed her husband upstairs, slightly encouraged by the lack of any type of strange sensations or cold spots, no feelings of being watched by some sort of invisible entity. In fact, it had been a relatively normal night: eat dinner, watch TV, go to bed. Not that there was anything wrong with that; she would rather have normal and boring over being scared half-to-death.

She got ready first, daring to use the bathroom by herself to test if the lack of an attack was only temporary. Five minutes of tense-but-quick teeth-brushing, toilet-using, and face cream-applying ended up…normal. She was still glad to be out of the bathroom when she was done, relinquishing use of it to Mark.

She changed into some soft cotton cutoff pajamas – which she custom-made by trimming the long pants down to a more-comfortable length. She loved the feel of them but couldn't stand to have her legs restricted while she slept. The result made it a little cooler during the night; however, that was why they had a heavy blanket. Mark slept in a pair of boxers, so it wasn't too hot for him either.

She crawled into bed, slightly shocked at the cool feel of the sheets against her skin. She checked all around in a quick frantic search, only relaxing when she didn't feel any specifically cold spots wherever she checked. The nights are definitely getting cooler – we may need to turn the furnace on soon. *She hated to be too hot when she slept, so she always waited until it was freezing in the house; she'd rather bundle up walking through the house than swelter in the heat the malfunctioning furnace gave off.* We should probably have it checked this year…well, when we get paid again.

She glanced at the crucifix hanging above the bed, the only one inside the house that had been there before she brought the others home. During her lunch hour, she visited the thrift store she frequented; she had seen whole collections of donated and

139

salvaged religious paraphernalia there every time she went but hadn't had a need of them before now. Luckily, today had been a yellow tag sale day, so she got them all half-price: all told, she only spent about $25 on the entire box. The two medals she found needed to be blessed again, but she was going to hold off on that part until it looked like they needed the extra protection.

As far as she could tell, it didn't look they were going to need it.

Mark finished up and came to bed, the thin carpet in their bedroom causing him to shiver as he hurried across the room before flinging himself inside the bedcovers. "Phew, that's cold too – you sure we can't turn on the heat yet?"

"Let's deal with it for a little bit longer; it's supposed to be warmer later this week. You know I don't like to run the furnace unless we're freezing."

"Yes, honey," he replied, in a fake-patronizing tone.

She didn't fake-hit him in the shoulder, however. "That's right – I'm in charge, and don't you forget it!" He laughed at her while he rubbed his shoulder and she joined along, her mood light and happy for the first time since she first felt a puff of air against her face a few days ago.

They lay down to sleep, a smile on her face as she was glad that everything had indeed worked out ok. If it all it took was a few prayers and some crucifixes on the walls to hold back whatever was doing all that stuff, it was worth every word and dollar she spent. She reached over and clicked the light off, closed her eyes, and was out before she knew it.

Chapter 16

Something was wrong. She jerked awake, heart beating super-quick in her chest as she opened her eyes. Trying to figure out what was happening with her blurry, sleepy eyes, she looked at the clock on the nightstand next to her. 2:13am. I must've had a bad dream or something; I hope I can get back to sleep because I need the rest. *She rolled over on her back, staring at the ceiling as she tried to will her eyes to close and fall back asleep.*

Why can't I sleep? I've never had this problem before. In fact, I normally have the opposite problem – I occasionally sleep too much. Look at Mark sleeping like a baby over there – he's rubbing it in my face. So what if we haven't had anything but drunken sex in the last month? That doesn't mean he doesn't love me anymore – right? Maybe he doesn't think I'm good enough for him anymore. Well, maybe I'm not; I haven't given him the kind of attention I used to when we were first married. But our relationship is still strong...maybe?

Depressive thoughts and questions swirled around in her brain for what felt like hours, though when she finally looked over at the clock, she saw that only about a half-hour had passed. She gave up thinking about trying to get to sleep, and, of course, that was when her body decided that it was ready to get some more rest. Her eyes started closing of their own accord, but before they could completely shut, she saw something out of the corner of her eye toward her closet.

*Andrea whipped her head around, eyes wide in fright as she looked toward the direction that she swore she saw some movement. It was indistinct; she didn't see a form so much as the barest hint of movement. Her heart was beating even faster than it was when she woke up, as she searched the entire room for whatever had caught her attention. She sat up in bed to get a better look, tracing her eyes along the floor looking for a mundane explanation like a mouse or even a rat – though she despised the filthy vermin. However, she would rather it be **something** instead of her overactive and stressed imagination.*

She didn't see anything, however – everything was quiet, and the moon from outside shining in and the nightlight they had out in the hallway reflected nothing through their open bedroom doorway. They used to close it every night, but then, inevitably, one of them would need to pee during the night and wake the other up when they opened the squeaky door; now, however, she wished they still kept it closed – the silent, open space looked out into the hallway. The few dark shadows she saw, illogically turned ominous as she imagined they held whatever she had seen out of the corner of her eye.

Her spastically beating heart gradually stopped trying to rip itself out of her chest, as nothing seemed to be out of place. She glanced over at Mark, seeing him completely undisturbed; it was that, more than anything, that allowed her to lie back down and close her eyes in another attempt to get some more sleep.

She didn't think she would be able to sleep after the fright she just experienced, but she was so exhausted she could feel it creeping up on her within a few moments of resting her head against the pillow. Right on the cusp of oblivion, a loud *thump* came from the hallway near the bathroom. Opening her eyes and lying completely still, she stared at the ceiling, afraid to look at the hallway as she listened for signs of anything else.

Nothing. She listened for a few more minutes before shutting her eyes for what felt like the millionth time that night, thinking about what it could be. Probably just the pipes again; this old house really needs a complete renovation – it's starting to fall apart. Starting with the furnace of course, but when we get enough saved up, we should replace the plumb—

Thump

This time, she sat bolt upright, opening her eyes as she did and stared toward the hallway. She saw nothing; but that didn't prevent the stab of terror assaulting her as she heard another *thump* out in the hallway, this time seemingly closer than the first. It wasn't coming from the bathroom, and she didn't think there were any pipes running through the floorboards; besides, the sounds were more akin to heavy footsteps than noisy pipes.

A third *thump* reverberated throughout the house, nearer than the others. Her hands clasped the top of the comforter in a painful grasp, as she was immobilized in absolute horror. She couldn't move anything but her eyes, and it was only with a tremendous force of will that she was able to tear her gaze away from the empty hallway to look at her husband, blissfully sleeping through the horrendous explosions of footsteps making their way toward the bedroom.

Her mouth opened and closed like a fish out of water and...no sound came out. She wanted to scream, to yell for help from Mark, and to even, belatedly, say a prayer – but her voice was gone like it had been ripped out of her throat. Giant, ragged breaths were heaving in and out of her lungs; her heart was thumping against her ribcage, threatening to part ways from her; her body felt chilled to the bone, though she couldn't feel any specific cold spots like she had felt before – it was figuratively frozen in fear.

Andrea still couldn't move as the footsteps continued; her body started to shake uncontrollably as they entered the room, each step bringing the dreaded sounds closer to the bed. They were slow in their inevitable approach, prolonging the horrific experience as they inevitably and irreversibly approached the side of her bed...where they stopped. She tried to force her head to move, to look at whatever was there, but it refused to move; only her eyes were able to look out of their periphery, seeing nothing there.

Nothing happened for what felt like an eternity; it was hard to tell how long she sat there, shaking nonstop with her aching hands clenched so hard against the covers she wouldn't be surprised if they were bleeding. Her hand started to unclench as the fear started to recede, allowing the barest movement as her frozen body started to thaw. She turned toward her husband, looking to see if he was awake during the cacophony of footsteps that were akin to gunshots in her mind; he was asleep. How he was able to sleep through everything was confusing to her, and she felt betrayed by his lack of awareness of her plight.

Through great struggle – as her whole body was still shivering wildly – she reached over to shake him awake—

An invisible finger ran itself over her face; it started with her left cheek, trailed down to underneath her jaw, leisurely made its way over her collarbone, and faded just before it reached her left breast.

The ice covering her vocal cords shattered as the finger's touch dissipated, allowing her to scream at the top of her lungs. The rest of her body followed suit, as she frantically rubbed at her face, trying to get rid of the feeling of...whatever...had touched her.

Strong arms wrapped around her, prompting an even louder shriek to emerge from her throat as she ineffectually tried to extricate herself, thrashing and scratching at the skin of the demon who was attacking her. Hands then grabbed her wrists, halting her wild self-defense; she started to kick her legs out, moving the sheets out of her way so that she could try to escape.

Which stopped the moment she saw Mark's face in front of her, as he threw her back on the bed and held down her hands above her head. Throwing his lower body on her spastic legs to stop them from kicking him, his visage appeared in her eyes, bleary-eyed and confused — but also a little frightened-looking as well.

All resistance drained from her at that moment, the entire ordeal causing her already tired body to lose all its strength. "What's going on!? What the fuck happened!?"

*Absently, she noticed that he had cursed, which he rarely, if ever, did; it was a measure of how frightened, angry, and shocked he was. She belatedly realized that she had woken him up from a deep sleep; that would put **anyone** on edge.*

The fear that had sunk so deep into her mind was starting to disperse in the face of his question. It returned full force as she answered him, unconsciously fighting him again in a panicked response to the recent memories of the footsteps and the invisible finger-touch. "There was someone in here! They stormed down the hallway, into our room, and touched my face!"

"Who? I don't see anybody here? Calm down!" he yelled at her, breaking through her frantic need to escape. She stopped struggling again and all the effort siphoned off any of the adrenaline that infused her body. She collapsed back on the bed, a weak puddle of skin and bones. He still didn't let her go, though.

"Now, who was it that you saw and what did they look like? Never mind, let me go search the house and see what I can find — stay here and I'll be right back."

Some of the energy surged back into her as she cried, "NO! Don't leave me here all alone! I don't know what they look like because...they were invisible. But I **know** what I heard, and I **know** what I felt!”

He let her go, rolling off her lower body as he stared at her face. “So what, you’re saying a ghost of some sort walked in here and touched your face? That shouldn’t happen – we’re protected by our belief in God. There hadn’t been a lick of anything else that happened tonight, so why would it start now?”

She had no answer for him; seeing this, he continued, “And why didn’t I hear it? If whatever you think you heard ‘stormed’ down the hallway, don’t you think I would’ve heard it?”

Hesitantly, she offered up an explanation. “Well, maybe you were in too deep of a sleep to hear it – I just happened to be awake at the time.”

He considered this for a moment. “That could be true, but I think the more likely explanation is that you had a nightmare. You only **dreamed** about it and thought it was real; that makes more sense than an invisible presence walking in and touching you.”

“But what about the stuff that went on the night before? How do you explain that? What if this was more of the same, just worse?” Her explanation sounded hollow even to **her** ears.

"I'll acknowledge that some...strange...stuff went on last night, but we're protected now. The evil force that assaulted us last night has no power over us if we pray and keep God in our hearts and mind. Besides, I don't know why it would've affected you and not me – we both said our prayers before bed, so there shouldn't be...any...reason...you did say your nightly prayers, didn't you?"

Andrea started sobbing, realizing that she hadn't said them; she thought everything in the house was sufficient, as well as their prayers earlier. Mark grabbed her and brought her into his arms, comforting her as she cried out her fright and frustration. "Shh...it's ok...it's ok...we'll say a prayer now, and everything will be fine."

He led her through another protection prayer against evil, as well as the nightly prayer she should've said earlier. When they were done, she felt...better. Not completely free of the paralyzing fear she felt earlier, but...better.

By that time, it was so late – or early – that it wasn't worth trying to get back to sleep, so they got up and went downstairs to the couch. Infomercials and old movies were about the only thing on so early in the morning, but they didn't care; it was better than trying to sleep in the bed where she had such a frightening experience.

Or did I? What if Mark is right? What if it was all a bad dream? A really, really, bad dream. I have been tired lately, and the stress of the incidents yesterday had been wearing on my mind. *She thought it **might** be possible that she dreamt it; however, it felt so real that she had a hard time picturing her imagination being that detailed.*

Before she knew it, 5am rolled around and they decided to get up...and get ready for work.

Chapter 17

Not even the combination of all the previous night's worth of fear could compare to the intensity Clive felt that night. Each step of the way, the concentration of emotions ramped up until he felt like he was swimming in an ocean of glorious insanity. There were a few times he almost lost control of what he was doing, but a small part of his mind was able to hold on long enough to get what he had planned done.

He wasn't expecting to be able to do anything that night; it was only after they had gone to bed and he stared at their floating numbers that he saw an opportunity. Before bed, the man had offered up a whispered prayer, bolstering his already dropping Resistance – not so the woman. Either she had forgotten, or she didn't think it was necessary; nevertheless, the result was a vulnerability he could exploit.

Around midnight, her FEAR Level started to rise as her defenses faded – along with her previously strong Resistance. He waited longer, however, so that she would be primed for his attacks before he started his assault. After no change in everything – after watching intently for about 20 minutes around 2am – he decided that she had bottomed out.

Andrea Stone

FEAR Level: 12 - (2 Temporary Reduction) = 10

Resistance to FEAR attacks: 5 + (2 Temporary Boost) = 7

Weaknesses: Depression

Perception: 1/10

Fatigue: 80%

He wasn't sure if he would be able to wake her up, since her perception was so low, but it was at least higher than the husband's 0/10. He had nothing to lose, though, especially if he only used some less powerful attacks to "test the waters". Fortunately, his first attempt was enough to wake her up.

Blowing a strong Errant Breeze in her right ear – perfectly placed as her head lolled to the side as she slept – the sudden introduction of an outside stimuli shocked her awake. The sudden introduction of an emotional feedback hit him like a sledgehammer: he honestly wasn't expecting it to work right away. As soon as he saw that it was successful, he immediately activated a Depressive Miasma that encompassed the entire room. He let it linger for a while as she settled down, her FEAR Level slowly dropping as nothing else happened to her.

Watching intently and easily ignoring the small amount of emotions that lingered from her sudden awakening, he waited until her eyes were almost closed before he triggered the

Peripheral Anxiety attack that he hadn't had a chance to try before.

The sudden increase of feedback from the strongest attack Clive had used to date overwhelmed him in its intensity; he was swept away in the tsunami of fear and anxiety, floundering in the flood of magnificent emotions. Coming back to himself, he changed his decision to take it easy that night – the outrageous success of his first assault of the night spurred him on to attempt even more of his newer abilities.

Even though he was swimming in emotional bliss, he was conscious enough of what needed to be done – and do it right. At first, he was going to just make some random footstep noises around the room; however, to his logical mind, this wouldn't make sense. They needed to come from somewhere: hence, starting them from the hallway, making their way to the side of the bed closest to the woman.

As a result, each footstep he produced boosted the fear he experienced, plateauing until another one rose it even higher. By the time he ended the last one by her side, the emotional onslaught coming from her was almost painful – and that made it all the better.

He almost lost the opportunity to strike again – as he was literally lost in the orgy of fear, anxiety, and pain coming from her – as the wife recovered enough to try to wake up her husband. With powerful concentration, he managed to use his other new ability, quickly running a small "finger" down her face and neck, before running out of Spiritual Force to go any further.

Her scream and the subsequent spike in her FEAR Level (as well as a small amount that came from the man) was so extreme that he lost connection with the world around him; he spent an indeterminate amount of time just...*feeling*. Nothing else mattered at that moment.

His focus returned to the bedroom when he felt a significant reduction in the emotions rolling off the wife. He observed them praying again, reinforcing their defenses – and reducing their FEAR to manageable (at least, for them) levels. He was tapped out, though, so he didn't have a problem with that.

He lazily watched them get out of bed and sit downstairs watching TV, his reactions slowed from the glut of feelings he was still...trying to digest, he guessed would be the correct phrase. It was like he had eaten a massive meal and was trying to think about anything other than how full he was. When he was much younger, one year his parents insisted that he eat a little of everything that was served at Thanksgiving dinner; he never did that again, however. He couldn't feel the pain of his distended stomach, but the explosive way it came out both ends later that night wasn't worth obeying his parental units concerning his diet afterwards.

By the time 4am rolled around on the various clocks displayed in the house, he had fully "digested" the feelings and was back to normal. Well, as normal as being a Spirit Core could be.   The numbers hadn't changed on his victims from their increased protection measures; not that he could do anything more to them that night, anyway. They left for work later that morning, leaving earlier than usual and looking even more tired than the day before.

Attack Period #5

<u>Results</u>

SF Used: 1950/2000

FEAR Generated (Andrea): 10(EB) + 30(PA)*4(DM) + 125(AHF)*4(DM) + 15(SpTo)*4(DM) = 690

FEAR Generated (Mark): 30(CI) = 30

Total Bonus Correlated Incidentals: 30(Mark) = 30

Total FEAR Generated: 720

Lifetime FEAR: 1100/550

SF Earned (Andrea): 100(EB) + 1200(PA) + 5000(AHF) + 600(SpTo) = 6900

SF Earned (Mark): 0 = 0

Total SF Earned for next attack period: 6900

Congratulations!

Your Spiritual Level has increased to 5!

Your Spiritual Level has increased to 6!

Your Spiritual Level has increased to 7!

Max and Nightly SF Recharge has increased! (X3)

New FEAR-based attack available! (X3)

Clive looked over the results of his work last night, and if he were capable of the emotion he would've been pleased; as it was, he took everything as just more information and pulled up his Core Status once his victims had left for work.

Spirit Core Status – Transformed Soul of Clive Logan
Spiritual Level: 7
Lifetime FEAR Generated: 1100/1225
Spiritual Force (Current): 3500/3500
Spiritual Force (Nightly Recharge): 400

Although Clive had done well that night, his overachievement left a lot of the Spiritual Force he had earned to go to waste. He had produced almost twice the amount of what his maximum was; added to that, his nightly recharge wouldn't help him, either. *Well, if I keep up this meteoric rise in levels, I guess that it doesn't matter.* And he knew he needed to keep it up, otherwise he wouldn't be in a position to eventually hurt or kill the married couple.

Since it wasn't a question of whether or not he cared (he was incapable of the emotion) that his abrupt escalation of his assaults was a cause for concern, he didn't worry about it (again, incapable). All he understood was that what he was doing was working; not only that, but a look at his new FEAR-based attacks gave him an even greater arsenal to use against the husband and wife.

5. Wide-range Temperature Change (WTC):

Description: *Create a significant increase or decrease in a room's ambient temperature, lowers all targets' FEAR Resistance*

Magnitude: *1 entire room inside your Area of Influence, lowers FEAR Resistance by 25%*

Duration: *20 minutes*

SF Cost: *500*

Target FEAR Requirement: *Level 22*

Max Generated FEAR: *50*

Unmodified Reward Upon Successful Attack: *500 SF*

6. Electrical Manipulation (EM):

Description: *Distort, disrupt, suppress, or manipulate the flow of electricity in a single object*

Magnitude: *1 object powered by electricity, whether AC-powered or battery-powered*

Duration: *Variable – 1 second to 10 minutes, depending upon SF used*

SF Cost: *Variable – 200 to 3195, depending upon duration desired (200 for the first second, 5 for each additional second)*

Target FEAR Requirement: *Level 25*

Max Generated FEAR: *300*

Unmodified Reward Upon Successful Attack: *200 SF*

7. Auditory Hallucination – Whispers (AHW):

Description: *Causes a single target to hear the sound of faint, largely indistinguishable whispering, with the only distinguishable word they can understand being their name*

Magnitude: *1 single target*

Duration: *Variable – 5 seconds to 30 seconds, depending upon SF used*

SF Cost: *Variable – 500 to 3400, depending upon duration desired (500 for the first second, 100 for each additional)*

Target FEAR Requirement: *Level 30*

Max Generated FEAR: *340*

Unmodified Reward Upon Successful Attack: *500 SF*

Looking at his ever-growing list of FEAR-based attacks, Clive knew that he now had enough to keep things mixed-up enough to prevent any repeats of the first night. He also resolved to be a little less heavy-handed with his attacks, though he wasn't sure if he could control himself while in the midst of any future emotional feeding frenzies. Looking back at the last couple of nights, he couldn't afford to waste potential Spiritual Force that could be used to help him increase his Spiritual Level, the leveling-up of which was important to his work.

While there wasn't necessarily a time limit that was imposed on him by the Goddess of the Underworld, he reasoned that the longer he spent getting to the point where he could kill them, the more likely she would reconsider his existence as a Spirit Core. Spending eternity in that emotionless void was not something that he thought would be preferable to his current form.

With his arsenal locked-and-loaded for the upcoming nightly assault, Clive waited in the living room, staring at the front door like he was trying to magically force his victims to come home sooner.

It didn't work.

Chapter 18

Clive needn't have bothered waiting for his victims to come home; although they came home at their "usual" time – at least from what he had observed – his preparation and the Spiritual Force burning a hole in his aethereal pocket did no good. It seemed as though the married couple had come prepared for a fight.

Even though she didn't come home with another box of crucifixes to decorate every wall in the house, the wife (along with her husband) came armed with verbal spiritual protection. His attacks last night must've changed something fundamental in her mind; at least once per hour, the two previously "part-time"-Catholics were saying their prayers as if it were going out of style. Since he couldn't do anything until 8pm, he couldn't see what effect it had, but when he did – his plans hit a wall.

Mark Stone

FEAR Level: 20 - (19 Temporary Reduction) = 1

Resistance to FEAR attacks: 15 + (40 Temporary Boost) = 55

Weaknesses: Spiders

Perception: 4/10

Fatigue: 50%

Andrea Stone

FEAR Level: 60 - (58 Temporary Reduction) = 2

Resistance to FEAR attacks: 5 + (30 Temporary Boost) = 35

Weaknesses: Depression

Perception: 3/10

Fatigue: 60%

And the situation only got worse. Instead of a steady drop in the wife's protection like the night before, the constant renewal of her defenses lasted the entire night through. Even while they were sleeping, the spiritual shield they had erected continued to operate – with very little degradation. Clive spent the entire night waiting for it to drop enough that he could take advantage of any chink in their armor; as 4am rolled around, he realized that the entire night was wasted.

He had all this power...with nobody to use it on.

The next night, he decided to use the only attack he had available to him: Localized Cold Spot. It was relatively inexpensive to implement – at only 50 SF per use – but he got almost no result from it.

They felt it – their reactions were impossible to miss. However, as soon as they did, their instincts turned from fear to prayer, eliminating any gains he may've made. It would raise their base FEAR Level, but any advancement in it would be negated by their own spiritual response. Since it was the only thing he could use based on their current FEAR, he had no choice but to continue to use it at random intervals during the night.

Attack Period #7

<u>Results</u>

SF Used: 750/3500

FEAR Generated (Andrea): 1(LCS)*10 = 10

FEAR Generated (Mark): 1(LCS)*5 = 5

Total FEAR Generated: 15

Lifetime FEAR: 1115/1225

SF Earned (Andrea): 100(LCS) = 100

SF Earned (Mark): 50(LCS) = 50

Total SF Earned for next attack period: 150

The advancements Clive had made during the first few nights had ground to a screeching halt. Although he could generate small amounts of FEAR, it ultimately had no lasting effects on his victims.

He had a net loss in his Spiritual Force that night, though his normal recharge that he gained back each night would help alleviate some of it. He had to watch what he did in the future, however, so that he didn't end up using everything he had – and not be able to capitalize on any lapse in their protections.

He could raise his Spiritual Level, at least – and that is what he did over the next month and a half. Balancing his available

Force, his natural nightly recharge, the amount he would earn from his attacks, and his penchant for keeping a hefty reserve in the potential case where it was needed, he gradually increased his Lifetime FEAR. Averaging around 15 FEAR points a night, he was eventually able to get his level to 10.

Congratulations!
Your Spiritual Level has increased to 10!
Max and Nightly SF Recharge has increased!
New FEAR-based attack available!
New Special Ability available!

That's new. Clive opened up his Core Status first to see where he was at.

Spirit Core Status – Transformed Soul of Clive Logan
Spiritual Level: 10
Lifetime FEAR Generated: 1800/2125
Spiritual Force (Current): 2550/5000
Spiritual Force (Nightly Recharge): 550

Nothing new there, other than the expected increases in my Maximum SF and recharge rate. Next, he pulled up his newest FEAR-based attack he had earned by reaching level 10. Level 8 had given him a Heavy Fog attack, which filled up a room with a thick, heavy, room-temperature fog; at level 9, he received

164

another Auditory Hallucination: Giggling Children. He wasn't sure how that would be scary, but it didn't matter – he couldn't try it out on anyone.

10. Shadow Form (SWF):

Description: *Creates a stationary shadow form of something vaguely human-shaped, an inky blackness that swallows all light around it; the form is completely opaque, blocking sight of everything beyond its shape; cannot intersect with targets – if one comes into contact with the shadow form, it will instantly disappear*

Magnitude: *1 shadow form that is visible to all targets*

Duration: *15 seconds, but may be dismissed before time limit*

SF Cost: *2000*

Target FEAR Requirement: *Level 50*

Max Generated FEAR: *200*

Unmodified Reward Upon Successful Attack: *2000 SF*

Just like the others that he had received, it was way beyond his ability to use – especially against their protections. He was beginning to think that he was going to spend eternity ineffectually creating cold spots around the small house he was trapped in. *Maybe when they die of old age, I can level-up enough to kill whoever moves in afterwards.* Unfortunately, he wasn't going to be able to do it anytime soon.

One side effect of his constant use of Localized Cold Spots was the gradual lessening of his victims' base FEAR Levels. As they grew more accustomed to his repetitive attacks, they started to lose their fear of it; as a result, as soon as he hit level 10, he also received some unfortunate news.

Caution!

Your constant repetitive use of the FEAR-based attack, <u>Localized Cold Spot</u>, has created an immunity to it within these specific targets. <u>Localized Cold Spot</u> now will generate 0 FEAR, as well as providing no Spiritual Force.

With his inability to generate *any* FEAR now, he was at a loss of what to do. Without any real expectation of salvation, he mentally thought about the Special Ability he had received after his level-up. It took him a moment, since he had never seen anything about it before, but it eventually popped into his mind.

10.1 Special Ability – Spiritual Nullifier

Once every 6 days, 6 hours, and 6 minutes, you can destroy all spiritual constructs within your area of influence for 30 seconds. Spiritual constructs include protections as well as your own FEAR-based attacks.

Cost: 4500 SF

Duration: 30 seconds

Cooldown: 6 days, 5 hours, 33 minutes

Just the answer he was looking for. It would take another five days or so before he had enough to use it and be able to do something productive, so the cooldown leading up to when he could use it wouldn't go entirely to waste. He wasn't sure yet what he would do with just 500 SF, but he had plenty of time to think about it.

Now all he needed to do was wait.

Chapter 19

Fortunately, he didn't have to wait that long. While Clive was busy over the last month and a half randomly creating cold spots for his victims, he was searching for something that would disturb their routine nightly prayer protections; with limited options, he couldn't think of anything that would work. Time marched on, with the Spirit Core oblivious to the passing of the seasons...and the approach of the holidays.

Unbeknownst to him, his answer came in the form of an alert.

Alert!
(1) Mortal approaching your Area of Influence!
Location: Front External Door
Automatically transfer to alert location? Yes/No

Lately, he had been ignoring these alerts and almost looked into somehow turning them off since they weren't helpful anymore. His uncaring attitude toward them, fortunately, worked in his favor; one night after 9pm, when everything was as "normal" as usual, the doorbell rang.

Before this, the man and woman had had some things delivered to the house which prompted the alert, but this was the first time he had seen someone other than the prayer duo (he didn't count the handyman outside, since he didn't actually enter the house). The husband appeared just as surprised as the woman when the doorbell went off, especially given what time of night it was.

Clive tried to get a look at who it was, but he didn't have a proper angle to see onto the doorstep; the best view of it would've been through the peephole, but the man was there before he could think to peer through. Apparently, he knew who it was, because he instantly opened it up and invited the woman with tear-stained, mascara-running face inside.

*   *   *

Thanking the nice, elderly woman who allowed her to hitchhike the last 30 miles to her sister's house, Jessica wished she had some money to give her to show her gratitude. Unfortunately, she left her wallet and her purse in her ex's apartment – and there was NO FUCKING WAY she was going back there. She didn't want to run into that whore she found in bed with him; there was a very good chance someone wouldn't live to see another day. And she didn't plan on dying...or going to jail.

With no money other than a 10-dollar bill she found in her jeans pocket (which she already spent on food), and her waitressing job barely getting her by, there wasn't much keeping her in Nashville anymore. Hitchhiking the 500 miles to her sister's place wasn't exactly horrible, but it wasn't pleasant either. She shivered when she remembered the truck driver near the border that was a little too "handsy". Her fingers were still a little stiff from the retribution she enacted in response.

But now that she was at her destination, she couldn't do it. She didn't want to face the disappointment Andrea would throw her way – like she always did. Ever since their parents passed away, she rarely measured up to her older sister's expectations; the "good" sister could never seem to understand that she **liked** not being tied down in any one place. The freedom she experienced was refreshing: she could pick up her things and go anywhere she pleased. Though she usually planned it a little better than this.

Andy (her sister hated it when she called her that, but the nickname had stuck since she couldn't say her real name properly when she was a little kid) worked in a law firm, although she wasn't a lawyer. Jessica thought she was something called a paralawyer or paralaw or...paralegal! That's it! All she knew of it was her sister was as dry and straightforward as the law books she was always reading in high school.

So she hesitated on the sidewalk, staring up at the cute little house Andrea and her husband Mark owned in South Carolina. Whereas they used the money from the sale of their parents' house to put a down payment on their future, Jessica had blown it by not working for a couple of months, as well as a revolving series of bad relationships with deadbeats that couldn't pay for anything.

*But that was in the past. If there was anything that the last few days had taught her, it was that not having money **sucked**. Not only that, but having her own, permanent, private place to stay was becoming more attractive the older she got. She resolved to get a job, get a place, and swear off men forever.*

Or at least until she found one that could pay for dinner once in a while.

She sat down on the curb, her head in her hands as she thought about what she wanted to do now. Her first thought when everything...went down...at her ex's apartment was that she wanted to get the hell out of there. It was only when she had managed to find a ride out of town that she realized she didn't have any type of backup plan. The only possible source of a place she could think to stay was her sister, so she told her ride to head east.

But now that she was here – without any possessions or anything else to her name – she couldn't help but look back at what she had been doing. She had been getting by in life; but she hadn't been **living**. *It was fun at times, but she ultimately had nothing to show for it. In short, she was a bit of a mess.*

Before she knew it, she was sobbing uncontrollably; the stress of finding her cheating boyfriend pounding away at some slut in their bed, traveling to another state essentially broke, and having to beg her last remaining family member for help had finally broken her.

When she had gotten ahold of herself the best she could, she got up and headed toward the front door of her sister's house. Normally fiercely independent, Jessica hated being a leech – but she didn't have a choice. She was out of options...well, legal ones at least.

Mark opened up the door in a t-shirt and some lounge pants, looking older but almost exactly like she remembered when they had met...at their wedding. She didn't realize until now how long it had been since she had seen him, or her sister either. They talked on the phone once a year on their respective birthdays, but the conversation was always stilted and didn't last long. Saying, "Happy Birthday, hope you're doing well...I gotta go, talk to you in a few months," doesn't take that long.

Behind the shocked and concerned face of her brother-in-law, Jessica saw her sister standing near a comfortable-looking couch. I wonder if they'll let me crash there for a little bit – doesn't look too horrible. *She knew she must look a mess, with her make-up running down her face, but that didn't change the fact that she soon found herself enveloped by her sister in a massive hug.*

"It's so good to see you, Jess – but what are you doing here? And at this time of night? What happened?"

Jessica started bawling again as her sister led her to the couch, where she let her whole story pour forth from her mouth without conscious thought. An indeterminate amount of time later, she felt as if a weight that she hadn't even known was on her shoulders had been lifted. Unburdening oneself of all one's troubles was an excellent way to feel better.

"Is there any way I can stay here for a couple of days? I really hate to impose, but I won't be too much of a burden, I just need to find someplace to work and stay. And get a replacement driver's license, and find some clothes other than what I'm wearing..."

Her tears had dried enough by then that she was able to see the strange look that exhibited a whole host of silent communication exchanged between her sister and her brother-in-law. While she waited with bated breath, she looked around the house for the first time. She had never actually been inside before, but she had seen pictures on social media when they had first bought it; she didn't remember there being so many crosses on the walls.

Now that she had a better opportunity to look, she could see them on each wall in the kitchen and hallway – the stairway even had three of them. She knew that they were raised Catholic, but from what she remembered, they weren't really "practicing Catholics". Jessica, for her part, hadn't been to church since the last time their parents made her go as a pre-teen, but something must have changed in her sister after getting married. Maybe they had some sort of "come to Jesus moment" or something.

Her inspection of the house was interrupted when Mark finally gave up, sighing heavily before heading off to the kitchen. "What was that about?"

Her sister turned to her after watching him retreat in defeat. "Sorry, it's just been a little stressful around here for the last few months. Anyways, we would love to have you for as long as you need to stay, especially with Thanksgiving coming up so soon. And afterwards, I'm sure there are some places nearby needing seasonal help for the holidays – at least until you can find some steadier work."

Jessica hadn't even realized what time of year it was, her waitressing double-shifts leaving very little time to think about things like that. She was tempted to ask about what was so stressful about the last few months, but she didn't want to push her luck; their agreeing to her staying there was enough for now. I'll have to dig into it later – I'm too tired to care about it right now.

*"There's just one thing...we do things a little differently in this house. It might not be what you're used to, but it is **very** important that you follow our rules and instantly obey when we tell you to do something," Andrea told her with a very serious look on her face.*

Jessica started to get a little nervous, as the extreme stress she had been under was lending itself to picture the straight-laced, obviously super-religious couple asking her to do some freaky sex dungeon stuff. She shook her head in disgust, trying her best to dispel the vision of her sister holding a whip while her husband was strapped to a rack. "Uh...what do you mean?"

"Pray, oh sister of mine...just pray."

Chapter 20

Clive held off on doing anything to the newcomer, although his first glance at the numbers around her told him that she was ripe for his attacks.

Jessica Baker

FEAR Level: 8

Resistance to FEAR attacks: 5

Weaknesses: Unknown

Perception: 3/10

Fatigue: 70%

Jumping right into an all-out assault was what got him into trouble before. Taking time to look back at his first few days as a newly-minted Spirit Core – with the free time he had most days and nights, lately – he was starting to comprehend the mistakes he had made. Logically (to his mind), what he did was exactly right; but fear was turning out to be highly illogical.

He couldn't help but think that if he had taken it slower, spread out his attacks so that they weren't so intense, and built his Spiritual Level up over weeks or months instead of days, he might have gotten to the point where he could effectively hurt or kill them before they started to invoke their prayer protections. That, and he should've left the husband for last, as he seemed more resistant to his attacks from the beginning. Isolating the wife was looking like it would've been the better call.

There was nothing he could do about the past few months; of course, that didn't mean he couldn't learn from his misjudgments.

So that was why he left her alone while he listened to her tell her story. Trying to attack her in front of her…sister, apparently…would only set himself up for failure. A knee-jerk reaction to the wife telling his new victim about the prayers they performed every hour almost made him pull out all the stops right then and there, with the intention of getting as much FEAR accumulated as possible, but he stopped when the new woman laughed at her.

After the laughter came amused exclamations. "What? You're kidding me! Did you turn this place into a church or something when I wasn't looking? That's ridiculous!" And then a little softer, so that only her sister could hear (and Clive, of course). "Is he making you do this? Just say the word and we can run away together; I can teach you how to survive on the move."

"No, nothing like that, Jess. This is just what we do here, and it is very important that you do it too if you want to live here, albeit temporarily. If you can't do it, that is perfectly fine, but unfortunately, I won't be able to let you stay," she calmly responded, before adding, "and that's *me* making that decision, not Mark, so don't blame him if you can't abide by the rules. I want you here, but not if your saf—...spiritual well-being is at stake."

The exhausted and tear-stained face of the sister looked incredulous, but she agreed to the stipulation regardless. Not one to put off the protection of her family, the wife led her in a prayer and Clive watched his new victim stumble through the unfamiliar words.   Dispassionately, he again looked at her floating numbers, expecting them to be as boosted as the married couple's.

Jessica Baker

FEAR Level: 8 - (2 Temporary Reduction) = 6

Resistance to FEAR attacks: 5 + (1 Temporary Boost) = 6

Weaknesses: Unknown

Perception: 3/10

Fatigue: 75%

He was momentarily mystified at the appearance of such lousy protection, but then he remembered the wife's first attempt at prayer. While their protections were almost equal now – though occasionally the woman would have a stronger one at times – her reductions and boosts were pitiful at first, allowing Clive to take advantage of them. He equated this to that experience; though on a much greater scale. In the end, he figured that she didn't really *believe* in the protections.

I guess I'll just have to find something else for her to believe.

* * *

He didn't do anything to her that first night for a couple of reasons. First, he thought that letting her settle in without trouble would lure her into a false sense of security. Since it didn't seem like his resident couple were too keen on sharing the details of his former assaults yet, he didn't think it was a good idea to give them a reason to.

And second, her Fatigue was so high that he would waste too much Spiritual Force trying to get through to her. He was sure that he eventually would, but it wasn't worth it.

She settled into the guest room upstairs after taking a long shower, the wife lending her some old underclothes and pajamas since they had similar figures (though the still-dieting woman was slightly bigger). The small difference in size didn't matter too much, though, as it fit her well enough.

Clive watched her climb into bed, falling asleep within minutes of lying down. Unlike the couple down the hallway, the sister hadn't followed instructions to pray before bed; as a result, all of her protections had faded earlier even before she got into bed. *Apparently, she has no Faith in her spiritual defenses.*

Despite knowing that it was a bad idea, he was tempted to take advantage of the vulnerability he saw in her. Knowing that this pressure on his victim was what messed up his previous assaults, he had to restrain himself. *There is plenty of time, remember – eternity, even.*

Her numbers didn't change at all that night, other than her Fatigue slowly dropping by the time 4am rolled around and her stats disappeared from his sight. It was only the second night since he had become a Spirit Core that he didn't generate at least a little FEAR during his attack period. He didn't think it was that big of a deal, since he was planning on starting up again the next night, but his benefactor didn't seem to think so: he finally had another visit from the Goddess of the Underworld.

Later that day, while the married couple were at work and the sister was out...doing something, he somehow sensed an abrupt change in his mind, as if he was in a crowded elevator and someone else was trying to shove themselves in.

"Hello, Clive. How has it been working out for you? The Spirit Core is great, isn't it?"

Before he could respond to the invasion, more questions hit him from the Goddess. "Look, I'm not here on a social call. I noticed that your production of fear is down lately; I receive a portion of any emotions you generate down here – did you know that? Anyway, you're going to have to step it up if you expect me to preserve your presence here. It is expensive in terms of my power to keep you existing as a Spirit Core and maintain the connection between you and the Underworld. Your first few days were very good, providing more than enough to replenish me after your creation, so try to repeat whatever you did. Better yet – kill one of them; that will keep you going for at least a year or more."

Clive quickly told her about the problems he had experienced, and how he had been stymied by the prayer-filled protections.

"Damn my sister! She decreed eons ago that Faith and belief in any type of spiritual higher power – not just this Catholicism these people practice – will protect them from anything I try to do. It sucks when I send one of my demons to possess someone, only to have them exorcized by some sort of clergy soon after. They're not infinite, you know?

"You acted too quickly and raised some red flags; try not to do that in the future. Well, there's not much you can do to get past their protections except...yep, you've unlocked the Spiritual Nullifier now, so that might be your only chance." Her voice started to fade, reminiscent of when he had first arrived at the house. "I have to go, I've spent too much already by sending part of me here to communicate with you."

Clive tried to ask a question about what Spiritual Level he needed to be to be able to finally kill one of his victims but was cut off before he could finish the thought, "No time—" her voice was whisper-quiet now— "just remember – DON'T CALL ATTENTION TO YOURSELF."

181

He still didn't know what that meant; replaying the conversation, he came away with more questions than answers. Even if the Goddess of the Underworld had ultimate power over the souls in her domain, was able to create the Spirit Core he now inhabited and could send demons to possess people – she wasn't great at answering questions.

Perhaps she doesn't know – she did say that I'm the first one to survive the Coring process. In the end, it didn't matter if he didn't have the answers to his questions, he would continue to operate how he had been, evaluating his previous attacks and the responses of his victims.

Now that he knew that his time there wasn't necessarily infinite, especially if he didn't produce results, he had even more reason to succeed. Not normally cautious, he had to adapt that "play-it-safe" mentality if he was going to survive.

Chapter 21

Jessica had spent the day working on replacing her driver's license and making a preliminary foray into looking for work. Fortunately – responsible adult that she was – her sister had kept a lot of important papers from their youth, including Jessica's birth certificate and an extra social security card. Those would prove invaluable to getting everything she needed replaced, so that she could legally get a job.

She had a little money saved up in her bank (which she was able to access once she got her replacement driver's license), but it was barely enough to buy a few sets of "new" clothes from the thrift shop and for a few weeks' worth of food – if she ate sparingly. It definitely wasn't enough for even a deposit on a new place, so if she expected to move out from her sister's place, she needed another source of income soon.

Now that she was under the watchful eye of her only remaining living relative, she somehow felt calmer and more confident in herself. Her resolve to clean up her act only strengthened, as she saw how stable Andrea and Mark's relationship was – not to mention having plenty of food and luxuries like a roof over their heads. She didn't care for their overly religious devotions, but she played along with it if it meant having a place to call home. At least for a little while.

As a small loan, which she had every intention of paying back even if her sister didn't look like she believed her, she persuaded her sister to get her a less-expensive, refurbished phone so that she could use it to look up available positions around the area. She still expected to have to hoof it around town, going from one place to another submitting applications, but some of them she could do online. She thought it strange that they didn't have a computer or even a tablet that she could use, but she expected they spent too much time praying to have need of it.

Early in the evening and after a dinner which they unhesitatingly shared with her, she felt awkward watching them curl up on the couch together to watch TV. She didn't feel right intruding on their private time, so she begged off citing she was tired from the day and went upstairs to play on her "new" phone.

Fortunately, despite their absence of any form of computer (other than their own phones), they had really fast Wi-Fi in their house. It made sense when she saw the various components attached to the TV in the living room, as she suspected that most of their *entertainment came from streaming movies (which needed a lot of bandwidth to maintain a high-quality experience).*

She took another shower, shorter than the previous night but just as refreshing, before changing into her nightclothes. She sat down on top of the mussed-up bed covers she had left from that morning, propped up by pillows as she spent the next hour looking for jobs and applying to a couple that looked like they were more than a temporary position. She had lots of experience doing different jobs, but she hadn't gone to college; a lot of the steadier, higher-paying work she saw required some sort of degree. At least I graduated high school, otherwise a lot of these might not be available to me.

Therefore, she was limited to positions that involved manual labor, entry-level sales, retail, and more restaurant work like the waitressing job she had previously. There were a few other likely prospects in different fields that were a little farther away, but transportation would be an issue as she would likely have to walk or take the bus to work. For now, though, she just wanted something that would pay the bills and allow her some independence and freedom.

Checking another job website that had a few positions that she hadn't seen anywhere else, she touched the "sort by distance" option and—

A slight breeze blew across the back of her neck, causing her hair to tickle her neck. She immediately froze as her eyes widened in shock; glancing at the window to her right, she looked to see if it was open. Chills broke out all over her body as she confirmed that it was closed, causing her to shiver at the unexpected movement of wind.

In her hand, the screen on her phone went blank as if all power had been cut from it, surprising her with its abruptness; she didn't think she had used all of the battery yet – it still said she had over 50% a few minutes ago. Why does this always happen to me? I hope this "refurbished" piece of shit isn't defective, I don't want to have to go back—

Frantically glancing around for any type of air vents where the moving air might have come from, she started to freak out until she saw a small one on the floor. She was about to get off the bed and inspect it for any type of air flow, but at that instant her phone restarted with a loud *beep*, shocking her even more than when it went off.

The strangled yelp she let out was loud to her ears; she hoped it wasn't loud enough to disturb her sister and brother-in-law. She heard them get ready for bed earlier, loudly saying their nightly prayers before silence reigned in the house. She sat there for a few minutes, the beating of her racing heart the loudest thing she could hear, as she listened to see if she had accidentally woken them up.

When she heard nothing out of the ordinary, she let out a sigh of relief as her tense muscles relaxed and her body thawed from the fright she experienced. She quietly laughed at herself, amazed that something so silly as a malfunctioning phone could scare her so much. Probably just a defect in it from using it so long tonight; if it happens again, I'll go back to the store to see if I can get a replacement.

The thought of potentially having another stop to make tomorrow convinced her that she needed to get some sleep – she had a busy day tomorrow. Not only was it less than a week until Thanksgiving, meaning that she only had a little time before most of the seasonal positions were filled, but her new housemates got up unbearably early. She was used to sleeping in every day, as her recent waitressing shifts had started later in the day and ran late into the night. It was going to take some getting used to; at least tomorrow was Saturday, so she hopefully thought that they might sleep in since it was the weekend.

She crawled underneath the covers and switched off the lamp on the nightstand, her planning toward the next day's activities filling her mind, overshadowing the fright that had occurred earlier.

*   *   *

Success!

His restraint had borne fruit as he watched the sister settle down to sleep, still fearful but unalarmed at his attacks.

Jessica Baker

FEAR Level: 94

Resistance to FEAR attacks: 5

Weaknesses: Unknown

Perception: 4/10

Fatigue: 60%

It was an impressive result from only using a couple of attacks, but it was boosted by the Depressive Miasma he was barely able to initiate before he used Errant Breeze. Shutting off the power to her phone was tricky at first, since he hadn't used that particular attack at first; he had to concentrate on it and specifically direct what he wanted done. The strain of maintaining the disruption in its power was new to him, and he was forced to let it go after 15 seconds. Fortunately, it had been off enough that it startled the woman when power was restored to it, netting him some additional FEAR.

Speaking of that, he watched her for the rest of the night, noting that her FEAR Level was rapidly dropping as she slept. By the time 4am rolled around, it was already around 20, though it had slowed in its nosedive toward the end. He thought that some of the lingering fear that he had caused would be present the next night; it would make the next step in his plan much easier.

As for the fear, he had nearly forgotten the intense feelings he could receive as emotional feedback; it had been quite a while since he had gotten more than the tiny pinpricks his Localized Cold Spots produced in his other victims. That was in part why he couldn't maintain his Electrical Manipulation for long: the fear she was exuding was intoxicating, leaving him only a little concentration for the strain the FEAR-based attack required.

Attack Period #55

Results

SF Used: 575/3100

FEAR Generated (Andrea): 0 = 0

FEAR Generated (Mark): 0 = 0

FEAR Generated (Jessica): 10(EB)*2(DM) + 27.5(EM)*2(DM) + 10(CI) = 85

Total Correlated Incidentals: 10

Total FEAR Generated: 95

Lifetime FEAR: 1895/2125

SF Earned (Andrea): 0 = 0

SF Earned (Mark): 0 = 0

SF Earned (Jessica): 200(EB) + 550(EM) = 750

Total SF Earned for next attack period: 750

Little by little, he was going to increase his Spiritual Level; now that he wasn't restricted to using just some random cold spots, it would go much faster. His ability to use his more expensive attacks meant that it would go even faster. If he was patient and prolonged her spiritual suffering, he expected to be able to get to the point where he could do some real damage to his victims.

Everyone slept in the next morning, since it was the weekend, though only until about 8am. Clive noted that not a word was said between the sisters regarding his attack, though the new inhabitant to the house hesitated a little when asked how she slept. From what he could see, she slept fine; she probably only remembered the fright she had beforehand.

While the sister said she was going out to look for work, the husband and wife left for a short time before coming back with a load of groceries – more than usual. Unlike their normal healthy foods for their diet (which appeared to be working, if his observations of them using the scale in the morning was any indication), they bought a plethora of Thanksgiving-related ingredients. Although he hadn't celebrated the holiday in years, he recognized the components for homemade stuffing, green bean casserole, pumpkin pie, and – of course – turkey. There were a few things that he didn't understand the importance of, but he thought it might have been a regional difference in the holiday preparation.

With nothing else to do but observe even after his attack period started, he patiently waited until the sister was again alone in her room.

Chapter 22

Another good, productive day, Jessica thought. She had spent almost eight hours going around to various shops, turning in application after application, finding numerous prospects for work. She was hopeful that she would be hearing from at least a couple of them soon, as they scrambled to find additional last-minute staffing for the holidays. None of the permanent positions she was hoping to grab were available until the new year, so she was going to have to settle for something seasonal.

In an honest conversation with her sister and her husband that night, Jessica told them what was going on. She asked them if she could stay there at least until the new year, where she would be able to get a more permanent position, which would lead to her getting her own place.

She felt bad about imposing herself on them more than she already had, but they seemed to understand and were receptive to her situation; the only stipulation they had was that once she found work, she would help pay for some of the groceries and save the rest for when she needed to put a deposit down on a new apartment. An easy condition that she readily agreed to – she was just glad that they weren't charging rent (however, she was sure they would do that if she ended up staying for a longer period of time).

Feeling lighter in her heart and breathing a little easier as the stress weighing her down lately loosened up a little, she left her sibling to do her cuddling thing with Mark on the couch after dinner and headed upstairs to her temporary (though for a lengthier amount of time than she had originally planned on) room. Throwing her stuff on the bed, she pulled off her socks and her outer sweater she had been wearing as she picked up the towel she had been using and felt to see if it was dry yet. Good enough.

She grabbed her donated pajamas – thinking that she needed to wash them tomorrow – and headed to the bathroom outside her room. Closing the door behind her, her bare feet immediately started to freeze against the abnormally cold floor. I don't remember it being so cold in here yesterday.

She reached down with her hand to feel the difference; it was strange, as there seemed to be a layer of frigid air covering the tiny bathroom floor up to her shins. Above that, the difference in temperature was dramatically warmer. She felt all around the floor, trying to pinpoint the source of the freezing area, but couldn't find anything. Shrugging to herself, she figured it was a weird quirk of the house; the only thought she had now was to take a nice hot shower. It would just be my luck catching cold from a cold floor.

Before she undressed, she turned on the shower and flipped on the overhead fan, the steam from the hot water already filling up the room with a fine mist. Quickly chucking off her remaining clothing near the door, she entered the shower and felt as the heat from the gloriously hot water almost felt like it was going to burn her; her thawing feet tingled and almost hurt as they were bathed in the fiery torrent of the near-boiling water. Or, at least, that's what it felt like.

Soon enough, her whole body unthawed, and she enjoyed the rest of her shower, taking the time to wash her hair with some of the new shampoo she picked up the day before. The dirt, sweat, and product ran from her hair in a torrent, leaving her feeling cleansed like she hadn't felt in a long time. She felt as if all her cares and worries were all being washed away, swirling away down the drain in leisurely circles. Although she knew she still had a lot of problems to solve, for the moment she felt free of them.

All too soon for her liking, she shut off the water – she didn't want her sister to accuse her of wasting water and start to charge her for a portion of the water bill. It was enough, however; she felt refreshed and ready to see if anyone had contacted her about any of her applications yet.

Sliding the shower curtain to the side, she was greeted with a wall of heavy steam. Listening intently, she realized that the overhead fan had stopped working, leaving the steam to build up without any outlet. It was so thick she could barely see the hand she held up in front of her face. At least the room isn't that big – I just need to get to the door and open it a crack to let in some cool air.

Stepping out onto the bathmat outside the tub, she grabbed her towel from where she left it and wrapped it around herself. It wouldn't do to open the door just to flash my naked body to Mark standing outside. *The thought of how creepy that would be for him to be standing there waiting made her shiver a little, which caused her to look down in surprise.*

The floor wasn't cold anymore.

The heat probably forced all the cold air out of here. *She couldn't actually see the floor for all of the steam, but she knew approximately where she was in relation to the door. She held out her hand in front of her as she placed one of her feet onto the linoleum flooring. Suddenly, all the hair on her body stood up, as if she had just stuck her wet hand into a light socket.*

Petrified in fear, she couldn't move. Her rational mind told her nothing was there, but as she could barely see past her face, the rest of her brain told her something was waiting for her, just out of reach. Something instinctively told her if she didn't move, it couldn't get her. So that was what she did.

A few minutes later, the feeling faded, allowing her to move for the first time since she felt her hair stand on end. As she put her weight on her forward foot, it slipped out from underneath her, the condensation coating the floor causing her to topple forward and hit her head on something she couldn't even see, knocking her unconscious.

*   *   *

Clive watched her hit her head, the wet floor inadvertently causing her to lose her balance. It wasn't something he had planned, but the resulting pain from the impact was a welcome spike in the emotional feedback he was experiencing. Unfortunately, with her now unconscious, he couldn't do the last attack he had prepared for her. Which was probably a good thing, as any more would've probably been too much; he was still working on restraining his attacks when everything was going well.

As the *thud* of her head against the vanity and the boneless collapse of her body against the floor reverberated through the house, he canceled the Heavy Fog he had created and returned power to the fan that he had been suppressing.

8. Heavy Fog (HF):

Description: *Creates a thick, opaque room-temperature fog in an enclosed room for a limited amount of time; all doors and windows must be closed; may be cancelled at any time by user*

Magnitude: *1 entire enclosed room inside your Area of Influence*

Duration: *3 minutes*

SF Cost: *1000*

Target FEAR Requirement: *Level 35*

Max Generated FEAR: *100*

Unmodified Reward Upon Successful Attack: *1000 SF*

He found that it was much easier to use his Electrical Manipulation on a simple switch-based mechanism like the fan on the ceiling of the bathroom; the resulting strain of keeping the power to it off was much, much less than the night before. The wet floor was an accident; the Localized Cold Spots (which, fortunately, *she* wasn't immune to) were there just to ramp up her FEAR a bit more so that he could use his other attacks, but they ended up cooling the actual steam that was created by the shower.

He watched the husband and wife head rush upstairs at the noise, calling to her outside of the bathroom. "Jess, are you alright? We heard a noise and thought you might be in trouble." When there was no answer, the woman tried to open the door —

which her sister had locked. The man took over and said through the door, "Jessica, we're coming in, so stand back – I'm going to have to break my way in."

A few slams of his shoulder against the door broke the mechanism holding it closed, sending the door flying open, narrowly missing the sprawled form of the unconscious sister. Fortunately for Clive, by this time the steam and fog had dispersed enough that it was just barely humid, though the water on the floor was still present.

The wife immediately went to her side and checked her vital signs – a clear indication to Clive that she had at least a rudimentary understanding of First Aid. "She's alive, but she hit her head – see here? It looks bad, but I can't be sure how bad it is. Quick, call 911...wait, hold on, she's waking up."

Covering her still-wet, semi-naked body up from where the towel had fallen away after she fell, the wife arranged her so that she wasn't flashing the whole world. The sister's eyes opened, unfocused; when they finally saw the wife, she jerked back in surprise before wincing in pain. She brought a hesitant hand up to her temple where she had hit the vanity, hissing in further pain as she touched what looked like was going to be a major lump on her forehead.

"What happened?" she asked, her words a little slow and slightly slurred.

"I'm not exactly sure, but from what we can tell you fell and hit your head. What do you remember?"

At the mention of we, the sister looked around wide-eyed, finally spotting Mark watching the proceedings from the hallway with concern on his face. She pulled at her towel some more, trying to cover up her nakedness. The wife looked back at her husband. "Can you go get the car ready, we'll take her to the hospital so that she can get checked out."

"No!" the hurt woman shouted, before clutching her head again from the outburst. "Sorry, wait, I think I'll be ok. I just need to rest for a second," she told them a little more calmly, "besides, I don't have any insurance right now, so I can't afford to go. I'll be alright, I'm just really tired right now."

"Are you sure? You may have hurt something that won't heal on its own. We'll figure out how to pay the bill later…"

But the sister wouldn't hear of it. "No, you've been nice enough to let me stay here, I don't want to be more of a burden. Really, I think I'll be fine."

The woman was silent for a moment, before sighing in defeat. "Fine, but I can't let you sleep yet; if you have a bad concussion, that could make it much worse. You need to rest, of course, and you shouldn't use your phone – the bright light and concentration needed to read anything will aggravate your injury. Here," she said, offering her arm, "let's get you back to your room where I'll lay you down and Mark here'll get you something with acetaminophen to help combat your headache."

So saying, Clive watched them work together to bring the sister to the guest room, helping her dress in some pajamas, and laying her on the bed. By the time she had gotten there, her eyes appeared a little more focused and judging by her Perception number, she was seeing everything better. It had been 0 when she was unconscious and had hovered around 2 when she woke up; now it was around 4 to 5, depending on the moment he looked at it.

"Now, what do you remember? Can you tell us what happened?" the wife asked, while concernedly looking at her husband, once the sister was settled and had taken some pills to help the probable pain in her head.

"No...I don't remember anything after...dinner tonight. I don't even remember taking a shower, to tell the truth."

The man had inspected the bathroom while the woman had been helping her sister get settled in her room; he offered up an explanation that worked for Clive, as it would lessen the suspicion toward his activities. "The floor was really wet, so you may have splashed a bit of it outside of the tub. I almost slipped myself when I was walking in there, so it's quite possible you just walked on it without realizing it was slippery. I'm going to get another couple of bath mats tomorrow so that nothing like that should happen again."

The wife looked relieved at the explanation, though she hid it from her sister. "Now, let's see what we can do to keep you awake until I'm a little more confident that you don't have a really bad concussion..."

Chapter 23

Attack Period #56

<u>Results</u>

SF Used: 3050/3100

FEAR Generated (Andrea): 50(CI) = 50

FEAR Generated (Mark): 20(CI) = 20

FEAR Generated (Jessica): 70(LCS)*2(DM) + 100(HF)*2(DM) +

85(EM)*2(DM) + 30(PR)*2(DM) + 35(CI) = 605

Total Correlated Incidentals: 105

Total FEAR Generated: 780

Lifetime FEAR: 2675/2125

SF Earned (Andrea): 0 = 0

SF Earned (Mark): 0 = 0

SF Earned (Jessica): 1400(LCS) + 2000(HF) + 1700(EM) + 600(PR) =

5700

Total SF Earned for next attack period: 5700

Congratulations!

Your Spiritual Level has increased to 11!

Your Spiritual Level has increased to 12!

Max and Nightly SF Recharge has increased! (X2)

New FEAR-based attack available! (X2)

The results of his 56th attack period was phenomenal. Not only had he leveled up twice, but the actions he took to earn the FEAR was forgotten by the injured sister. The downside was that, since she had forgotten why she was so scared, her FEAR Level had dropped dramatically during the night. What was at one point over 600, bottomed out at around 20, similar to the night before. So, no progress on her base FEAR; instead, he had tremendous progress on the Spirit Core front.

He took a quick look at his status and saw that his new maximum Spiritual Force was 6000, and his nightly recharge was sitting at 650; his extraordinary results from last night would provide a bit of excess, but he hadn't been expecting to do so well. He got lucky that she didn't remember what he did – he would have to remember that less was more. Unfortunately, it was hard to limit himself when he was in the throes of intense emotions.

With his new levels, of course, he received some new and interesting FEAR-based attacks; they still weren't able to harm anyone, but he could see that they were getting more and more physical in their form and function.

11. Glowing Eyes (GE):
Description: *Creates a pair of incorporeal red glowing eyes that can hover in place or can teleport to a different place when the target is*

distracted; contact with the target will cause the glowing eyes to disappear

Magnitude: *1 pair of eyes, the size of a human's, unlimited teleports (as long as the target is distracted)*

Duration: *1 minute, but may be dismissed before time limit*

SF Cost: *1500*

Target FEAR Requirement: *Level 55*

Max Generated FEAR: *150*

Unmodified Reward Upon Successful Attack: *1500 SF*

12. Object Manipulation – Open or Close Doors (OMOCD):

Description: *Allows for the opening or closing of unlocked doors at whatever reasonable speed chosen; locked doors must be opened with a different attack; doors may not physically impact your targets and cannot do any physical harm, otherwise the action will be cancelled*

Magnitude: *Close or open 1 unlocked door*

Duration: *Specified by user, speed of action dependent upon choice*

SF Cost: *1800*

Target FEAR Requirement: *Level 60*

Max Generated FEAR: *180*

Unmodified Reward Upon Successful Attack: *1800 SF*

With even more options at his disposal, he waited to see what the coming day would bring. Normally, it being Sunday, his usual victims came home from church with extra-strong defenses that usually lasted a couple of days. He just had to wait and see if it would be the same for his newest one.

Her head still hurt, but at least it was feeling better than it had the night before. Jessica was glad that she was able to blame her inability to go to church on her injury. She didn't relish sitting in a pew, listening to the priest drone on and on for hours. One, her head couldn't take it; two, she had enough of that when she was younger, and didn't think her dislike of it had changed over the years. She would go if it was necessary to stay on her sister's good side, but she'd rather not if she didn't have to.

Playing hooky from church wasn't the most fun, since she ended up sleeping most of the day. Every couple of hours she would get up and walk around a little, eat something and use the bathroom, but she always ended up back in bed, nursing her head with some more pain relievers. By the time night fell, she had slept so much during the day that she was wide awake when her sister and her husband went to bed.

That was why she was on her phone, its power cord plugged into it to make sure she didn't have any abrupt interruptions while she searched for more open positions. She hadn't gotten any bites from all her applications yet, although it hadn't been even 48 hours for most of them yet – and it was the weekend. She was hoping she would hear something the next day, or Tuesday at the latest. If she didn't hear anything by then, she probably wouldn't *until the next week when everything settled down after the Black Friday weekend.*

Which was fine, since she didn't really want to go into a job interview with a massive bump that looked like some sort of cancerous growth on her forehead. Her head was feeling much better, even if she had to look away from her phone every couple of minutes to avoid a headache. Despite that, she still thought she needed to rest as much as she could so that she would be in tip-top shape when she hit the job market hard again.

At one point during the night – after she had exhausted all the job postings on the major employment websites – she glanced over at the clock and was shocked at how late it was. 1:30! She was normally back from work at her old waitressing job by midnight, so it had been a while since she had voluntarily been up that late. She sighed as she thought, I better get at least a little sleep – who knows when Missus Prayer will get me up tomorrow?

She was checking one more thing on her phone when her toes suddenly felt like she had placed them in a snowbank. She had been lying atop her covers even though it had been cool in the house; her headaches didn't like too much heat. She hated to sleep cold, however, so she immediately shoved her legs inside her sheets and blanket, warming them instantly. She placed her phone on the nightstand next to the alarm clock and reached over to turn off the lamp.

Movement at the corner of her eye made her pause mid-reach, frozen in a panic as she wavered between wanting to see what it was and at the same time thinking, I REALLY DON'T WANT TO KNOW. *Eventually, her need to know there was nothing to be afraid of won out, and she turned her head enough to see...nothing. She laughed nervously at herself and collapsed back in bed, staring around her in confirmation that everything was fine.* This bump on my head must be making me see things.

She was about to turn and reach for the lamp again when she heard a click. Looking at where it came from, her body turned cold as she saw her door opening. The well-oiled hinges made very little noise as the door swung inward, but a few creaks seemed to echo throughout the mostly-silent house, making her jump whenever a particularly loud one disturbed the otherwise peaceful surroundings.

I must've not closed it completely...that's all it is...I should just go close it and get to bed. *Her body betrayed her as she watched it open completely, halting before it hit the rubber stopper. She couldn't move; worse yet, she couldn't breathe. The fright that encompassed her body was so intense she was having trouble letting her body perform its natural functions.*

The impenetrable silence was broken by the faint sound of whispering. She thought it was coming from her sister's room down the hallway, since they typically kept their door open all night. However, when she concentrated on it, she realized it was coming from the opposite side of the room from the door. She wasn't able to move her head, but her eyes traced over where she thought it was coming from.

Still nothing.

She was starting to see spots in her vision as the lack of oxygen to her brain was slowly making her vision distort. Will a great effort of will, she forced herself to expel the air that was in her lungs and sucked in a huge breath – right before something touched her injured forehead, causing her to flop back down, unconscious before she hit the pillow.

Unnoticed by her, the door slowly moved of its own volition, a faint click sounding as it closed again, leaving no evidence of anything that had happened.

Chapter 24

Well, that was unexpected.

Clive had lost control again; when the waves of fear hit him, he was almost inevitably swept away with them. He was still conscious enough of his actions to perform additional attacks, but he had only been planning to open the door – that was it. The cold spot, the Peripheral Anxiety, and the Depressive Miasma were all intended to bring her FEAR Level up from the 8 and 9 it had been hovering around – all so he could open the door. But the simple act of a moving door created more of the intense emotion than he had planned.

He didn't originally intend to create the whispers in her head or to Spectral Touch her injury on her forehead; that was all the result of his *need* for more powerful emotions. The fact that she didn't scream he put down to the fact that she, for some reason, had stopped breathing. He figured that was the real reason she had passed out and not necessarily because he touched her sore spot.

She didn't wake up again for the rest of the night; he watched her floating numbers and saw that her FEAR was steadily dropping, though it was slowing down just before the attack period ended. *If it continues to slow, her FEAR should be at a much higher base level for the next night.*

The one major thing that had changed, however, was that he now saw something that wasn't there previously.

Jessica Baker

FEAR Level: 545

Resistance to FEAR attacks: 5

Weaknesses: Object Manipulation

Perception: 0/10

Fatigue: 90%

Now I know why she was so affected by the opening door. Even though the reason why opening a door would cause so much fear was still a mystery to him, the fact of the matter was that the much more powerful reaction it produced was what made him lose control and attack her more than he should've. He was risking her taking the same sort of protective measures his former victims took against him.

And that wouldn't be good for his ultimate objective.

After looking over the results of the night, he found that he had generated just over 1,000 FEAR as a result of her Weakness. He ended up spending most of his Spiritual Force – especially with his extra expenditure closing the door after she had been knocked out. It was expensive because he didn't gain anything from it, but he thought it might alleviate some of the evidence of her attack.

The last thing he wanted was for the married couple to catch on to what he was doing.

Fortunately, his extremely successful assault on the sister had produced enough Spiritual Force that he was still going to be maxed out for the next night. Pulling up his Status, he saw that he had increased his Spiritual Level not only once or twice, but **three** times. Now at Level 15, he had access to even stronger and, theoretically, more powerful FEAR-based attacks.

Spirit Core Status – Transformed Soul of Clive Logan

Spiritual Level: 15

Lifetime FEAR Generated: 3685/4125

Spiritual Force (Current): 7500/7500

Spiritual Force (Nightly Recharge): 800

13. Visual Hallucination – Mirror Entity (VHME):

Description: *Creates a visual hallucination in a single target that will see an entity of user's choice in the mirror; the Mirror Entity cannot attack or physically harm target; Mirror Entity will disappear if target takes their eyes off of the mirror or after 10 seconds*

Magnitude: *1 Entity of user's choice*

Duration: *10 seconds or if target takes eyes off of mirror*

SF Cost: *2000*

Target FEAR Requirement: *Level 65*

Max Generated FEAR: *200*

Unmodified Reward Upon Successful Attack: *2000 SF*

14. Object Manipulation – Throw Object (OMTO):

Description: *Allows the user to quickly move an object from one place to another; object cannot impact any target(s) or inadvertently intercept the path of any target(s); no physical harm can be produced from the initial attack*

Magnitude: *Move 1 object that weighs less than 2 lbs.*

Duration: *Instant use*

SF Cost: *2200*

Target FEAR Requirement: *Level 70*

Max Generated FEAR: *220*

Unmodified Reward Upon Successful Attack: *2200 SF*

15. Spiritual Telepathy (SpTe):

Description: *Allows the user to communicate a short message telepathically to a single target; user can choose what type of voice to use – either the user's voice or the target's internal voice*

Magnitude: *1 Telepathic Message*

Duration: *Short message no longer than 3 seconds*

SF Cost: *2500*

Target FEAR Requirement: *Level 75*

Max Generated FEAR: *250*

Unmodified Reward Upon Successful Attack: *2500 SF*

Even though he had these additional attacks, Clive resolved to hold off on them until a later time. He had pushed his luck last night; only time would tell if it had been too much.

Jessica felt someone trying to wake her up, but she was still so tired that she had forgotten where she was. "Please mom, can't I sleep a little longer?" she slurred, barely awake as a hand shook her shoulder.

"I'm not our mother, and no, you should probably get up – being a little more active will help your recovery. But not **too** active; you still need to rest, but you don't need to be in bed all day."

The words of her sister, as not unkind as they were, finally reminded her of where she was. She had momentarily thought she was back home, her mother waking her up to go to school. The memory of the gentle way she used to rub her back in the morning, allowing her to wake up slowly, brought a small tear to her eye. She hid her face in her pillow, wiping it away before her sister could see; she didn't want her to think she was ungrateful for her attentiveness.

When she had schooled her features, she turned over and sat up, seeing her sister perched on the edge of her bed. "How are you feeling today? Is it any worse, or is it getting better?"

It feels like my head is going to split open... *"I think it's feeling better, but it's hard to tell so early in the morning. Once I get some more pain relievers, I'm sure I'll be fine. I just wish I slept better, I'm more tired than anything."*

"I'm sorry you didn't sleep good, was the pain keeping you up?"

No, but your voice is a little too chipper for...6am. *"No, I think I just had a nightmare or something, that's all."*

Her sister looked more concerned than the news of her bad dreams seemed to warrant. "Have you been saying your prayers like we've asked you to? Your faith in our Lord will help prevent...bad dreams. Look at me, for instance: ever since I've started praying every night, I haven't had a single bad dream!"

Woohoo, good for you...I need some drugs for my head now. *"Yes, I've been saying my prayers like you asked...it's probably just my head injury messing with me,"* she lied to her sister, not wanting to provide her with any reason to kick her out. *"I'm sure it's nothing – I'll be fine. And I was planning on calling a couple places today to check on my applications, so I'll be a little more active – but not **too** active,"* she added, a forced smile on her face.

"Ok, well you be sure to tell me if you have any more...nightmares or anything like that; I don't want you to feel uncomfortable here. Just trust in your faith in God and keep praying!"

Jessica told her sister that she would and watched her leave her room, shutting the door behind her. She knew that Andrea usually went to work early, so she planned on pretending to be up until she left and then getting a little more rest. Despite the amount of sleep she got yesterday, she really didn't have a very restful sleep during the night-time hours.

The nightmare she had was vivid in her memory: the way she thought she saw something out of the corner of her eye, her door opening all by itself, the strange whispers coming from inside the room...the feeling of suffocation because she couldn't force her lungs to breathe. It seemed so real, but she knew it couldn't have been; things like that just didn't happen. I think I was telling the truth about my head wound messing with my mind.

She tried to put it out of her head as she struggled to get up and get dressed, intent to get some more acetaminophen in her system to combat the headache. It wasn't as bad as it felt when she first woke up, nor was it as bad as the day before, but it was still uncomfortable. She wished she had access to some stronger stuff, but her sister didn't have any in the house and getting some from a doctor meant medical bills; therefore she was stuck with over-the-counter medication.

She got some breakfast from the kitchen which consisted of some coffee and some scrambled eggs, which Mark had made extra of that morning. She wasn't terribly hungry, but the caffeine worked to perk her up a bit, so much so that she didn't think she'd be able to get back to sleep once they left for work.

Which proved true for a couple of hours; as soon as they left, Jessica flopped down on the couch and watched some early morning TV – mainly news and some game shows. After 10am, however, her tired body fell asleep watching a soap opera she had no interest in on one of the big network channels.

Her phone woke her up later, the generic ringtone she hadn't had the inclination to change yet harsh to her ears as she shot upright from a deep sleep. Picking up the phone to stop the incessant ringing which was aggravating her headache, she saw that she had been asleep for half the day already.

Recognizing her sister's number, she tried to sound alert and awake as she answered, "Hey there, how's it going?"

"Sorry to disturb you, but I forgot to mention this morning – Mark and I will be attending a church function after work. We're

getting some stuff ready for all the kids for Thanksgiving, so that it can be ready to go before the holiday. We'll be back by...hopefully 9:30, so don't wait up if you need to get to bed. Oh, and there should be some frozen meals in the freezer if you're hungry."

Jessica thanked her for letting her know about everything before hanging up. Now that she was awake, she decided to get a little something done with her day. She shut off the TV and took some more stuff for her head; in a little bit she planned to start calling a few places about her interest in a job.

She wanted to at least be a **little** productive.

Chapter 25

Clive knew he had "dodged a bullet" when he heard the sister explain away what happened to her during the night as a bad dream; he could tell the wife was suspicious, however, which made it doubly important that he curb the reckless use of his abilities. Despite the prime opportunity to "raise hell" while the husband and wife were away until later in the night (he had no compunctions against listening to all of the sisters' phone conversations), he needed to practice his restraint.

It slowed his growth, but he knew that slow growth was better than no growth at all.

*   *   *

She didn't realize how creepy the house got at night when she was there alone. Andrea and Mark – though they weren't necessarily loud – had always been there at night, lending a bit of... security to the house, as if they were what held it together. She couldn't explain it, other than as a vague feeling that she was intruding upon their territory somehow.

She had spent hours calling stores and restaurants asking about her applications, but every place she called either told her no or asked her to contact them again after the upcoming holiday. It was reasonable to think that a lot of them wouldn't want to put up with hiring and training someone new during the busiest time of the year; if she had started a couple of weeks earlier, of course, there wouldn't have been any problem. That didn't help her now, since a couple of weeks ago she had a waitressing job back in Nashville.

Their rejections didn't really hurt her at first. She had gotten used to it over the years: from boyfriends, potential employers, and even co-workers. But something changed at some point during the night; while she was watching TV on the couch later that night, she suddenly broke down, the pain of her injury and the stress of trying to find a job when no one was hiring was too much for her.

"What is it about me that makes people want to hurt me? Am I not girlfriend material? Do I not work hard? Do I not work my fingers to the bone to support all the men I like? Why do they think they can take advantage of me? Why does this have to happen to me?"

She didn't even know she had started to speak aloud until the first words came out of her mouth and surprised her; after that, it all came tumbling out. All her fears, her insecurities, her disappointments in herself – everything. There was no one to listen to her except herself, so that was probably what made it easier to unburden herself.

She thought she would feel better after getting it all out, but that wasn't the case. In fact, she felt even worse, as if having all of that out in the open was having the opposite effect. The more she thought about her life, the more she despised her choices; she had made so many mistakes and wasted so much time that she didn't know if she would ever recover from it.

Grabbing a couple of blankets, she cuddled underneath them, miserable at the cold temperature the room seemed to get when she wasn't paying attention. When she breathed out, she could even see her breath. "Fucking cheap-ass motherfuckers – don't want to pay for the furnace to be on. Why does this always happen to me?"

You're a bad sister.

She froze in the process of grabbing a tissue to blow her nose. The thought had come unbidden to her mind, as if it had been dredged up from her subconscious. It was her voice, however, so she continued in her endeavor to remove the stuff clogging up her face as she thought about it.

Am I a bad sister? Am I taking advantage of her the way my exes took advantage of me? All I'm doing is staying here rent-free, eating her food (though I promised to help pay for some of it when I get a job), and injuring myself in the bathroom...oh my God, I *am* a bad sister. I'm actually worse than my exes – I'm taking advantage of *family*...the only family I have left, in fact.

The thought that she was acting just like those money-sucking leeches she always seemed to attract in her life made her bawl even harder. Jessica wondered what would happen if she had been in her sister's position: would I take her in without judgement, feed her, and let her stay free without having to pay a dime? *She'd like to think that she would, since it was family, but she was forced to admit that she probably wouldn't.*

Her sister had always been the "good" one, the one that could do no wrong; she would probably get a whole lot of satisfaction from seeing her laid low. She would probably take her in – at least for a little bit. But she wouldn't be as lenient with her as she had been with her ex-boyfriends: she would kick her out within a couple of days if she wasn't going to pay her way.

A quick look at the time told her that her sister was due back any moment. She attempted to dry her eyes and compose herself; although she was a bad sister, she didn't want Andrea to know that she knew that. Maybe if I don't verbally acknowledge it, it won't be real.

She thought she had done a good job of removing all signs of her distress, though she realized she was getting hot. The previously chilly room had warmed up again, which forced her to throw off the blankets to cool off. The abrupt change in the room's temperature didn't worry her; she was now more worried that she had a fever or something. Hot and cold, cold and hot: I usually only feel like this when I'm si—

The sound of quick, heavy footsteps above her head made her sit still as a statue, paralyzed in fear at the unexpected noise. She waited for what felt like an eternity before slowly grabbing the remote and turning off the TV.

She was listening intently for anything else…so she almost jumped out of her skin when she heard something from the front door, followed by its opening. Screaming loudly in fright, she only calmed down when she saw it was Mark (who jumped himself at her outburst), followed by a concerned-looking Andrea.

"What is it? What happened?" *her sister asked, not having seen her sitting there at first.*

Jessica's hand was against her chest, holding her heart inside and preventing it from leaping through her throat. She felt herself hyperventilating from the fear, which quickly dissipated as she started to laugh at herself from her fright. "I'm sorry, I forgot you were coming home, and I had been watching a scary movie," she lied. "Phew, you really got me good there!"

I must've heard them coming up the sidewalk and some sort of funny acoustics made it seem like it came from upstairs. *She thought her quick-thinking lie was pretty convincing from the way Mark reacted, but her sister had an unconvinced look on her face.*

"You shouldn't watch those types of movies when you're home alone. Besides, you should be in bed already; if I remember correctly, you didn't get a lot of good sleep last night."

"Yes, **mom**," she snappily replied, regret filling her instantly. I shouldn't have said that: mom is still a sore point between us. *Her sister frowned at her but didn't say anything else. Jessica* apologized, "Sorry, I didn't mean to say that — I was just all wound up from screaming like all Hell was coming for me."

"Don't joke about that — you never know who's listening. Now, go get ready for bed because we'll be right behind you. Whoever thought putting together craft sets could be so exhausting?"

Jessica watched her take off her coat and hang it up, with no other explanation of her cryptic remark. Shrugging, she headed upstairs and changed into her pajamas, her resolution to clean them that day forgotten until she put them on. I'll take a shower in the morning – I'm going to make another run to a couple more places. Hopefully they'll have a work opportunity for me.

Now that she wasn't downstairs, her mood had lifted. She didn't know what the difference was, but she attributed it to the fact that her sister was back inside the house. Jessica had rarely ever looked up to her sister as a role-model; she was usually jealous of the attention she received from their parents and at how well she did in school. However, her presence lately had been more akin to a rock or an anchor – something strong, confident, and sturdy. She felt buoyed up by her instead of being brought down like she used to feel; she was just what she needed at the time.

Well, I guess it's true what they say: any port in the storm.

Chapter 26

Clive spent the next few days repeating the restraint he evidenced on Monday night – which was successful if subdued. By watching and reacting to her actions, as well as being aware of the arrival of the married couple, he was able to manipulate things so that everything seemed natural. He was better at that than trying to figure out how she would react to the sometimes strange and illogical attacks he initiated against her.

He wasn't planning on using his new Spiritual Telepathy on her, but as soon as she started talking to herself, it almost seemed natural to add a quick thought to her mind in her own voice. He wasn't really imaginative, so "You're a bad sister", was the best he could come up with. Fortunately, it seemed to work; instead of screaming about a voice in her head, which he fully expected her to do, she seemed more thoughtful and eventually started crying some more. Completely illogical, but there it was.

He had been watching for the return of the man and woman – mainly so that he could have a good indication of how much longer he had before he had to stop – so he saw them outside through the window almost a minute before they got to the doorway. A spur-of-the-moment hallucinatory footstep attack seemed appropriate: he thought it could be excused away as them coming up the walk. As she didn't mention it, he assumed it had worked.

Attack Period #58

Results

SF Used: 3850/7000

FEAR Generated (Andrea): 5(CI) = 5

FEAR Generated (Mark): 25(CI) = 25

FEAR Generated (Jessica): 50(WTC)*2(DM) + 250(SpTe)*2(DM) + 65(AHF)*2(DM) + 50(CI) = 780

Total Correlated Incidentals: 80

Total FEAR Generated: 860

Lifetime FEAR: 4575/4125

SF Earned (Andrea): 0 = 0

SF Earned (Mark): 0 = 0

SF Earned (Jessica): 1000(WTC) + 5000(SpTe) + 1300(AHF) = 7300

Total SF Earned for next attack period: 7300

He even received some bonus Correlated Incidental FEAR from all three of them when she screamed at the arrival of the husband and wife. Since it ignored their Resistances, any FEAR he earned from it was welcome – he rarely got anything from them anymore. Which gave him an idea in the future...

For the next few days, though – he kept his attacks potentially explainable in nature on Tuesday and Wednesday. He used some random Errant Breezes as she was walking around, some more Localized Cold Spots on the floor of the bathroom whenever she would take a shower, and even shut her phone down twice when she forgot to plug it in while using it. The most successful attack he used on her was the one he received back when he hit level 9.

9. Auditory Hallucination – Giggling Children:

Description: *Causes a single target to experience the sound of young, giggling children*

Magnitude: *Choice of 2 giggling girls, boys, or one of each*

Duration: *Variable – 1 to 30 seconds, depending upon SF spent*

SF Cost: *Variable – 750 to 3650, depending upon duration desired (750 for the first second, 100 for each additional)*

Target FEAR Requirement: *Level 40*

Max Generated FEAR: 360

Unmodified Reward Upon Successful Attack: *750 SF*

For some reason, she turned out to be deathly afraid of children. He had spotted some kids playing outside the next-door neighbor's house late at night; although they were relatively quiet, he used them as a way to introduce the sound near the window of her room. After she recovered from her fear enough to move, she investigated where the sound came from and noticed the children outside. Clive was worried they would go inside before she looked, but they stuck it out long enough for the sister to see them.

Since that seemed to be another weakness of hers, it had ramped up her FEAR to unseen levels. He kept the hallucination going for the full 30 seconds it was able to be used, which essentially incapacitated him for the rest of the night; the inundation of delicious emotions warred with his ability to concentrate for hours. And, of course, it gave him the much-needed boosts in his Spiritual Level.

Congratulations!
Your Spiritual Level has increased to 20!
Max and Nightly SF Recharge has increased!
New FEAR-based attack available!
New Special Ability available!

Spirit Core Status – Transformed Soul of Clive Logan
Spiritual Level: 20
Lifetime FEAR Generated: 6250/6750
Spiritual Force (Current): 10000/10000
Spiritual Force (Nightly Recharge): 1050

20.1 Special Ability – Force Absorption
Once every 15 days, you can drain the batteries of all portable electronic devices with a charge within your area of influence; the amount drained from said devices will provide you with Spiritual Force; in addition, all Spiritual Force earned during the assault so far and for the rest of the night will be added immediately to your pool,

with a result that you will not receive any for use the next attack period (starts without a cooldown)

Cost: 0 SF

Duration: Instant

SF Provided: Dependent upon number of drained devices

Cooldown: 0 days, 0 hours, 0 minutes, 0 seconds

He received the new Special Ability as well as another four FEAR-based attacks, which would come in handy the next night. His first Special Ability was just now coming off cooldown and he had some special plans for it...

He was going to make this Thanksgiving one to remember.

Chapter 27

While she didn't have any luck with finding a job, she did have some promises from a couple that they would consider hiring her next Monday if she was still interested. One was for waitressing at The Slow Poke, a BBQ joint near the highway; she would take it if there was nothing else – she was tired of the industry, but she knew she could do it.

The other was at a grocery store, stocking shelves overnight. She hesitated when she heard the hours; she had never worked those types of hours before, and she didn't know if she could do it. However, it started with a higher pay and had the potential to turn into a full-time position. She wasn't sure what she wanted to do yet, but she still had a few days to decide: they told her to reapply after the weekend.

She put it out of her mind, though, because it was Thanksgiving! She offered herself up all day to help with the cooking; since she didn't help pay for it, she thought it might be a good trade-off to help cook it. She had actually gotten pretty good around the kitchen from working in the food service industry for so long –

there were some shifts when someone didn't show up and she was
"voluntold" to go cook for the night.

Her sister seemed relieved; she remembered that Andrea wasn't a
big fan of helping to cook big meals. For herself, she loved helping
their mom with the preparation. Hmm, maybe I can look into
getting a position as a cook somewhere and work on my skills. I
think I'd actually like to go to work then.

Therefore, while Mark watched football all day, Jessica toiled
away in the kitchen, preparing all the traditional foods: turkey,
homemade stuffing, green bean casserole, cranberry sauce, and
pumpkin pie. There were a few things their family usually made as
well: vinegar-soaked collard greens and some delicious corn
pudding. It was a ton of food; even if they had another dozen
people coming, they probably wouldn't run out. As it was, their
fridge would be stuffed with leftovers until Christmas.

For the first time that she had been there, they actually ate at the
dining room table. It was nice spending the holiday with family; it
had been too long since the last time. Normally she was forced to
work most holidays – most food service workers didn't really get a
day off. The thought of having to work the next Christmas
switched her thinking toward the stocking job; she had enjoyed
the last week with her sister and her husband and looked forward
to spending the next holiday with them. Going back to

waitressing would probably mean that she would have to either work late Christmas Eve or during the mid-shift on Christmas: newbies usually got shafted with the worst shifts.

The last few days had been good for her recovery, apart from a few times when she had the crap scared out of her. She didn't know why she was so jumpy; she figured it might be a result of her injury. Maybe my subconscious is trying to tell me to take it easy by being so paranoid.

*When she heard the laughing children coming from outside, she remembered peeing her pants a little. It was fortunate that she had another pair of panties and pajamas her sister loaned her, otherwise she would've spent the night feeling like she was five years old again. Not that she wet the bed when she was younger...well, not **a lot**. But she did remember it happening...once or twice.*

She was stuffed by the time they were finished, and she regretted having so many of the sides: she ended up not having any room for pie. Oh well, it'll be there tomorrow – I can pig out again for the next couple of days. *She didn't worry about putting on a few pounds; as soon as she started her new job, the exercise from it would melt the weight away. Unlike her sister, she didn't usually need to diet: a life filled with long work hours and not enough money for things like food normally contributed to a slim figure.*

It was only about 9pm, but she was tired since she had been up early cooking. *At least my head doesn't hurt anymore.* Her injury was still a little tender to the touch, but it had healed to the point where she forgot about it unless she bumped it into something. Her feet were sore from running back and forth in the kitchen all day, but she was used to that.

She took a quick shower before heading to bed; the sweat from the hot kitchen combined with various food debris from preparation made her feel a little icky. She was just glad that the heat from the marathon cooking had heated up the house enough that the floor of the normally freezing bathroom was nice and cozy.

Ten minutes later, she was in her bedroom, combing out her semi-wet hair as she got ready for bed. She originally wasn't going to wash it, but every time she brought a handful of it in front of her face, all she smelled was a mixture of turkey and...beets for some reason. Which was strange – they didn't have any beets for dinner. Fortunately, a thorough scrubbing with some deliciously scented shampoo was enough to get rid of the smell.

The house was warm enough – again, from all the cooking during the day – so she didn't care about going to bed with her hair still wet. Still, she didn't want it to be rat's nest in the morning, so she *took the time to gather it up in a bob on top of her head, securing it with some borrowed hair ties. She couldn't wait until she was able to make a little money and buy some things of her own again.*

Getting under just the sheets, as she was much too hot for the comforter, she lay down with a smile on her face and the smell of the shampoo in her nose. Things are really coming together; I'm glad I decided to come to my sister for help, even if I am taking advantage of her a little. I promise I'll make it up to her somehow. *With that internal vow echoing in her ears, she closed her eyes and was almost instantly asleep.*

*   *   *

It felt like it was only minutes later when something woke her up. She immediately sat up in bed; it had felt like some sort of explosion had hit her and everything around her. She couldn't be sure, but she thought she could hear a tinkling in her ears – though it could be that the house was so quiet and she had just woken up from a deep sleep.

A faint tingling was felt all over her body, like she had just exfoliated every inch of her skin and it was reacting to the outside air. She looked around the room and saw nothing out of the ordinary. Her phone was still where she had left it on the nightstand, her dirty clothes from cooking during the day were still in a bunch near the wall, and the door was closed – everything was normal except for the weird tingling.

Which stopped less than a minute later; how much less, she didn't know – but the clock hadn't changed from 12:01am since she first looked at it. With the absence of anything out-of-the-ordinary, she looked around for a moment before thinking, that was weird, I wonder what—

No sooner had she thought that when a click from the door called her attention to it; she watched as it slowly opened, creaking and popping every once in a while, which caused her to jerk in response to each one. This is just a dream, this is only a dream, this has to be a dream...

So faint that she could barely hear it, she heard a little girl laughing, coming from the hallway. She froze, petrified until she could barely breathe. She scooted back until she was up against the headboard in an involuntary response; she had heard the giggling become louder as the first laughing girl was joined by another. She couldn't see anything, but she could picture where it was based upon its progress as it entered her room.

The giggling stopped, and she held her breath, waiting for whatever was coming next. She felt the hair on her body stand straight up and it triggered a memory: standing outside the

shower in a fog-filled bathroom as her hair stood on end, her bath
towel wrapped around her. This has happened before? I can't
seem to remember...

"Jessica! Are you alright?" she heard her sister call from what felt
like miles away. Footsteps traveled down the carpeted hallway
until she saw a glimpse of her sister and Mark heading toward her
room. He was scraping at his face and yelling obscenities, which
shocked her with its rarity. She wanted to respond to Andrea, but
the fear that paralyzed her had gotten ahold of her throat.

The last glimpse she had of the happy couple was her sister
locking eyes with her and reaching out, before the door slammed
in her face.

Chapter 28

Andrea wasn't sure what was wrong, but something felt a little off. She woke up, sitting up in bed while she felt a prickling against her skin. She absently noticed that Mark was awake as well and sat up next to her. They looked at each other in confusion as she scratched at her arms, thinking she was having an allergic reaction or something. When he did the same thing, she really knew something was wrong. As soon as she started to say something, the feeling stopped.

She heard Jessica's door open down the hallway and expected her sister to walk out. She waited, but nothing came through the door. The hair on the back of her neck stood up as she remembered that night almost two months ago where she thought something was in the house with them; the anticipation of...something...happening was stressful.

Suddenly, a breeze blew past her face, moving some of the stray strands of hair that had escaped from her bun. The suddenness of it shocked her, and when she looked over at her husband, she could see the same thing happen to him. The fact that it had done something to them both worried her; it meant that their prayers were no longer working to hold back whatever was in the house. And if it was doing this to **them**, then what was it doing to...

"Jessica! Are you alright?"

Hearing no answer, she quickly threw off the covers as she felt every hair on her body try to escape, vividly reminding her of that night down in the living room. I have to get to my sister...if anything happens to her because I allowed her to live here, I'll never forgive myself. She was happy to see that Mark had the same idea, because she was right behind him as he hit the hallway.

A short yelp that came from her husband startled her, as she watched him slow down his head-long rush to the guest room in the attempt to get something off his face. He kept moving, however, even when he ran into something else invisible another few feet down the hallway. He screamed a little louder this time as he barreled through it, his ragged gasps of air betraying his fright.

He'll be fine – I need to get to Jessica. She pushed past her husband as he continued to pull off whatever seemed to be on his face and finally got a glimpse of her sister inside her room. She was sitting up, pressed against the headboard as she clutched the pillows on either side of her. Her eyes looked wild inside her white-as-a-sheet face, the shock of whatever was happening inside her room marring her otherwise delicate features. Andrea wanted to erase that look on her face and involuntarily held out her hand as she ran, finally locking eyes with her only living relative...before the door slammed shut inches before she got there.

She rebounded off the hard, wooden door – suddenly regretting that they hadn't replaced the old door with a hollow wood one like all the others. It had been a matter of insufficient funds at the time they moved in; they always said they would do it eventually, but it never seemed important. Until now.

She felt her nose as her forward progress was halted, briefly thinking that she had broken it when her hand came back bloody. Ignoring her own personal pain, she reached for the door before a massive solid *thud* hit it and rattled the entire wall. Grabbing the handle, she turned it and...it wouldn't budge. She placed her shoulder against it and shoved, budging it less than an inch.

Mark was there by that point and took over, his battering and kicking barely audible over the almost-inhuman scream that was coming from her sister. Less than ten seconds later, Mark had moved the door enough to squeeze through and she followed behind him.

The first thing she saw was Jessica still up against the headboard, screaming her head off with her mouth opened wide as she grabbed at different parts of her body. Andrea was reminded of the horrific finger that had touched her face and neck; if she was being touched all over, she didn't blame her for screaming.

As soon as she was far enough in the room, she realized that the entire room was as cold as her face was less than a minute ago. Her breath mixed with Mark's as they rushed toward the bed.

Before they could get there, the sheets were ripped off the bed, exposing Jessica's legs, and were flung across the room, landing in a heap against the closet doors. They froze, the sudden yank of the moving bedlinens had stopped them like they had run into a wall. Her sister stopped screaming but her eyes looked unfocused and like she couldn't see them.

At the foot of the bed, a large man-shaped shadow appeared without a sound, red-glowing eyes staring at Jessica. Spurred on by the appearance of whatever hell-spawned demon that was now assaulting her sister, she rushed to the nightstand with the intention of turning on the light. She hoped that the light would expose the dark shadow and bathe it in the Holy Light of the Lord—

The lamp fell to the side like it had been shoved, falling to the floor and shattering the lightbulb inside. She stopped in shock, her hand paused halfway to where the lamp used to sit. Looking down, she saw Jessica's phone and grabbed at it, only to have it shoot across the room, impacting the wall and breaking into two pieces.

Looking back, she saw the shadow disappear as her husband bravely jumped forward and grabbed for it; instead of any resistance, he fell right through it, hitting his head on the corner of the bedframe on the way down. She couldn't tell if he was alright, because at that moment the red-glowing eyes had moved to just inches in front of Jessica's face.

It stayed there, unmoving, for a few seconds before her sister shrieked so loudly Andrea thought her eardrums would start bleeding. It was so intense that she closed her eyes trying to block out the sound of her frightened sister's screaming, only to open them again when it stopped.

She couldn't see if Jess was alright, because as soon as she could see again, she saw a pair of red eyes staring at her from mere inches away. She fainted as the shock hit her system, falling in a tangled heap along the floor, her arm outstretched toward the bed in a final attempt to save her sister.

Chapter 29

The experience of taking a life through the use of intense fear was so gloriously overwhelming that Clive lost himself for a while. During his attack, he barely held onto his concentration while he was operating in two different places; he had done his best to ignore the emotions of fear that inundated him from multiple sources so that he could get done what needed to be accomplished.

And what an accomplishment it was.

If he could be proud of himself, he would be beaming from ear-to-ear; as it was, he replayed the events of the previous night over in his mind, looking for ways he could've improved his attacks to make them more effective. On further consideration, he realized that he had done pretty much everything he could've: especially considering that he wasn't planning on the married couple waking up so early.

His original intention was to eliminate all defenses that were put in place; although the prayers that the sister said didn't do much and were almost gone by the time he attacked, he couldn't have anything interfering with his plans. Additionally, once he had commenced his assault, he needed to ensure the man and woman in the other room couldn't use *their* defenses to somehow alleviate the FEAR Level in his primary target.

What he didn't plan for – since he hadn't ever used it before – was his use of the Spectral Nullifier to wake everyone up. He thought it would just do its thing and leave him to work uninterrupted. When the husband and wife woke up as well, he split his attention between the two rooms, instantly teleporting between them; it was a little disorienting at first, which actually helped to ignore the waves of fear he generated.

Acting on-the-fly, he decided to take advantage of their early presence; the additional Correlated Incidentals he generated between the various people helped to raise everyone's FEAR Level. The only problem he faced was keeping the rescuers away from his primary victim until he could finish.

He had to raise their FEAR Levels to be able to initiate his own defenses. The Localized Cold Spot helped to raise it enough to generate a Depressive Miasma, which in turn allowed him to hit them with a Piloerection Reflex. That didn't stop them, of course, but the two Spectral Cobwebs that he had placed to slow the man down worked extraordinarily well.

By that time, his use of his first Special Ability, in addition to his other attacks, had wiped him out of Spiritual Force. He activated his Force Absorption, draining the batteries of every phone in the house as well as the batteries in the TV remote controls (which he expected). What he didn't expect, however, was the plethora of battery-operated sex toys in the master bedroom giving him another unexpected boost. In addition to giving him the Force already earned from his attacks so far, he was stuffed to the gills with energy; apparently, his second Special Ability allowed him to hold more than his current maximum, though he was sure any excess would bleed away at the end of the attack period.

But he didn't intend to waste any of it.

He slammed the door in their faces, ensuring that they were able to see each other to heighten their fear. He used the attack he earned at level 16 to move the dresser in front of the door, delaying them long enough to continue his attack on the sister.

16. Object Manipulation – Move Furniture (OMMF):

Description: *Allows the user to move a piece of furniture from one place to another; object cannot impact any target(s) or inadvertently intercept the path of any target(s); no physical harm can be produced from the initial attack; no targets may be in physical contact with the piece of furniture*

Magnitude: *Move 1 piece of furniture that weighs less than 200 lbs.*

Duration: *Instant use*

SF Cost: *2400*

Target FEAR Requirement: *Level 80*

Max Generated FEAR: *240*

Unmodified Reward Upon Successful Attack: *2400 SF*

While they were busy trying to batter down the door, he turned back to the sister; he had started by opening the door, followed by the sound of giggling children: both weaknesses on her part. He had already initiated Depressive Miasma, which only heightened the fear she experienced. When he slammed the door and moved the dresser up against it, her FEAR had heightened to an all-time high. When he recovered from the joint influxes of emotional feedback from all three people who witnessed his Object Manipulation, he started Spectral Touching all over the sister's body, prompting the first screams she had voiced that night as she frantically grabbed wherever he touched.

The next minute was so intense he barely remembered it. He knew he used multiple attacks that were part of his victim's weakness of Object Manipulation. Two of them were new from Spiritual Levels 17 and 18: Bedsheet Pull and Light Fixtures. Accompanied by throwing the now-dead phone across the room, each of these actions only made the Shadow Form with Glowing Eyes all the more effective.

The last thing Clive remembered doing was moving the Glowing Eyes around the room, sticking it in the faces of the two women when they were distracted. He vaguely recollected using his Spiritual Telepathy to say something to the mind of the woman on the bed, but he couldn't remember precisely what he said. All he knew was that whatever he had said was enough to push the adrenaline surge through her heart, stopping it with a flood of concentrated fear.

That was the last thing he knew as the backlash of the sister's final breath hit him with such intensity that his vision went dark; he experienced such an awesome feeling that it rivaled the Spirit Core-making process. *If that is what it feels like, I can't wait until I can kill the others.*

Toward the end of his near-orgasmic wallowing in a sea of fear and death, he started paying attention enough to see the results of his successful assault. He still couldn't visually see anything, but he was able to evaluate the Spirit Core's report on his activities.

Attack Period #61

<u>Results</u>

SF Used: 3850/10000

FEAR Generated (Andrea): 4(EB) + 9(PR) + 15(CI) + 20(CI) + 180(OMOCD) + 240(OMMF) + 50(WTC) + 230(OMBP) + 200(SWF) + 150(GE) + 210(OMLF) + 220(OMTO) + 150(CI) = 1678 (Depression weakness negated by selfless acts)

FEAR Generated (Mark): 3(EB) + 7(PR) + 25(SC)*2(Weakness) + 24(SC)*2(Weakness) + 180(OMOCD) + 240(OMMF) + 50(WTC) + 230(OMBP) + 200(SWF) + 150(GE) + 210(OMLF) + 220(OMTO) + 80(CI) = 1668 (Depression negated by selfless acts)

FEAR Generated (Jessica): 180(OMOCD)*4(DM+Weakness) + 180(AHGC)*4(DM+Weakness) + 180(OMOCD)*4(DM+Weakness) + 240(OMMF)*4(DM+Weakness) + 40(SpTo)*2(DM) + 50(WTC)*2(DM) + 230(OMBP)*4(DM+Weakness) +

200(SWF)*2(DM) + 150(GE)*2(DM) +

210(OMLF)*4(DM+Weakness) + 220(OMTO)*4(DM+Weakness) +

250(SpTe)*2(DM) = 7140 (FEAR threshold reached)

Total Correlated Incidentals: 215

Bonus Death FEAR: 500

Total FEAR Generated: 11201

Lifetime FEAR: 17451/6750

SF Earned (Andrea): 0 = 0

SF Earned (Mark): 0 = 0

SF Earned (Jessica): 0 = 0

Total SF Earned for next attack period: 0 (all SF gains negated by use of Force Absorption)

Congratulations!

Your Spiritual Level has increased to 21!

....

Your Spiritual Level has increased to 34!

Max and Nightly SF Recharge has increased! (X14)

New FEAR-based attack available! (X14)

New Special Ability available!

There was a lot there, but what he took from the breakdown of his attacks was that the bonus he had expected from the Depressive Miasma was eliminated in the husband and wife because they were concerned for the sister. Their selflessness in trying to save her overrode any depressive feelings they may have had, even if it didn't prevent their FEAR Levels from rising.

The other thing he saw was that he had met the FEAR threshold on the sister, resulting in her death – which was his goal. He wasn't entirely sure if he would be able to reach it because the information given hadn't been thoroughly explained, but he had already seen that he could scare her so much that she stopped breathing; it was only logical that he would be able to escalate that.

He didn't get a chance to look at anything else, because at that moment his vision returned to him. It was already midday by the light coming in from the windows, which meant that he had been out of commission for at least 12 hours – possibly more if it wasn't the same day.

An evaluation of the former-sister's bedroom confirmed that he hadn't been gone *that* long, however.

Chapter 30

"That'll do fellas, let's wheel it out of here."

Clive had just got a glimpse of the top of his victim's hair as they zipped her up in the body bag, which had already been placed on top of a gurney. The rest of the room looked similar to when he left it, though the dresser had moved close to where it had been before to allow better access to the room. On the floor, the bedsheets he had ripped off the bed had a large bloodstain on it; he absently thought that it didn't look like enough to kill someone, but whoever it belonged to probably wasn't having the best day.

Two men who had jackets with CORONER written on the back of them pushed the gurney outside the room and down the hallway. He followed them as they collapsed the wheels at the top of the stairs, bringing it down manually, before letting them unfold again at the bottom. He ignored them after that, other than to note that they were heading out the wide-open front door.

The husband was sitting on the couch, his head wound being attended to by someone with an EMT badge on her uniform. From what Clive could see, it didn't look too serious –

but might require a stitch or two to fully close up. *That must be where the bloodstain came from.* He had been so inundated with emotional feedback last night that he didn't even remember how it happened.

The wife was hysterically crying, which only intensified as she saw her sister's body being wheeled past. A police officer of some sort was sitting with the couple, asking them some questions about what happened.

"Look, if you want to know what happened, let's go to the station – I don't want to spend another minute in this house right now," the husband interrupted the uniformed officer, whom Clive suspected was a detective, "otherwise, I'm leaving with or without your consent."

"Fine, if that's the way you want to do it – by all means, let's go."

So saying, the married couple followed him out, trailed by a few other cops that had been standing nearby. *I'm going to guess that they think those two had something to do with the sister's death.* He didn't think they would get in trouble, however; while there was no doubt that they were present when she died, there was no evidence pointing to their guilt other than that. In fact, since no one had actually touched her, it would be hard to prove they had anything to do with her death.

Not that he cared either way, but he still had to kill them – which he couldn't do if they were incarcerated.

Once they walked out the door, Clive looked outside; at least a dozen police cars were parked nearby with their lights flashing, and he saw at least a half a dozen news vans set further back. The sight of all the hoopla reminded him a little bit of when he had been captured. He hadn't seen any of the news footage, but he had heard in passing that the media circus was the craziest anyone had ever seen before.

Of course, this time, he got away with his murder without consequence. At least, he thought so. While it was true that the married couple had a general idea of what had happened, there was no way for them to prove it. Nor, from his limited knowledge on the subject, would anyone actually believe that a "ghost" or "evil entity" killed her.

Roaming around the house, he worked to avoid the dozen police/investigators who were still inside the place looking at *everything*. They were even more thorough in their investigations than Clive was when he first got there; they opened everything and took hundreds of pictures of what they found. Nothing they found would help prove or disprove their innocence, he couldn't help but notice.

Too late he realized that one of the people taking photographs was taking pictures of the walls of the room he was in – which just happened to be the master bedroom. He froze as the flash blinded him a little, since he had been staring right at it.

Warning!

Image Capturing has advanced to the point that with the right type of circumstances, IT CAN SEE YOU! Avoid visual detection by staying out of sight of any of this type of equipment.

Warning!
You have been visually detected by a mortal wielding sufficient technological equipment! Vacate your immediate location before the sighting can be confirmed!

Before reading any more, he saw that the warning had been correct. The man who had been taking pictures looked down at his camera with a confused look on his face, before attempting to clean the digital screen. Clive immediately teleported himself to the living room, where he fortunately found no one using a camera there.

Detection Confirmation can lead to penalties to your FEAR-based attacks. Since they rely on the *belief* that something *unknown* is causing the fear they experience, knowledge of your existence can lead your victims being less inclined to *believe* in the attacks you use against them.

Well, now I know. He realized that he was fortunate that none of the residents of the house had been big picture-takers; he might've inadvertently revealed his presence unknowingly. He cautiously crept back upstairs, ensuring that he didn't run into anyone wielding any type of camera, to see the same guy who had been taking pictures continue on with his job, oblivious to the what he may have just captured.

He floated slowly back downstairs, staying out of the way for a couple of hours until they were done with their investigations upstairs. Which was fortunate, as he caught wind of a conversation between two non-uniformed-but-obviously-police men as they entered through the front door. The one who was speaking was younger and was nervously reading from a small notepad, informing an older and clearly more-experienced man with a thick, bushy mustache.

"...and that was just the initial call. The neighbor said she heard horrific screaming coming from the house and was concerned that someone was hurt. The call afterwards from the husband, a Mr. Mark Stone, was only a few minutes later. When units arrived on the scene, the wife, a one...Mrs. Andrea Stone, was still unconscious. Mr. Stone had a small laceration to his forehead, which was treated by one of the EMTs after it was determined that the scene was safe. Soon after the other EMT was able to see to Mrs. Stone, she was able to be revived.

"Due to the hysterical nature..."

"Hold on – don't say hysterical. I'd rather you put it down as...distraught. 'She was visibly distraught'...and so on and so forth," the older man interrupted the recitation.

"Uh, ok...Upon seeing the body of her sister, a one...Ms. Jessica Baker, located on the second bedroom bed, she was...visibly distraught...and had to be restrained from touching the body and contaminating the evidence. She was then brought down here to the living room, where she and her husband were held while Detective Long began interrogating them."

The older man chewed on his mustache while he thought about what he had heard. "Change that to 'questioning' them – we don't want to assume guilt, and 'interrogating' sounds like we already assume they are guilty. Proceed."

After scratching out the word and replacing it with the new one, he continued, "After refusing to answer any questions, they eventually requested to be..." he scratched out another word, "questioned down at the station, stating that that they didn't want to stay in the house anymore.

"The victim was found fully clothed in a two-piece pajama set with no visible defense wounds, propped up by the headboard and slumped over in rigor mortis. She had a small contusion to the left side of her forehead, but that apparently had nothing to do with her death; it was almost a week old, judging by the coloration. The ME will be performing a full autopsy later, but the initial report was that she expired from cardiac arrest."

"A heart attack? Really? Am I supposed to believe that a seemingly healthy 24-year-old girl had a heart attack in the middle of the night with her family next to her? Who just happened to be knocked unconscious at the same time?"

The younger man closed the notebook before looking hesitantly at his superior. "What? What is it? Spit it out."

He cleared his throat and shuffled from foot-to-foot, apparently nervous or embarrassed about what he was going to say next. "Did you see her face?"

"What? Who – the wife's? Yeah, I saw her."

"No...sorry, I should've been more specific. The dead girl's, I meant."

"Can't say that I did; the coroner was done before I got here. I've seen enough dead bodies to last a lifetime, though, so I don't see any reason why I need to see hers."

"Now, I'm no doctor, and I can't say that I've seen as many dead bodies as you have, but her face...her face...there was a look of such horror frozen on her face that I wouldn't be surprised if she was literally scared to death."

The older man was silent for a second, before bursting out with laughter. "Hahaha, that's a good one! I've never heard that one before, rookie." His face instantly transformed a few seconds later, however. "I wouldn't let anyone hear any of those crackpot theories – we work on cold, hard facts: not suppositions that someone can die from hearing a ghost story. C'mon, let's get back down to the station to see if they've made any progress with those two."

Clive had heard the younger one's theory and noticed how it had been shut down immediately by the senior officer. *Just like I supposed.* Having it known that someone had died of fright in the house might make it harder to continue his work – at least, once his current victims were dead and gone.

He watched them leave with indifference, seeing how the younger one turned back inside before exiting, a look of confusion on his face. Clive guessed that he was trying to figure out another explanation for the death of the young woman now that his theory had been shot down.

It was ironic how right he was – and that no one would ever know it.

Chapter 31

For the next week, the house was figuratively infested with investigators and various police who were checking out one thing or another, taking additional pictures, and generally looking for any more evidence that may have been missed. Unfortunately (for Clive), they never stayed past 6 or 7 in the evening, so he never got a chance to use any of his attacks on them.

Not that he had a lot to use.

His nightly recharge was bringing it back up from the bottoming out it did after his successful night; it was only toward the end of the week when he felt he was adequately equipped to attack the husband and wife when they came back.

If they came back.

He was still sure that there was nothing that the police could charge them with, so he expected them back any day. Planning for their defenses – which he suspected would be more formidable next time – occupied most of his nights, while watching the quickly dwindling surge of authority figures pawing through the house occupied his days. By the end of the week, not a single person had come into the house; he suspected that they had run out of things to look for and were going to release his victims soon. It turned out that he was right: they were back the next day.

But they didn't come alone.

*   *   *

Alert!

(5) Mortals approaching your Area of Influence!

Location: Front External Door

Automatically transfer to alert location? Yes/No

He had seen and ignored the alert too many times to count over the last week. This time he paid attention; not only had the influx of police and police-adjacent figures stopped coming, but they usually didn't come in such a large group. He still said **No** though.

There wasn't a need since he hadn't moved from the living room.

The sight of the familiar faces of his future victims came in first; they looked haggard and tired, the wound on the man's head healing but still had a way to go until it didn't look like he'd been in a fight. Which he supposed it was – though not in the usual sense. Clive was the one doing all the attacking.

They were accompanied by a trio of what appeared to be some sort of priests, clad in fancy clothing. One had on fancier clothing and seemed to lead the others, who assisted him by carrying inside a few bags. Although he attempted to look inside one when it was put down on the dining room table, for the first time since he had become a Spirit Core, he couldn't pass through the outside of it. Instead, he rebounded off like he had hit a wall.

He backed up and retreated to the far wall, watching intently at the three obviously religious individuals as they set up for something. He didn't have enough knowledge to know what they were doing, but he *did* understand that he might be in trouble. He had already seen what their prayers could do to protect them from his attacks; with the extra help from these other church people, he didn't think it boded well for his future.

They started with a whole bunch of prayers, which wasn't unexpected; when they started throwing water around and rubbing oil all over the walls, doors, and windows, however – something changed. A pressure was created in the very air itself, starting in the first room (which was the living room). It seemed to squeeze him out, forcing him retreat to the kitchen; and then to the hallway as they "blessed" (a common word they continually used over and over again) that room as well.

They finished up the first floor before hitting the basement, shutting off all the lower areas from his access. He attempted to teleport or even gradually try to enter them; the teleport didn't work at all and the other method was like trying to move through thick mud, eventually ending with his being shot backward like he had run full-tilt into a giant rubber band.

By the time they finished the top floor, including the bathroom, he was relegated to an existence in the attic. Which, fortunately for him, they didn't touch. He thought it might be because it wasn't an actual living area like the rest of the house; in the end, though, it didn't matter: he was effectively locked out.

Attention!
Your targets have enlisted help from their local religious/spiritual representatives to perform some sort of spiritual banishment ritual. While it cannot actually "banish" or hurt you, it does come with the following restrictions/obstacles:

- **Your Area of Influence now consists of the only area not covered by the spiritual banishment ritual: The Attic**
- **Your current Spiritual Force reserve has been lost**
- **Your nightly Spiritual Force recharge has been reduced by 95% until the banishment period has ended**
- **Your Lifetime FEAR has been drained, leaving you with: 0/17425**
- **The Spiritual Level of your Spirit Core remains unchanged: 34**
- **You still maintain possession of your FEAR-based attacks and Special Abilities**
- **Your Spiritual Nullifier Special Ability will have no effect on the new protections placed around the house**

- During the banishment period, any targets residing inside your former Area of Influence have a permanent FEAR Level reduction and FEAR-based Attack Resistance boost of 100.
- Banishment Period will end in: 5 months, 29 days, 23 hours, and 59 minutes.

Well, this is bad—

Warning!
Increased attention from religious organization may result in harsher banishment rituals and/or an exorcism. If under threat of a Spirit Core-destroying exorcism, please contact your local administrator.
Current Local Administrator: Goddess of the Underworld

The phrase "Spirit Core-destroying exorcism" floated around his mind for a while. He was under the impression that he couldn't be harmed, though based on the last day it was obvious that they could at least do *something* to him, even if no harm was done. To step up the penalties seemed logical, however – at least based on his own spiritual attacks.

Rather than wasting time bemoaning his situation, he focused on the words "local administrator". He held it in his mind and concentrated on it, trying to do whatever he needed to do to contact the Goddess of the Underworld. He had some questions for his "benefactor".

After an indeterminate amount of time, he finally got the response he was waiting for.

Her voice was faint at first, but quickly grew stronger the greater the connection between them strengthened. For some reason, it sounded like he had interrupted a party going on; she was laughing like she was having a good time and she was distracted at first, only paying attention to him when he addressed her.

"Ah, there he is – our conquering hero! Congrats on your first kill as a Spirit Core! I've been...feasting...on the glorious torment I've been able to inflict on your latest victim. I have to say, it's even better than I had imagined! The sweet, succulent taste of an innocent soul is a treat I don't get very often – so keep 'em coming!"

The Goddess almost sounded like she had been drinking, though he suspected it was more of a gluttony thing than any type of intoxication. He could understand it a little; when he was in the throes of excessive ecstasy, drinking in the waves of fear coming from his victims (and the latest death, of course), he would probably sound the same way.

Despite the fact that she appeared to be grateful for his latest exploits, he had no compunctions about telling her about the consequences he was now experiencing. That sobered her up immediately.

"What did you do? Please tell me you didn't cause this by showing your abilities off to some mortals – and then letting them live? That is the worst thing you can do; that kind of attention could get you killed, and then I'll be out all the power I spent on creating you. Not only that, but you would bring attention to *my* activities, which is something I absolutely cannot have. I took a risk disrupting the balance between my sister and I by placing you there; if word gets out about it, then she might try something like this as well."

So what should I do? He had no idea what she was talking about concerning her sister, but he was at a loss; using his FEAR-based attacks got him into this situation, but how was he supposed to kill his victims without using them? It seemed counter-intuitive, to say the least.

"First, you need to lay low for a while – which shouldn't be too hard considering you're stuck in that attic for the time being. After that, you need to *subtly* use your abilities to affect your victims. Theoretically, they shouldn't even know you are there; that's a bit out of the question now, since you essentially showed yourself to them. However, I think you can still salvage the situation.

"The Spirit Core system you are part of is unique; not only are you one-of-a-kind, but I designed it to adapt and tailor your FEAR-based attacks and Special Abilities to the situation. It may not seem like it at first, but everything you have access to has been granted to you based upon your victims. You have what you need to do this – now you just need to figure it out."

How do I do that?

"I can't tell you that because I have no idea; all I know is that you'll figure it out at the time. There is no right way to do it...but as you've seen, there is a **wrong** way. You've gotten this far without me and I have confidence you can do it – now go get me some more souls!"

The connection was abruptly cut off as she presumably went back to torturing the soul of the young woman that he had killed a week ago. Clive roamed around the attic as he looked to see if he had missed anything there from the first and only time that he had seen it months ago. Nothing in general had changed, though he did notice that the family of mice he had seen before was gone. Other than a few spiders and a variety of other small bugs, he was alone in the attic.

Fortunately, he couldn't get bored or lonely.

Chapter 32

Clive wasn't completely cut off from the world. Through some vents in the siding, he could look outside, though his view wasn't very extensive. He could see the street in front of the house and the backyard of the house behind him, but they rarely held anything of interest. Despite that, he spent most of his days over the next six months looking outside, absently watching cars drive by. His nights were a different matter.

While he couldn't push through the barrier preventing him from entering the rest of the house, he could press against it and see down into the top floor. It was like placing his face into a pool of water and looking down into a whole new world. He couldn't hear anything, as if watching a TV program with the volume muted, but he could roam around the attic and look down into every part of the second floor. It helped to pass the time looking at his victims even if he couldn't interact with them.

Even though he couldn't hear anything, it was obvious that the wife had...changed. *I'm guessing her sister's death affected her emotionally.* It was the only explanation he could think of; she appeared to cry by herself at least every other night, seemed prone to instigating hand-waving arguments with the husband,

and a few times he saw her arrive home later than usual, stumbling and disoriented as she dragged herself to bed.

The six months until his exile ended went by quickly, and before he knew it, Clive was back. It was in the middle of the day when he was finally allowed access to the house, so he took the time to explore everything, almost repeating what he did when he had first arrived as a newly created Spirit Core.

He had noted that the guest room had been cleaned and the bed was made up again with a new set of bedsheets and comforter. The door had been replaced after it had been damaged during the night of his attack, as well as a new lamp. However, after that was done, the dust he saw over everything (as well as his own observations from the attic) showed that they hadn't been in there since. He also noticed that the wife had nothing to do with any of the repairs and, from what he could tell, refused to even go inside the room.

The downstairs wasn't much different except for the lack of its previous cleanliness; stacks of dishes were piled up in the sink, the floor throughout the kitchen and living room were dirty as if they hadn't been vacuumed or cleaned in months, and dust had settled over almost everything. As for the basement, other than the laundry area having been obviously used, the storage area was still in disarray, having been moved and searched through during the police investigation half-a-year ago.

From what he could see, the only thing that appeared upkept was the living room couch and coffee table, as well as the upstairs bathroom and master bedroom. Clive suspected that the husband kept them clean because he spent the most time in those places, whereas the rest went by the wayside as the wife didn't contribute as much to the upkeep and cleaning as she used to.

After a thorough inspection of everything, he waited in the living room like he used to, expecting the arrival of his victims at any time. He didn't have long to wait.

Alert!

(1) Mortal approaching your Area of Influence!

Location: Front External Door

Automatically transfer to alert location? Yes/No

He had almost forgotten about the alerts; he had been locked up in the attic so long that he hadn't seen any lately. Since his Area of Influence was only the attic, neither the man or woman had been anywhere close to entering it. He selected **No**, and then waited for the wife to walk in.

Contrary to normal (or at least the normal of six months ago), it wasn't the woman who came home first, but the man. He couldn't really get an accurate view of him while he was stuck in the attic, but he could see that he had put on some weight; his belly was a little bit pudgier and his face had filled out. Of the head wound he had received during Clive's attack, there was now only a very small scar that was barely noticeable.

He walked in with a bag full of groceries and shut the door behind him, locking it securely before heading to the kitchen. Clive noticed the look of resignation as he saw the dirty dishes in the sink, which he tackled with a big sigh once he put everything away that he had brought home from the grocery store.

With his arms up to the elbows in soapy water, the woman finally arrived home, negligently throwing her purse and keys on the couch once she was inside. She appeared a little disheveled and lost, with big dark circles under her eyes betraying a sleepiness Clive could see in her whole demeanor. She immediately went upstairs and changed out of her work clothes into some loose-fitting loungewear, throwing herself on the couch and turning on the TV.

Opposite of the husband, the wife had somehow lost weight. The formerly well-fitting clothing she had been wearing when she came home – as well as her current sweatpants and ratty t-shirt – hung on her frame as if she was all skin and bones. Which she practically was, as he had watched her quickly change; she appeared unhealthily thin and frail now.

By that time, the husband was done in the kitchen, frowning at the appearance of his wife sitting on the couch. He looked at the door and his frown grew deeper. "Honey, you've got to remember to lock the door. I know I was here at the time, but it's better if you get into the habit—"

"Don't start with me today, ok? I had a bad day at work and I have a headache, I don't need to hear your incessant nagging."

Instead of looking offended at her comment, he appeared to be used to her recent attitude and took it in stride. "Ok...so what do you want for dinner? We can go out if you want to, or I just bought some stuff at the store – I'll cook it all and clean up, so you don't have to worry about it."

"No thanks, I'm not hungry."

He crossed over to the couch and sat next to her, grabbing the remote and muting the TV, prompting her to protest, "Hey, I was listening to—"

"Andrea, we need to have a talk. I'm worried about you not eating; in fact, I can't remember the last time we ate dinner together. The small snacks you have on the weekends aren't enough, especially if you want to stay healthy. I mean, you're practically a skeleton now!"

"What, you want me to eat and get fat like you? No thanks, I'm fine with the way I look now; I can even fit into those skinny jeans I've had in my closet since high school."

"Honey, this isn't about eating enough to get fat, I'm talking about staying healthy. I know you haven't been sleeping well, and I fear it's because there's something wrong. I think you need to see someone about this," he responded without any trace of anger at her calling him fat.

"What, like a shrink? What can they do about my sister dying in the same house we can't afford to move out of? What will they be able to do about the fact that every time I think about that night, I wish I had been stronger, that I regret ever letting her stay here even though we knew it might be dangerous, and that I didn't even think about asking for help from God at that moment? And what can they hope to do about the crushing realization that the only living relative I had left was killed just feet away from me by some evil entity and the police *still* think we had something to do with it?"

He was silent for a moment, as if he was gathering his thoughts. "Honey, you can't keep blaming yourself for what happened. It's not your fault; we had no idea the kind of power this demon had, otherwise I wouldn't have agreed to let her stay here as well. If anyone is at fault, it is the demon Father Larkin helped to banish from this place – not you or I. It's gone now, so everything will be ok."

"But...but...I can't help but feel that it's all my fault, no matter what you say," she started, before bursting out in tears. The husband gathered her up in his arms, letting her cry herself out, soaking his work shirt that he hadn't even changed out of yet. Eventually, she stopped sobbing and he let her go, leaving her with continued assurances that everything would be ok. She didn't look convinced, but she attempted a smile anyway.

He made them a quick and healthy dinner of grilled chicken and salad, accompanied by some sort of thick natural-looking green juice. She couldn't even finish half of it; her stomach had probably shrunk so much from her malnutrition that she couldn't fit much in. By the end of the meal, however, they both looked satisfied.

Just like old times, they snuggled up on the couch and watched TV for the rest of the night, though the wife appeared to have nodded off early in the evening. The husband didn't disturb her, instead letting her sleep up against him, a smile on his face as he looked down on the waifish, sleep-deprived woman.

His attack period finally started at 8pm, and Clive was able to see their numbers for the first time since he had been banished.

Mark Stone

FEAR Level: 2 - (1 Temporary Reduction) = 1

Resistance to FEAR attacks: 15 + (40 Temporary Boost) = 55

Weaknesses: Spiders

Immunity: Localized Cold Spot

Perception: 5/10

Fatigue: 40%

Andrea Stone

FEAR Level: 50 - (18 Temporary Reduction) = 32

Resistance to FEAR attacks: 5 + (5 Temporary Boost) = 10

Weaknesses: Depression

Immunity: Localized Cold Spot

Perception: 1/10

Fatigue: 90%

The numbers floating around the man was what he had expected; the prayers that they continued to say together during the night had bolstered his Resistance and cut in half his already really low FEAR Level. What he hadn't been expecting was the difference in the woman.

Apparently, the same protections and defenses that the prayers used to give her were weakening. He wasn't sure if it was the same as the lack of "belief" he had seen in the sister, or if something else was at work, but he had to restrain himself from jumping into the same pattern as before. Her current vulnerability made him almost reflexively use some of his lower-strength FEAR-based attacks to once again feel her fear; he had been entirely emotionless for the longest period since he had been incarcerated (not counting his youth where he hadn't learned about the euphoria he experienced when he killed someone), and the need to feel something again almost tipped his hand.

He had a lot of time to reflect on his previous actions, however, so it was only through a small effort that he was able to hold off on attacking that night. The first reason was that the wife was so Fatigued that it wouldn't be as effective; the second reason was he didn't want the fully protected husband to be anywhere near his assaults. Looking back, Clive thought it might

271

have been a mistake to include him on his attacks: he was the one who implemented the prayer protections in the first place.

He had been having much more luck with the wife alone, just as he had with the sister. If he hadn't included the married couple in the final attack, there was a distinct possibility that none of the banishment situation would've ever occurred. He was going to have to work slowly and figure out how to eliminate her without arousing suspicion. The last thing he could afford now was to be banished again so soon after obtaining access to the house again.

Or worse: exorcism.

Chapter 33

Spirit Core Status – Transformed Soul of Clive Logan

Spiritual Level: 34

Lifetime FEAR Generated: 0/17500

Spiritual Force (Current): 17000/17000

Spiritual Force (Nightly Recharge): 1750

Although his Spiritual Force had quickly topped off once the restrictions had been lifted due to his increased nightly recharge, he didn't spend any of it for the first week. He patiently assessed the situation, gaining more insight on how he could effectively isolate the wife without gaining the attention of the husband; he knew he couldn't use most of the previously experienced attacks like the Errant Breeze, since he was sure they would arouse suspicion. Instead, he looked into both his new ones that he received after he killed the sister and some of the ones he hadn't used before or only on the sister.

He started out slowly, using his Depressive Miasma in almost every room of the house. It was a large expenditure of SF that didn't have any obvious returns at first, but he was recharging more than enough each night to make up for it. The change in the already clearly depressed woman was apparent, however. Although she didn't become more fearful, she became even more withdrawn, refusing to eat unless her husband forced her to, and even stayed home from work a few days when she couldn't find enough drive to get out of bed.

Her health declined in the process as well, though Clive didn't intend for her to die from malnutrition-related issues – her death wouldn't help him because it wouldn't be a FEAR-based attack that caused it. He was saved from having to stop his Depressive Miasma regimen by the man taking her to the hospital for a couple of days when she passed out in the middle of the day, pumping her full of fluids and other nutrients, with instructions to maintain a high-protein, high-fluid diet for the next few months until her weight stabilized. He couldn't go with them to the hospital, of course, but when she came back, she looked healthier and more alert.

By forcing her to eat and stay healthy, the husband inadvertently helped Clive. He had been seeing diminishing returns on his Miasma, mainly because her Perception and Fatigue had been affected by her deteriorating health. He needed for it to be going strong for the next stage of his plan.

Events out of his control sparked a major change in those plans.

One day during the middle of the week, a day that was slowly becoming like many others, he was alerted that someone was near the back door. Knowing that no one ever went through there other to take some trash out, he immediately transferred to the location.

He arrived just in time to see someone kick open the door. It was a heavy wooden door leading to the outside, but the lock and deadbolt on it were weak; a good, strong kick by a heavy boot near the handle was all that was needed to bust it in. Since there wasn't an alarm system, the owner of the boot walked right in without hesitation.

When Clive thought about what a thief or a robber looked like, he pictured a man clothed all in black, wearing a ski mask, and carrying some sort of weapon and a big empty sack that he planned to fill up with valuables. Contrary to those expectations, this person looked like any other average man you would see on the street.

A dark-green polo shirt, dark jeans, sunglasses, short hair, leather gloves, and a pair of hiking boots completed the outfit, and he immediately attempted to kick closed the now freely swinging door. The only thing out of the ordinary was the smirk on his face as he took a look around the kitchen; he quickly checked the drawers and cabinets for anything of value, dumping their entire contents out on the counter or in the sink. He even checked the freezer, dumping things out without a care.

He didn't waste any more time as he went to the living room, unhooking all of the components underneath the TV and throwing them on the couch. Clive expected him to take the large flat screen TV too, but he ignored it as he went down to the basement.

A few minutes knocking things aside in the unfinished basement netted him a few small choice items; immediately, he haphazardly carried an armful of various knickknacks and antiques upstairs and threw them on the couch next to his previous items.

Rushing upstairs as if he was being chased, he went from room to room, pulling out drawers and emptying closets all over the floor in the search for…whatever caught his fancy, apparently. The jewelry the woman owned was an obvious item, but he also took a few shirts from the man's closet as well. Before he left the upstairs, however, he stripped the sheet from the main bedroom, tossed his items from upstairs inside, and gathered it all up until he had an impromptu bag.

Rushing downstairs, he plopped it on the couch, opening it enough to add the stuff he collected before his search upstairs. Running out the back door with a sack full of stolen merchandise over his shoulder like Santa Thief, Clive realized that the intruder was in and out of the house in less than 10 minutes.

Everything was a mess, with all of the neatly organized areas of the house scattered all over the floor and broken dishware littering the kitchen. He couldn't do anything about it by the time his victims came home – not that he felt any inclination to – so he was there to see the wife's reaction when she came home.

To say that she was – if he remembered what the detective had said before – "visibly distraught" was putting it mildly. One look at their violated house made her run out the door, where she didn't step foot in it again until the husband had cleaned it all up. A day later (he wasn't sure where she spent the night), she was back in the house, appearing hesitant to sit still, stating to the man that she didn't feel safe and that she wanted to leave.

Based on what he knew of their finances, at least from over-the-shoulder looks at different financial statements (and how they discussed the real-estate market), they weren't going anywhere. The wife had been fired from her law firm after the whole "scandal" where she was still a suspect in the eyes of the authority, so she was forced to take a much lower-paying job in an office somewhere else. They were barely making ends meet, though he did see that the husband had a couple thousand squirreled away in a secret account.

Which, some days after the break-in, he used a small amount of as he bowed to the wishes of his wife and bought a gun.

The final piece clicked into place and he started his quiet assault the next day.

Chapter 34

Andrea didn't feel safe anymore. Even though the priestly blessing Father Larkin performed on the house got rid of the demon that killed her sister and protected the house spiritually (and made them a topic of much backroom conversation at their church), it couldn't prevent the physical dangers present in the world. When she came home from a long day of work to find that their house had been broken into and trashed, she felt violated – not only the place where she lived, but personally. She had no reason to believe that it was personally targeted toward her, but she thought it might be the Lord's punishment for her actions (and non-actions) concerning her sister's death.

She convinced Mark to buy a gun, stating that it made her feel safer in her own home: just in case someone broke in while they were there. They couldn't afford a security system; well, they could – since there were multiple deals out there that came with free equipment and installation – but they were strapped for cash the way it was and couldn't afford the monthly fee. She didn't know where her husband got the money for the gun, but he said he had a small emergency fund stashed away

for...well...emergencies like this. She didn't care, so long as
something *made her feel more secure.*

Fortunately, their insurance company paid to replace a lot of their stolen items, which they used to replace some important things, but they stashed the rest of the check away for the future. She was still hoping to move away at some point, and they needed to save as much as they could; the housing market sucked in this part of the state, unfortunately. And a little exploratory searching for possible real-estate agents had them politely refusing to help, stating that they didn't want to be associated with those that were still under investigation for murder.

*She almost wished she or her husband **were** responsible for Jessica's death. The horror of how she actually died was still fresh in her mind after nearly a year, and nothing could make the memories stop. Lately, she had even been plagued by vivid dreams of that night, though some of the details were strange. It almost appeared as if she was looking at the entire scene from up high in the room, as if she were a security camera watching her sister's murder by the shadowy figure with the red-glowing eyes. She shuddered again as she thought of the demon that was literally straight out of her nightmare.*

She sighed as Mark intently watched her eat, making sure she ate and drank the required amount to keep her happy and healthy.

Well, at least healthy. She had never been so skinny, which was a dream of hers, but it came at a cost; she still remembered being so weak and frail from malnutrition that she could barely walk without falling down. That had been months ago, of course, and she had filled out again: some of the fat she had gained back had filled in her bra again! So at least some things were looking up.

After dinner, Mark invited her again to watch a movie, which had been their major source of entertainment since they didn't have a lot of extra money to go out. No horror movies though; they lived through the scariest thing they could ever imagine – they neither needed a reminder of it or any other fuel to add to the fire.

She tried to put a brave face on the situation, but the fact of the matter was every time they lay down on the couch to watch a movie all she could think about was how it all started. Even though it eventually led to a life that was closer to their Lord and Savior – with their constant prayers and devotions – the couch was also a reminder of the events that followed. She had begun to lose her faith; she couldn't help but think that, just like the break-in, they were being punished for past sins.

After a funny romantic comedy involving two married couples and sixteen goats (she worried at first at the description, but fortunately no bestiality was involved), she actually felt a little better, as she had laughed louder and harder than she had in what felt like years. She brought their dishes to the kitchen while her husband headed upstairs to get ready for bed first.

As soon as she walked toward the sink, she tripped and dropped one of the cups when the power in the house suddenly went out. It was dark-ish inside the kitchen, but she could still see the shattered remains of her favorite porcelain coffee mug they were using all over the floor.

"Are you ok?" Mark shouted from upstairs.

"Yeah, I just dropped my favorite cup and broke it. I'll be up in a second – I'm sure the power will be back on momentarily," she shouted back. She placed the other plates and cups in the sink, before she bent over to pick up the scattered pieces of the mug. As she gathered all the pieces, she stood up too quickly and felt a little dizzy. Suddenly, in the shadows near the back door, she saw something move out of the corner of her eye.

She stared at the place she thought she saw...something...as her head stopped spinning. Must be my head and this stupid power outage playing with my eyes. *When she didn't see anything, she shrugged it off and placed the shards in the trash, vowing to remember to pick up any pieces she missed in the morning. She was just glad tomorrow was Saturday, so they could both sleep in* and she could take her time cleaning up the poor remnants of her mug.

Before she even got to the stairs, the power suddenly came back on. She tripped again at the suddenness of it, catching herself on the couch before she could hit the ground. She laughed at her clumsiness, relieved that she could easily see again and refusing to acknowledge how being alone in the dark kitchen had scared her. She walked through all the rooms, beating back the fear that was still making her heart beat fast as she turned all the lights off.

"See, I told you it would be back on soon," she told Mark as she saw him come out of the bathroom, apparently finished with his nighttime rituals. She admired the way his chest looked without a shirt on and just some loose-fitting lounge pants – he was looking **good** lately. He had filled out quite a bit while she had gotten thinner; after her stint in the hospital, however, he had started eating better and she suspected that taking care of her (and even initially having to carry her places) had tightened up his muscles. He also said that he had been using the office gym on his lunch breaks to tone himself up a little.

She might just have to jump his bones – she wasn't overly tired, and they could stay up as late as they wanted. The thought was extremely tempting because they hadn't been "intimate" since the...incident. Thoughts of that night again intruded on her mind, but she pushed it away, tired of it ruining her night – and her life.

Before she headed to the bathroom, she stopped by her closet to grab a little something special. A lot of her "fun" clothes had been thrown all over the floor during the break-in – prompting her to immediately throw them away, as she didn't like the thought of the one who had pawed all through their stuff having touched them. Fortunately, there had been a few that didn't look like they had been touched, and it was one of these that she brought to the bathroom.

She knew it would probably be a little big for her now, but the sexy light-blue teddy she picked out probably wouldn't be on long enough to matter. It was all about the initial presentation; she knew as soon as he saw her, he wouldn't hesitate to take it off as soon as he could.

She told him that she was going to take a shower first before she left the bedroom, which brightened his face up, giving her a not-so-sly wink. It wasn't normal that she took a night-time shower, so he knew what it meant. She laughed at him, heading to the bathroom with a smile on her own face, while he finished resetting their bedside clocks that had been reset during the power outage.

She closed the door behind her and undressed, shivering at how cold it was in the bathroom. She absently remembered that it was late fall, with all the chilly evenings that came with it. She reminded herself to ask Mark about that emergency fund of his, and whether he had enough in there to fix the furnace; she was tired of freezing her ass off whenever she took a shower anytime past September.

The shower was nice and hot at least; as she scrubbed herself all over, she felt the figurative ice that had covered her after entering the bathroom melt away in its steamy glory. By the time she got out of the shower, the room had warmed up enough that she was able to step out onto the wide range of bath mats that they had placed after Jessica fell and hit her head. The memory dampened her mood, but she again pushed all thoughts of her sister away. Tonight was just between her and her husband.

Drying off, she placed the towel back on the rack when she was done and walked to the sink naked. The steam had fogged up the mirror, so she took a nearby washcloth and started to wipe it away – she wanted to check herself out when she put on her "fun" clothes. She was halfway done with it when she caught the sounds of whispering at the edge of her hearing.

She paused, listening intently at what sounded unintelligible to her; I wonder if the power coming back on earlier accidentally turned the TV back on downstairs, and it's only now that I'm hearing it. Or maybe Mark got bored while I took a shower and is occupying himself. *She figured she'd check it out when she got out of the bathroom.*

She started to clean off the mirror again and, just as she finished, the power went off again. Now that she was in a completely enclosed room, the only light she could see came from underneath the doorway, which was faint in and of itself since there weren't any windows nearby letting in moonlight. She paused and reached for the door to at least be able to see something, when she froze; the faint whispering she had been hearing was now ringing in her ears.

That's not the TV, is it? *The indecipherable whispering grew louder and louder, until it seemed as if it was practically shouting in her ears. She dropped the washcloth she had been holding and covered her ears, but it didn't stop. It was almost becoming painful when it abruptly stopped, the tense "calm-before-the-storm" feeling making her shiver uncontrollably.*

With the whispering shut off, she turned to the door again and reached for the handle, only for the power to be restored at that moment. A sense of movement out of the corner of her eye made her look at the mirror.

Jessica was standing behind her, dressed in the same clothes she died in, her mouth open in a silent scream as she glared accusingly at her sister. In her head, she heard Jess scream out, "Andrea! SAVE ME!"

Whirling around in confusion and panicked fright, she looked for the place her sister was standing, only for no one to be there. A quick look back at the mirror showed nothing, the spot where Jessica had been was empty in both places. She wanted to scream, but her throat was closed up tight; by the time her voice was freed from the paralyzing fear, she had calmed enough from the vision that she was only breathing raggedly.

Goosebumps had broken out all over her body as the shock of seeing a vision of her sister rattled her to the core; belatedly, she also realized that the room had grown cold again while she had been standing there.

Abandoning her fun clothes, she quickly dressed in her pajamas again and rushed out of the bathroom, not wanting to spend another moment in there. My mind is playing tricks on me; I'm still not over that night. I wonder if she blames me for her death – I know I blame myself.

She practically ran into the bedroom, seeing that it was past 10:00pm on her nightstand alarm clock, before jumping into bed without looking at her husband. In the midst of opening her mouth to tell him about the strange vision of her sister in the mirror, her mind went blank as she experienced a sharp pain in her head. She was confused for a moment, but then she suddenly threw the covers over her and turned away from Mark. His gentle hand on her arm startled her. "Hey there, honey. Do you want to—"

"Not tonight – I have a headache," she cut him off before he could continue. He moved away to his side of the bed, and she instantly regretted how abrupt she had been with him. As she settled down more comfortably into the bed, she felt a tear slowly roll off her face and hit her pillow.

Chapter 35

The Goddess of the Underworld had been right. All of the FEAR-based attacks he had earned before he had been banished were working; with a combination of some of his older abilities, he was able to further his plan a little bit every day.

The most important one he had been using was, of course, Depressive Miasma. It was consistently making her depression deeper, which he took advantage of using something he had acquired at Spiritual Level 32: Dream Control.

32. Dream Control (DC):
Description: *Allows the user to slip into the dreams of a single target, inserting their own dream sequence of their choosing; cannot last for more than 10 minutes; only one use of Dream Control can be used on a single target per attack period; may be canceled at any time*
Magnitude: *1 Complete dream sequence*
Duration: *Variable – 1 second up to 10 minutes based upon user's choice*
SF Cost: *3500*
Target FEAR Requirement: *Level 240*
Max Generated FEAR: *350*
Unmodified Reward Upon Successful Attack: *3500 SF*

Fortunately, for the FEAR requirements, the wife was drowning in it: ever since he started to passively use the Miasma, her already inflated FEAR Level was boosted with every little bump or sound she heard (which wasn't even his doing, the house was just settling). Once he started in with a gradual regimen of specifically targeted dreams, he knew he was getting somewhere when her FEAR Level reached a base of about 500, plus or minus about a hundred depending on the situation.

While they still maintained their prayer rituals, the effectiveness of it was wearing thin on the wife; it now gave very little protection, and even that was gone in less than half an hour. There was no change in the husband: he was still essentially untouchable, and the Spirit Core meant to keep it that way for now.

As for the previous night, he had stepped up his assault, utilizing a mixture of old and new FEAR-based attacks and his new Special Ability he had earned at Spiritual Level 30.

30.1 Special Ability – Power Surge
Once every 10 days, you can shut off all incoming electrical power to your Area of Influence for up to 1 minute, though you can end this before the time limit if you choose to; does not affect cordless or battery-operated electrical objects; generates no FEAR
Cost: 1000 SF
Duration: Up to 1 minute
Cooldown: 9 days, 13 hours, 34 minutes, 16 seconds

He also knew that with the visual appearance of his Mirror Entity, his attacks were hitting another level; he ran the risk that she would say something to her husband. Therefore, before he even contemplated doing it, he made sure he had an answer in the form of the very last FEAR-based attack he received at level 34. It was an invaluable, if expensive, ability that was the only likelihood that he could pull everything off.

34. Short-term Amnesia (STA):

Description: *Destroys 99% of the memories of the last 2 minutes of a single target, eliminating most knowledge of any FEAR-based attacks that they may have suffered at your direction; eliminates all Lifetime FEAR gains and SF earned during those 2 minutes and provides no SF, but maintains the FEAR of the target; may cause a minor headache in the target when activated and increases their Fatigue; dream-like echoes of the attack will affect the target during times of stress*

Magnitude: *2 minutes of memories are erased*

Duration: *Permanent*

SF Cost: 8500

Target FEAR Requirement: *Level 280*

Max Generated FEAR: *0*

Unmodified Reward Upon Successful Attack: *0 SF*

The benefit of "memory wipe" was that he didn't have to rely on the possibility that she would keep her mouth shut and it still increased her FEAR Level. In addition, the "echo" of her traumatic experience would emerge at a time where it would be the most beneficial.

Of course, the major downside to it was that he didn't get any return on his investment: no increase in his Lifetime FEAR and Spiritual Force. That didn't matter to him, since he was sure he had everything he needed; the raising of her base FEAR Level was the most important part. That, and inundating her with visions of her sister and her death while she was both awake and in her dreams.

All in all, a successful night, even if he didn't earn much for it.

Attack Period #380

<u>Results</u>

SF Used: 16925/17000

FEAR Generated (Andrea): 30(PA) + 50(WTC)*4(DM) + 120(AHW)*4(DM) + 22.5(EM)*4(DM) + 200(VHME)*4(DM) + 250(SpTe)*4(DM) + 50(WTC)*4(DM) + 0(STA) = 2800

FEAR Generated (Mark): 0 = 0

Total Correlated Incidentals: 0

Total FEAR Generated: 2800 – 2570(STA) = 230

Lifetime FEAR: 10030/17500

SF Earned (Andrea): 300(PA) + 2000(WTC) = 2300

SF Earned (Mark): 0 = 0

Total SF Earned for next attack period: 2300

He had accumulated some of his Lifetime FEAR back from seven different instances of using his Dream Control attack. He had been spacing them out at irregular intervals to mix it up a little; he expected that if he did it every night, it might become suspicious. Overall, however, it was looking like it was working.

His goal was set now – it would only take time. Fortunately, he had plenty to spare.

Chapter 36

"Are you sure you have to leave? I don't want to stay here by myself tonight."

*She saw her husband sigh in exasperation, his normally even temperament obviously starting to fray from her incessant insistence that he not leave her for the night. She didn't care, though: she honestly **didn't** want to stay there tonight by herself.*

"Honey, I told you I have to go to this meeting down in Orlando; I'd take you with me, but we don't have enough to pay for your hotel room. Since you convinced me that the furnace needed fixing, my emergency fund has been drained – I'm just lucky my company is paying for the trip," he repeated to her for probably the hundredth time. She knew all that, but she was still hoping he would change his mind.

*"Look, it's only one night; I think you'll be okay. You're protected here in this house – if anything, you should be worried about me," he added with a strained smile. He didn't want to leave either, but he **had** to go for his job – there wasn't an option if he wanted to*

keep his job. And they needed his job now, as her current one was starting to lay people off after a merger last week. She didn't know for sure, but she suspected she was on the chopping block; from what she had heard from the others that had been fired, they were giving out generous severance packages — but it would only take them so far.

"Fine, I know you have to go, but I'll miss you."

"I'll miss you, too — and I promise to call you whenever I'm free." With a final kiss, he headed out the door with a small suitcase in his hands. He wasn't going to be gone long, luckily, so he only needed a basic change of clothes and some personal effects. Nevertheless, as soon as the door closed behind him, the house suddenly felt emptier and more menacing. She realized that she hadn't actually been alone in the house for more than a couple of minutes since Jessica had died, and now she was going to be spending almost two full days.

It was really early Monday morning — just past 4am — and Mark was taking an early flight out from Charleston International Airport to Orlando International Airport in Florida. It was a short flight of just over an hour, so that meant that he would be spending most of the rest of the day (and more than half of the next day) in meetings. He would be coming home late in the evening Tuesday night, so at least he wouldn't be gone too long.

One night was long enough.

*She apathetically got herself ready for work, wearing some of her old clothes that she had spent a few evenings tailoring herself to fit better. Now that her frame was a lot slimmer than it used to be (though it was filling out little by little) her old clothes were **way** too big. Since they couldn't afford to buy her a whole new wardrobe, she had taken the time to alter her existing clothes; watching some videos online helped her to make them look better than it would've otherwise, and she was moderately proud of her work.*

But with the worry about Mark being gone the next night, the early morning start, and the horrific nightmare that she had last night concerning her sister's staring eyes looking at her accusingly while she was burning in the fires of Hell – all of it kept her from getting much sleep last night. The three cups of coffee she had already had that morning didn't touch her exhaustion; she hoped that the stronger stuff they had at her office would help.

Once she started to move around, she felt a little better. Within an hour of having the strong, concentrated coffee that she immediately grabbed as soon as she got to work, she managed to forget the empty house that was going to greet her later when she got off work. In fact, she forgot about it until she pulled into their

driveway.

The exhaustion seemed to hit her like a ton of bricks when she put

her car in park. She hesitated on picking up her purse; maybe I

can just drive around, park somewhere, and sleep in my car? *The*

fact that she even contemplated that just went to show how much

she didn't want to go inside the empty house.

With a great effort of will, she grabbed her bag and got out of the

car, walking up the walk until she got to the door. Nervousness hit

her as she fumbled with her keys, dropping them twice before she

was able to get the key in the lock. The door opened with a creepy

squeak that reminded her of those old black-and-white horror

movies; she hadn't really noticed it until now.

Now angry at herself for being such a chicken-shit, she stomped

inside and threw her purse on the side table next to the door. She

headed for the kitchen before she turned around, heading to the

door to lock it. Mark would never forgive me if someone broke in

and murdered me the **one** day he wasn't here.

She spent the rest of the day and early evening jumping at noises

before her exhaustion caught up with her. By the time 9pm rolled

around, she was practically asleep watching some boring news

program on the couch. She hadn't eaten dinner because she couldn't find the energy, even though she knew she would catch some flak for it when her husband found out; he had made it his personal mission to make sure she stayed healthy.

Before she headed upstairs, her phone rang, startling a small scream out of her at the abrupt loud noise. Giggling and shaking with fatigue, she talked to Mark for almost a half-hour before she started to nod off in the middle of their conversation. After the second time he had to shout into his phone to wake her up, he let her go to get some sleep – he promised he would call the next day.

She managed to get herself upstairs, leaving the lights on around the first floor because of two reasons: 1, she didn't want to stumble around alone in the dark if she needed something in the middle of the night and 2, she was too tired to take the few steps it would take to get to them.

She wasn't sure how she made it to the bedroom, but after a quick stop off at the bathroom to pee, she took off the work clothes she hadn't bothered to change out of when she got home and collapsed on the bed in just her bra and panties. Since they had the furnace fixed, the house was now cozy but not too hot, so she had taken to sleeping barely clothed lately.

As soon as her head hit the pillow, she was lost to oblivion.

What is Jessica doing here? Mark let in her sister, who was standing at the door with wet mascara running down her cheeks, following what appeared to be tear streaks. She enveloped her in a massive hug and led her to the couch, where Jessica immediately told her a sob story that was as per usual for her unstable lifestyle. Although she loved her sister, she didn't understand how she could live her life the way she did. She would go crazy if she didn't have a steady job and place to live – not to mention the awesome husband she had.

At that thought, she looked at him and smiled while Jessica continued to bawl her eyes out as she told of her unfortunate circumstances. Suddenly, the recounting of the story abruptly stopped, and Andrea looked back at her sister.

Her sister's face had such a look of fear on it that she flinched back and felt chills run down her spine. Jessica just stared at her and everything seemed to stop; she looked for her husband to find that he was gone. Turning back to her sister, she saw her mouth start to open, growing wider...and larger...until it encompassed most of her face.

She couldn't move or say anything as Jessica's eyes continued to look at her, though now with a glare that portrayed accusation *along with the fear she saw in the rest of the face. Her sister bent forward, as if she was intending to fit Andrea's head inside her mouth and bite it off. She stared inside the gaping blackness that gradually worked its way toward her, somehow feeling herself swallowed whole until everything around her grew dark.*

As her own fear and self-accusation hit her like a shot to the heart, she heard her own voice yell into her mind, "I killed her!"

Chapter 37

She jerked awake, the nightmare she just experienced so real and vivid still in her mind. As she opened her eyes, a bead of sweat rolled down her forehead and fell into her left eye. Whoa! That was so intense it had me sweating. I wish these goddamned dreams would stop already. *She went to reach up with her hand to wipe it away...*

But it wouldn't move.

In fact, as she tried her other arm — thinking that she must be sleeping on the first and all the feeling was gone — she started to freak out as it wouldn't budge either. Her panic intensified as she couldn't move anything: her legs and feet, her fingers and toes, her hips and back, and even her neck. The only thing that she could shift was her eyes, which roamed wildly around the room as her breathing intensified.

She wasn't sure how long she lay there in the bed — paralyzed, panicked, and completely helpless as she heard a noise in the too-empty house.

Click *Click*

She was lying on her side and was staring at the wall, so she couldn't see toward the hallway, but the noise seemed to be coming from downstairs. She wasn't sure what the clicking was, until she heard the same creepy squeaking she had heard from the front door as she opened it coming home.

Maybe Mark is home early! Though I'm sure he would've called first...

She still couldn't move, but she was suddenly filled with a little bit of hope as she listened intently to verify if it was her husband walking through the door. Which was soon crushed as she heard as the drawers and cabinets in the kitchen being slammed open violently, one after another. She didn't hear anything hit the floor and break, fortunately, but with the way it sounded, she wouldn't be surprised if there was some damage to the storage units themselves.

What am I going to do? I can't move and there is someone in my house! Struggling mightily with the paralysis plaguing her, she managed to grunt out an incomprehensible sound, but that was the extent of her victory. She stopped fighting it as she heard the sound of heavy footsteps coming up the stairs.

One after another, they unhesitatingly made their way up, a dozen long strides in total before they stopped at the entrance to her room. An icy chill crept up her spine as she felt the gaze of whoever it was standing there looking at her; before long, every hair on her body shot straight up as she experienced the intense anxiety of waiting for the proverbial "axe to fall". She wanted to shout out for whoever was staring at her to leave, take whatever stuff he desired, and to leave her alone! But her mouth and voice were frozen solid just like the rest of her body.

Just when she couldn't take it anymore – the anticipation was almost literally killing her – the presence seemed to fade from her perception. The feeling of someone standing there, watching her, was gone; she heard the same footsteps recede down the hallway and down the stairs, leisurely taking their time like their arrival.

She let out a breath that she hadn't known that she was holding, the burning in her chest accompanying the hot tears spilling from her eyes. Another minute went by before her tense body relaxed, the suddenness of returning feeling and movement shocking her.

But not for long.

She immediately rolled over to her husband's side of the bed, grabbing at the drawer where he held the gun he had bought not so long ago. Shakily, she brought forth the handgun from the recesses of the nightstand, holding it with a death-grip until her hand started to hurt. Pointing it toward the hallway outside her door, she sobbed and shivered uncontrollably as she tried to keep it steady.

*She waited there for a good 15 minutes, until her shaking and tears stopped long enough for her to search for her cell phone. I left it downstairs on the couch! She had been so tired she didn't even think to bring it to bed. Of course, **now** she was wide awake.*

Knowing there was no help for it, she kept the gun in her hand trained in the general direction of the doorway while she dressed in the clothes she had haphazardly thrown off when she got to the bedroom earlier. Tiptoeing to the door, she could see that it was empty; sticking her head and the gun in her hand out, she looked around the corner of the doorway into the bathroom, not taking any chances that whoever had broken in had hid in there, waiting for her to come out.

Fortunately, it was empty – and so was the guest bedroom (Jessica's old room) when she checked it as well. She stayed as light on her feet as she could as she gingerly walked down the stairs, her eyes wide open and frantically roaming all around the parts of the living room she could see. Expecting someone to be hiding around the corner, or behind the couch, or underneath the dining room table, she cautiously (with gun pointed always ahead of her) got to her phone, which she was pleasantly surprised was still there and hadn't been taken.

The front door was wide open, showing no signs of having been forced. I know I locked it earlier – I made particularly sure I did. She thought that someone either had a key (which wasn't entirely **impossible** *but wasn't likely) or they had picked the lock. And the deadbolt.*

A quick glance at a portion of the kitchen showed that every cabinet and drawer she could see had been opened and were sticking out, as if someone had wanted to check them all at the same time. She didn't look any further than that, as she immediately grabbed her keys from next to the doorway and ran to her car. Flinging the gun into the passenger seat, Andrea threw the car into reverse and took off, only stopping to call 911 when she was parked in front of the nearest gas station.

Chapter 38

The sight of police back in the house reminded Clive of the events surrounding the death of his first victim. At least his first victim as a Spirit Core; if he were to count the victims of his killing spree when he was alive, it would've made the sister #363. And he remembered every single one.

They didn't find anything, of course; there was nothing for them to find. And the fact that nothing was gone, coupled with the lack of forced entry, caused the police (who were *still* suspicious over their complicity in the aforementioned murder) to blame the event on juveniles who found an unlocked door and wanted to scare her before running away. Harmless teenage fun...or at least that's what Clive heard one of the uniformed police officers say behind their back.

The husband had come home from his trip early, after apparently receiving a phone call from both the wife and the police. He seemed angry more than anything and demanded that the cops do everything they could to find the perpetrators; even Clive, with his lack of experience with understanding some particular social interactions, could see that the assurances they were given were said in a sarcastic tone.

The wife was a wreck — exactly what he had planned. It was going even better than that, in fact; they were both so caught up in mundane matters that they started to neglect the spiritual. The man was still well-protected most of the time, but the woman appeared to have given up trying to maintain any type of faith in her prayers. Most of the time any small boosts they gave her were gone within minutes.

His newer FEAR-based attacks, combined with some of his older ones, had gone over well. After the latest assault, he reviewed what he had attacked with — and what he could do better in the future. Fortunately, her FEAR Level at the beginning of the night was so high that he didn't have to worry about any protections or any of his attacks' requirements.

Andrea Stone

FEAR Level: 982 - (2 Temporary Reduction) = 980

Resistance to FEAR attacks: 5 + (1 Temporary Boost) = 6

Weaknesses: Depression

Immunity: Localized Cold Spot

Perception: 1/10

Fatigue: 85%

He started the night (or early morning, depending on how you looked at it) with another use of Dream Control, which — accompanied with the Spiritual Telepathy that woke her up — further entrenched the thought into her mind that it was all her fault that her sister died. After that came the lynchpin in his plan that night: Sleep Paralysis.

31. Sleep Paralysis (SP):

Description: *Must be initiated while target is still asleep; when the target wakes up, they are completely immobilized for up to 10 minutes, allowing for only the movement of their eyes; does not physically harm the target, and if any external harm is experienced, the target will regain all mobility*

Magnitude: *Full-body paralysis following a period of sleep, with only eye-movement permitted*

Duration: *Up to 10 minutes, can be cancelled at any time*

SF Cost: *2700*

Target FEAR Requirement: *Level 220*

Max Generated FEAR: *270*

Unmodified Reward Upon Successful Attack: *2700 SF*

With her unable to move, she couldn't see to verify what was happening in her house; added to that, she was forced to experience everything imprisoned in a body that refused to obey. Once she was paralyzed, Clive used another of his newer abilities to start the next part of his plan.

29. Object Manipulation – Unlock Door (OMUD):

Description: *Use of this ability must be out of visual sight of any targets; fully unlocks 1 door with manual locks; does not affect doors with electronic keypads or other technological defenses (use of*

Electrical Manipulation is needed to deactivate them before using this ability); does not generate FEAR or Spiritual Force

Magnitude: *Unlock 1 door that has manual locks*

SF Cost: *800*

Target FEAR Requirement: *Level 190*

Max Generated FEAR: *0*

Unmodified Reward Upon Successful Attack: *0 SF*

Once the door was unlocked, it was an easy use of his Object Manipulation – Open/Close Doors attack to open the front door. That done, another of his abilities – that he had earned at Spiritual Level 22 – came into play.

22. Object Manipulation – Open All Cabinets and Drawers (OMOACD):

Description: *Use of this ability must be out of visual sight of any targets; one-by-one or all-at-once, open all of the cabinets and/or drawers in a single room; generates FEAR, but does not provide any Spiritual Force; does not apply to appliances*

Magnitude: *Open all drawers and cabinets in a single room*

SF Cost: *3000*

Target FEAR Requirement: *Level 120*

Max Generated FEAR: *300*

Unmodified Reward Upon Successful Attack: *0 SF*

Both that and the previous FEAR-based attacks didn't provide him with any Spiritual Force, but at least the more expensive one brought her FEAR Level up. There was no explanation for the lack of SF, but he suspected that it was because it was something visual that was done out of sight of his victims.

After that, it was basically just a liberal use of his Auditory Hallucination – Footsteps with a little Piloerection Reflex thrown in for good measure. All of which shot her already heightened FEAR shooting to nearly 3,000; not nearly enough to kill her, though at points she appeared as if all she wanted to do was die to make it all stop. That wasn't his goal at that point, however.

Attack Period #393

Results

SF Used: 17000/17000

FEAR Generated (Andrea): 350(DC) + 270(SP) + 250(SpTe) + 180(OMOCD) + 300(OMOACD) + 125(AHF) + 125(AHF) + 10(PR) = 1610

Total FEAR Generated: 1610

Lifetime FEAR: 11990/17500

SF Earned (Andrea): 3500(DC) + 2700(SP) + 2500(SpTe) + 1800(OMOCD) + 1250(AHF) + 1250(AHF) + 100(PR) = 13100

Total SF Earned for next attack period: 13100

He deliberately didn't use the Depressive Miasma that night; although the use of it most likely would've killed her, he had been getting better at restraining himself. Although the emotional feedback was still intense, he was continuing to learn how to concentrate on the bigger picture. It was something that would've been helpful while he was still alive; if he hadn't been so focused on killing at random, he might've been able to plan things better so that he wouldn't have been caught.

No, the wife needed to stay alive a little longer – she was to play a vitally important role in her husband's downfall.

Chapter 39

Thanksgiving – definitely not a time to give thanks in their household.

A year ago, Andrea's sister Jessica had been killed by the evil entity that had inhabited their house. With everything that had happened over the past twelve months, they didn't have a whole lot to be thankful for: held by the police and – still – suspects in the murder of her sister, losing her job and being forced to find a lower-paying one, the break-in and theft, the horrible nightmares, the guilt that came from her last relative's death, and finally the recent invasion of their home by some unknown person.

Mark thought that she had left the house unlocked and some kids got in, terrorizing the "murderess" who lived in the house. He thought it wasn't a coincidence that it happened when he wasn't there; they wouldn't try it with him around. No matter what she said to protest his assumption that she left the door unlocked, he didn't listen. He had gotten more distant and standoffish since he had come home from his meeting in Florida; she knew that, as a result of his having to leave early, he was facing a lot of pressure at work.

But she knew that it wasn't all him – it was in a big part her fault. She found herself down in the dumps almost every night, sniffling and sobbing uncontrollably while she continued to blame herself for the death of Jessica. It seemed like the only thing she could think about, awake or asleep; especially when the one-year anniversary of her horrific murder started creeping up on her.

And it **was** a murder, despite the fact that the murderer was an invisible presence.

She knew she wasn't the best person to be around when she was figuratively beating herself up every day, but he had stuck with and supported her like the awesome husband he was. Eventually, though, she could see that he was getting worn down dealing with her issues; she wished she could stop, but she just couldn't. Even if she wanted to go to therapy to help with her (what she was almost positive it was) depression, they couldn't afford even the co-pays seeing a mental health specialist would cost.

She refused to self-medicate with mood-altering drugs or alcohol; although her sister wasn't involved with them when she came to see Andrea, she knew there was a history of their abuse in the *past. That was the last thing she wanted to do to uphold the memory of Jessica.*

So she dealt with it, consciously trying not to drag Mark down into her depressive depths with her. She (as well as her husband) thought things might be calmer after the holidays, when the time of year everything happened was over. Everything she saw, from the happy commercials and special episodes of various shows on TV of people enjoying a feast on Thanksgiving, to the Black Friday advertisements she saw in the stores already, they all contributed to fouling the memory of the once-enjoyable holiday.

Come January, she expected (and fervently hoped) that it would be better. She was tired all the time from the sporadic nightmares she still had, her unconscious mind screaming at her that it was all her fault for not recognizing her sister was in danger, and for letting her stay there in the first place. The only thing she was glad of these days was that the...demon...was gone.

When Thanksgiving came around, they both agreed that they would go out instead of staying in. There was no way Andrea was going to cook; after the delicious dinner her sister made last year, she couldn't and didn't want to top it, and it brought back too many memories. They had saved up a little bit to be able to have a nice dinner – nothing extraordinary – but it was a nice treat since they didn't have a lot of chances lately to go out on the town.

Hmm, maybe we can make this a new tradition for the years to come, *she thought, as she walked arm-in-arm with her husband out to the car after a delicious and "non-depressive" dinner. It always seemed that all her negative feelings intensified while she was at home; she resolved to find some things to do outside of the house with Mark in the future (that didn't cost anything or at least very little, of course). The night out was just what they both needed to take their minds off of the holiday.*

Her spirits dampened a little when they got home, though by the time she took off her heavy winter jacket after walking through the door, the heat from the furnace warming up the house comforted her. It had been unseasonably cold lately, so much so that she almost thought it might be chilly enough to snow. In their part of the country, however, it was rare; it was more likely they'd have freezing rain than anything. When she thought about it, she couldn't remember a time when she'd seen more than a dusting of snow, even on the coldest nights.

It was late by the time they got home, so with an unspoken agreement they decided to head straight to bed. The sooner this day is over, the sooner I can hopefully start to heal. *She knew it* might be wishful thinking, but it was the only thing she had going for her at the moment.

Nothing out of the ordinary happened while they were getting ready for bed, even though she (and even Mark) was silently worried that the evil demon would rear its ugly head. She was **not** disappointed when the night was as calm as every other one that they'd had since the house had its priestly blessing.

For some extra insurance, she made sure to triple the prayers she said that night, though she still couldn't manage to find the will to believe that they were working.

*   *   *

Something woke her up; as she struggled to wake up fully, she couldn't decide if it was the awkward way that she was sleeping finally hurting her back, or if it was because it was freezing inside their room. She could see her breath when she breathed out; a sudden spike of fear assaulted her, until she realized that it was silent. Too silent – she couldn't hear the low hum of the furnace through the few air ducts running through the house.

She didn't know jack about how to fix it and wasn't going to try her hand at it now. Making sure she stayed underneath the comfortably warm covers, she wiggled over to the other side of the bed and woke Mark up. "Mark. Mark. Mark!"

She didn't mean to shout, but the last utterance of his name came out a little sharper than she had intended. Luckily, it had the desired effect.

"What is it?" he mumbled, barely awake and coherent enough to formulate the question.

"I think the furnace is on the fritz. I thought you said it was fixed."

"What? Yes, I feel it now, it's freezing in here." He seemed more awake now. "And yes, it **was** fixed – but it's old. We couldn't afford a new furnace, so it was the best solution available to us at the time. Things break, honey; I just hope it's something easy like the pilot light going out." He started unfolding himself from the bedsheets and comforter. "At least the guy showed me what to do if there was a problem with the thermocouple...well, at least if there isn't a complete malfunction in it."

He yawned as he got up and put some socks on, as even the carpeted floor appeared to suck up the heat from the room. As he was going down to the basement, she heard him put on his shoes from the living room; if it was chilly upstairs, it was probably a freezer in there.

*The news said it was going to be cold, but she didn't think it was going to be **this** cold. It wasn't even winter yet, but the meteorologist on Channel 5 said that a storm from out of the west had pushed all the cold air to the coast. She didn't understand all of it – all she knew was that she wasn't ready for the cold weather yet.*

Chapter 40

She lay there in bed for a while as she tried to keep warm. She wasn't keeping track of the time, but she thought that it couldn't have been more than ten minutes before she heard the rumbling of the furnace coming back to life. Its gentle hum was joined by some warmer movements of air against her face. The heat she started to feel was welcome after the icy coldness their room formerly had.

She was beginning to drift off, fully intending to wait for her husband to come back but failing miserably, when she heard a loud *thump* from downstairs. Jerking awake, she sat up in bed as her husband yelled something unintelligible down in what she thought was the living room. Throwing her blankets aside, she got up and ran to the doorway of the bedroom, where she stopped, listening intently to...something...downstairs.

"Mark, are you alright? I thought I heard something?"

The very air seemed to take a breath as her voice echoed through the house, before everything happened all at once. She could hear some grunts along with the sounds of someone straining, followed by the impacts of something heavy hitting the floor.

"Andrea! Run! There's someone he—" was all he said, before she heard him scream out, a bone-chilling yell that was as much surprise as pain. It pierced her mind with a spike of helplessness and sympathy, before it was abruptly cut off. Silence reigned throughout the house, before she heard some eerily familiar footsteps walking around the living room.

Oh shit oh shit oh shit, Mark! What in the hell happened? Is he dead? Worried that she already knew the answer, the footsteps seemed to break the paralysis she felt when she heard him shout, allowing her to rush over to Mark's nightstand and open the drawer. With shaky hands, she pulled out the handgun, and unsteadily turned toward the doorway.

Andrea was shaking so badly at this point that she didn't think she'd be able to hold the gun steady; in fact, she ended up pulling the trigger accidentally. Luckily, the safety had still been on, so no harm no foul. She managed to grab her gun hand with her other, using them both to steady herself as she stood in front of the bed, facing toward the hallway.

Thoughts of closing the door beckoned her, as well as a quick glance back to her phone on her own nightstand, and she took a half step toward it before she heard the familiar heavy footsteps on the stairs. Instead, she stayed where she was, full of false bravado, the fear and worry she felt for her husband calming her down enough to remember the brief training her husband had given regarding using the gun.

She clicked the safety off as a figure wearing a baggy, dark-colored hoodie and black jeans walked up the stairs, taking its time to get to the top. The figure made no noise other than its substantial tread, which seemed to reverberate through her soul the closer it came to her. As it got to the top of the stairs, the figure appeared to pause as it saw her there pointing a gun in its direction. After a moment, though, it started moving towards her with its hands upraised, as if it was trying to reassure her that it meant no harm.

"Who are you?! What are you doing in my house?! Where is my husband?!" she practically screamed out, the hysterical note in her voice obvious even to her. She didn't care though; she really was generally hysterical with fear for both herself and her husband by that point. The figure didn't answer, though it did pause after her outburst at the threshold of the bedroom.

She tried to look under its hood to see its face, but it was completely dark; it was almost as if the shadowed dark itself was hiding its identity. She assumed it was a he, but she could be mistaken because the overall form was very slight; it was always possible it was a woman in oversized clothes.

"Don't step any closer! I **will** shoot you!" She didn't know if she really could or not, but the stranger wouldn't know that.

With arms still outstretched in front of it, the hooded person slowly – with deliberate steps – crossed the distance to her until it was only inches away from the end of the gun. I can't do it, I can't do it, I can't do it. Tears ran down her face as she shouted, "Get away from me!"

Hands that she hadn't even seen start to reach for her gun when she yelled at the figure paused, before resuming their slow and cautious journey to her weapon. At this point her arms were jolting spastically with fear; when a hand came down on her own, the icy chillness of it shocked her so much that she pulled the trigger in reflex.

The shot was so loud and powerful that she jerked back with the recoil, surprise warring with her fright shutting down her outer senses for a few seconds. When she recovered enough to look, she could see the figure on the ground, groaning in pain and clutching at its chest. Although she couldn't see anything on its dark clothes, she could see red staining its delicate-looking hands as it attempted to stem the tide of lifeblood draining from it.

The hood had fallen back from its head, showing a face straight out of her nightmares: Jessica. She was writhing in pain and fear, all while looking unflinchingly at Andrea's eyes with an accusatory stare. Pale in the bloodless look of death, her skin had a waxy appearance to it, only heightened by the few spots of blood that were flung up from the wound in her chest.

And then the same voice from her dreams invaded her mind. "I killed her!"

This has to be another nightmare! That's all this is, another stupid dream! Oh God, why do you do this to me! Haven't I suffered enough?! *She collapsed to her knees next to the dying body of her sister, watching her bleed out from the wound she caused in her chest. Jessica's accusing eyes still stared at her, making her feel guilty for killing her, even though she realistically knew her death wasn't really her fault. It didn't stop the tears from falling down her face, mixing with the blood starting to pool on the carpet.*

Andrea looked at her sister slowly dying and thought, Why won't this nightmare just end? Am I forced to watch the entire time while she dies? *She looked down at the forgotten weapon in her lap, her hand absently holding it even through all the despair she felt. In the midst of throwing it away in disgust, she paused.*

Don't they say if you die in your dream you'll wake up? *She knew it was a sin to commit suicide, but since this was a dream, it didn't count.* Right? *She couldn't take it anymore, she didn't want to watch as her sister died right in front of her eyes for the umpteenth time in a nightmare. She just wanted all of the self-flagellation and guilt to end...so she brought the slightly warm tip of the gun to underneath her chin.*

With a final prayer that this would be the last of the nightmares she would experience, she pulled the trigger.

*   *   *

Mark was fed up with their stupid furnace. He knew it was old, but the service technician that had installed some new parts told him that it should last at least another five years before he had to seriously consider replacing the entire unit. Which was good, since they definitely didn't have enough in their budget for a whole new furnace, or even a refurbished one.

The hit to their finances they experienced when Andrea lost her old job was still something they were recovering from, but he had hopes that he would still be up for that promotion at work. Despite leaving the shareholders meeting in Florida where he was supposed to present a new idea he had, he thought that if, even after everything that had happened, he could secure the position, the pay raise would more than make up for the deficit they were currently experiencing.

He grabbed his shoes on the way down, knowing that the cement floor in the basement would be like walking on literal ice. When he got to the basement and turned on the light, he saw right away that the furnace was indeed not working. In fact, it looked as if all of the power going to it had been shut off for some reason. He grabbed a flashlight from one of the storage racks and tried to turn it on, but the batteries had died at some point.

Fortunately, he thought there was another one further down the rack...right there! He grabbed it and turned it – dead as well. He was going to have to make sure he bought some new batteries when he got enough money – D-cells were expensive. It wouldn't do to have no working flashlights, especially if they had another power outage like they had almost a month ago.

With no external light, he fumbled around the furnace, looking for a reason why it stopped working. He fiddled with the plug, thinking it had been jiggled loose over time. He touched and wiggled some other parts, pretending to himself that he actually knew what he was doing, but in the end nothing worked. He was about to give up and tell her wife that he would call someone tomorrow to fix it (though he wasn't sure how they would pay for it), when it suddenly kicked back to life.

He stood there looking at it for a couple of minutes, making sure that it really was working and wasn't going to shut down when he looked away. He couldn't feel much difference in the chilly basement, but when he was close enough to the vent leading away, he could feel the heat radiating off of the old, leaky ducts. Another thing we need to get fixed or replaced.

He quickly ran back up the stairs to the living room, where he kicked off his shoes so that they landed near-ish the door. Looking forward to getting back to sleep, he walked upstairs and heard a weird *click* come from the bedroom. It didn't really occur to him what it was until he saw Andrea standing in front of the bed, wide-eyed and shaking – with their gun pointed straight at him.

"Whoa, honey – what's going on? Did you hear someone else downstairs? Put that thing away, everything is fine," he softly said, not wanting to startle her. When she didn't respond, he slowly walked toward the bedroom with his arms outstretched in as non-threatening a manner as possible. I think all of the stress has finally gotten to her; no matter what it takes, I've got to get her to a doctor. *Of course, he had to get the gun away from her first, before she hurt someone – or even herself.*

"Who are you?! What are you doing in my house?! Where is my husband?!"

What is she talking about, can't she see I'm right here? He continued to speak reassuringly to her, to get her to put the gun down – but it was like she couldn't even hear him. From what he could see, she appeared to be lost in her own fantasy world, the nightmares she didn't like to talk about – but he knew she was having – were manifesting themselves while she was awake. She's worse off than I thought.

*"Don't step any closer! I **will** shoot you!"*

She didn't react other than to shake even more violently when he started to inch closer to her, intending to slowly relieve her of the weapon before something bad happened. His soft patient voice seemed to be helping, so he kept it up as he reached for the gun, only to jump in fright as she shouted, "Get away from me!"

She didn't pull the trigger, so he thought there was a good chance she wouldn't. Mark knew his wife, and she wasn't a killer; it was a consideration that he thought about when he bought the gun in the first place. He was pretty sure she wouldn't ever fire it, but if having it in the house made her feel safer and more secure, he was all for it.

He would do anything for his love.

Mark's hands continued their journey to the deadly weapon in the hands of his wife, his everlasting love, his soul mate; but his freezing hands that were messing with the furnace downstairs hadn't warmed up yet, and the shock of his cold fingers made her flinch and pull the trigger.

He didn't remember falling; the first thing he remembered was looking up at the ceiling above, noticing the few areas where the acoustic covering it was stained and needed replacing or some new paint. He felt a huge weight on his chest, but there was no pain. He brought his hands up to feel a warm wetness against his fingers; the light coming from the hallway showed they were covered in differing shades of red. And that's when the excruciating pain of being shot point-blank in the chest hit him.

He tried to cry out, but he just couldn't seem to find enough air. He coughed a couple of times, feeling liquid coming up in response. I think I'm dying. He knew he should be panicked, but all he could think of was his wife.

She was standing over him, looking on in horror at what she had done. Collapsing to her knees, the gun hanging limply in her right fist, she started sobbing uncontrollably. He tried to ask for her to call 911, but all that came out was gurgles and bubbles from his lips. Spots started to cloud his vision as he saw her start to throw away the gun, only to stop and stare at it for a moment.

The next thing he knew, she had the barrel stuck underneath her chin; silent prayers that he thought he should recognize formed on her lips, before the sudden gunshot made him jump in surprise – which made all his pain fade away as he saw the blood and brain matter spatter against the same ceiling that he was just looking at a few moments ago.

He couldn't move, he couldn't breathe, his wife had shot him and then killed herself; but that wasn't the worst part. As the light faded from his eyes, he felt the barest of winds caress his face as if mocking him. No! We blessed the house! It should have no power—

But he couldn't finish the thought as it emptied from his mind, like the last trickling of his blood joining the ever-growing pool underneath the bodies of Mark and Andrea Stone.

Chapter 41

Clive wasn't sure how he held onto his concentration after the woman shot herself, but he remembered a part of his calculating mind absently notice that the FEAR Level of the man was just barely high enough to affect with his Errant Breeze, knocking it up a notch before he expired as well. Once that was done, he surrendered to the sweet experience of fear, pain, and death he received from the emotional feedback.

He floated in an ocean of bliss, the joyous feelings of **something** other than his normal absence of emotions was better than he had ever experienced. The death of the sister had been overwhelmingly awesome, but two together had topped it in terms of sheer enjoyment and unending euphoria. It was as close to heaven as he was likely to get, and he reveled in the infusion of the charged emotional pleasure.

Even when he came back to himself, hiding in the corner of the main bedroom, he could still feel everything like a jolt of adrenaline through his non-existing veins. He imagined it was like the high that drug users felt; he had never tried them when he was alive, but he had heard about it. *If this is what it felt like, it's a wonder that **everyone** wasn't addicted to them.* He didn't want it to end, but he could sense a lessening of it when he was able to see again.

I must've been out of it for a long time. Expecting to see police, he was instead greeted with an empty room, the carpet ripped out down to the floorboards and a fresh coat of paint over the walls and ceiling. He broke out of his self-imposed static placement and roamed around the house. Everywhere he looked, it was empty: the guest bedroom, the bathroom, the living room, the kitchen, the basement. Even the walls were bare, but he could see where the pictures had hung previously. In short, it appeared as if it had been completely stripped and abandoned.

He looked outside to see a "For Sale by Bank" sign in the front yard, though he doubted there would be any takers in the near future. A thin layer of dust over the surfaces in the kitchen and bathroom counters hinted at the fact that it had been a while since the house had been emptied.

With nothing better to do, he floated in the middle of the living room and looked at the notifications from his guide-assist that he had ignored in favor of assessing his current situation.

Attack Period #395

Results

SF Used: 17000/17000

FEAR Generated (Andrea): 350(DC) + 250(SpTe) + 50(WTC) + 300(EM) + 400(AHC) + 125(AHF) + 125(AHF) + 500(VHC) + 200(CI) + 250(SpTe) = 2550

FEAR Generated (Mark): 20(CI) + 3(EB) = 23

Total Correlated Incidentals: 223

Bonus Death FEAR: 1000

Total FEAR Generated: 3773

Lifetime FEAR: 16813/17500

SF Earned (Andrea): 0 = 0

SF Earned (Mark): 0 = 0

Total SF Earned for next attack period: 0

The rest of the attack periods following were blank, though he noticed from the number of them that it had been at least three months since he had killed his victims. He didn't receive a lot of Lifetime FEAR from the night, but that had never been his initial goal. He would've spent the necessary Spiritual Force if she hadn't killed herself to ramp up her FEAR Level enough to kill her like he did her sister, but it turned out to be unnecessary.

He still couldn't believe how well everything had worked out, especially with all of the variables involved.

It all started with another Dream Control (which he had been using liberally lately, as it primed her for the night), followed by a Spiritual Telepathy to wake her up. Before that happened, he shut down the furnace using his Electrical Manipulation and cooled down the house with some Wide-range Temperature Changes. When the husband went down to fix their malfunctioning heating system, he started the most-tenuous part of his plan.

When the man was done in the basement (he just let the time expire on his Electrical Manipulation attack), he activated his Force Absorption Special Ability to acquire as much SF as possible and used something new on the woman.

21. Auditory Hallucination – Custom (AHC):
Description: *Causes a single target to hear a custom auditory hallucination for predetermined amount of time; the custom auditory hallucination can be whatever the user decides; does not block out other sounds and can be cancelled at any time*
Magnitude: *Single target*
Duration: Variable – from 1 to 30 seconds (depending upon SF spent)
SF Cost: *Variable – 375 to 4000 (375 for the first second, 125 for each additional second)*
Target FEAR Requirement: *Level 110*
Max Generated FEAR: *400*
Unmodified Reward Upon Successful Attack: *4000 SF*

Clive was able to create the sounds of a struggle in the living room while the husband was still down in the basement. As soon as he came upstairs, the hallucination was cut off after he made it seem like the man had been killed or silenced by someone. Two uses of hallucinatory footsteps sent the wife running for the gun like he thought she would, and then two more new attacks finished everything off.

28. Silent Void (SV):

Description: *Creates a bubble of silence around the head of a single target, preventing them from hearing anything outside of it; will move with them, though the more they move the shorter it will last; does not distort or prevent sounds they make from reaching outside sources; if another target physically touches the invisible bubble, it will immediately be canceled; may be cancelled at any time by user; generates no FEAR or SF*

Magnitude: *Single target*

Duration: 3 minutes

SF Cost: *2900*

Target FEAR Requirement: *Level 180*

Max Generated FEAR: *0*

Unmodified Reward Upon Successful Attack: *0 SF*

33. Visual Hallucination – Custom (VHC):

Description: *Creates a visual hallucination to a single target of whatever the user desires; the more believable and life-like the hallucination, the more effective it will be (rewarded SF dependent upon effectiveness); does not create auditory hallucinations (must use a different attack for sounds); if a target interacts with the hallucination, they will pass right through it; can be cancelled at any time*

Magnitude: *Single target*

Duration: 3 minutes

SF Cost: *5000*

Target FEAR Requirement: *Level 260*

Max Generated FEAR: *500*

Unmodified Reward Upon Successful Attack: *100 SF*

They were what allowed Clive to place the image of her sister over the advancing form of the man, and also block out his attempts to communicate with her. She fortunately didn't notice that she couldn't hear anything but herself talking; her FEAR Level was jacked up so high by that point that all she could concentrate on was the figure in front of her. Everything after that point just flowed naturally.

So...now he was done with his objective. He wasn't sure what—

Congratulations!
You have succeeding of capturing the souls of not only 2, but 3 innocent victims! Your current local administrator sends their regards for your success!
Consequently, for your efforts, you have been awarded an additional 10,000 FEAR toward your Lifetime total!

Congratulations!
Your Spiritual Level has increased to 35!
....
Your Spiritual Level has increased to 43!
Max and Nightly SF Recharge has increased! (X9)
New FEAR-based attack available! (X9)

New Special Ability available!

Uh, ok...that's good to know, but what I am supposed—

Additionally, you have also earned the right to choose your next course of action:

1. Stay in your current Area of Influence, expanding it to include the outside sections directly adjacent to the residence; every time you complete an objective you may choose to expand this territory to include nearby residences as well

   - The downside of this choice is that there will be an unpredictable amount of time until more victims decide to move into your Area of Influence
   - In addition, you will keep the current FEAR-based attacks and Special Abilities that you have acquired, though whether or not they will be suitable for your new victims is unknown at this time

2. Move to a completely new location, transferring your Spirit Core to someplace entirely at random; currently, you cannot choose where you will go, though with enough objectives completed in the future, you will be able to do so (Objectives Completed 1/5)

- The downside to this option is when you are transferred to a new location, you will lose all of your Lifetime Fear, your Spiritual Levels, and your current FEAR-based attacks and Special Abilities; essentially, you will start over
- However, for choosing to brave the unknown, you will receive a bonus 10% more Lifetime FEAR after using your attacks, though this will not affect the actual FEAR generated by your attacks; this bonus will increase with subsequent location transfers
- In addition, all of your FEAR-based attacks that you acquire in your new location will be tailored to your current targets

Hmm...that's a hard decision. Play it safe – keeping everything that I've earned so far, or "brave the unknown", as it says.

Clive wasn't one for normally taking risks, he preferred to have everything laid out and straightforward (breaking into houses and killing the people inside didn't count as a risk to him – he knew exactly what he was doing). He lived his whole life making decisions not based on emotional "feelings", so he wasn't planning on starting now.

Nevertheless, he was still "high" on emotional feedback...which may have influenced his final decision...

Epilogue

Although it wasn't *quite* as painful as the initial transformation into a Spirit Core, it was still enjoyable enough to Clive that he realized he made the right decision. *If I can experience that every time that I complete my objectives, it just gives me more motivation to kill my targets.*

Opening his "eyes", he found himself in a large dark space, the only light entering through the cracks in a doorway at the top of some unsteady-looking wooden steps. It didn't matter too much, though, as he didn't need it to see his new Area of Influence.

The cement foundation making up the walls of the space indicated that he was in a basement; a dirty, spider-infested basement filled with random disorganized piles of old furniture, toys, and various sports equipment. *Quite a change from the last place.* After exploring the entirety of the dingy basement, including the new-ish furnace (which only had a very small layer of dust compared to everything else), he floated toward the exit.

Indeed, the old wooden stairs were a little rickety, though he did see that some effort had been made to add braces to them recently. Given the new furnace, he assumed it had been done during the installation so that no one would fall through them carrying the heavy appliance.

At the top of the steps, he floated through the thick wooden door, only to find himself in a very large, sparsely decorated living room. The house was completely silent, other than the ticking of a clock he could hear in the distance and the low hum from the kitchen he could see through the nearest entryway. As opposed to his former "residence", this one appeared to be much, much larger. Vaulted ceilings with dark wooden beams running across showed that it was at least two stories, though even that might be deceptive. It was entirely possible that there was a third level that he couldn't see from his current location.

The furniture that was there was well-used but not dirty or destroyed; instead, it looked lived-in. There was no TV in the room that he could see, but what he did see caught his attention.

On the wall next to the entrance, he saw multiple photographs hanging on the wall, depicting what he assumed were the residents of his new Area of Influence. Various baby pictures of a boy and a girl – different ages – started on the right side, with their stages of growth and accomplishments evidenced the further left he perused. The latest pictures showed a girl with waist-length blonde hair – approximately 10 years of age, and a boy who appeared to be around age 8 with light brown hair. Of the parents, there was no sign of them; it was apparently just a wall to showcase the kids.

Alert!

(1) Mortal approaching your Area of Influence!

Location: Front External Door

Automatically transfer to alert location? Yes/No

This should be...what is it they say...fun?

End of Book 1

Author's Note

I hope you have enjoyed Core of Fear!

I always wondered, when watching paranormal-themed horror movies, what the motivation was behind the "spirit" or "ghost" or "demon". I know that, most of the time, the gradual ramping up of their scare tactics was for the benefit of good pacing in a movie – but what about real life? Would a real spirit act the same way if they had a choice? If they were able to do enough to kill the residents of the house that they "haunted", why didn't they do it right away? Was there some sort of spiritual system set up that required them to, "just scare them a little bit for a couple of weeks, then you can see about killing them"?

I'm not saying that I answered that, because, really, no one really could. But this is just my interpretation set in a structured, logical (at least to me) form.

As for the ruthless, uncaring nature of the "protagonist", I didn't want to fall into the pitfalls I see time and time again of an "evil overlord" showing a caring side, sparing his victims because, like the Grinch, he/she grew a heart. No, Clive is not one to do that; he was deliberately created to shrug off what most people might worry over – killing "innocent" people.

I originally struggled to figure out how a normal man or woman could get transformed into a Spirit Core and kill people they didn't know. It could be done, but I always ran into the literary equivalent of a wall: morality. Could they kill other people to save someone they love? Eh...yes. But what about when that person is safe? Would they keep going, or would they stop, ending the story? Clive Logan solved that dilemma.

Again, thank you for reading and I implore you to consider leaving a review – I love 4 and 5-star ones! Reviews make it more likely that others will pick up a good book and read it!

If you enjoy dungeon core, dungeon corps, dungeon master, dungeon lord, dungeonlit or any other type of dungeon-themed stories and content, check out the Dungeon Corps Facebook group where you can find all sorts of dungeon content.

If you would like to learn more about the Gamelit genre, please join the Gamelit Society facebook group.

LitRPG is a growing subgenre of GameLit – if you are fond of LitRPG, Fantasy, Space Opera, and the Cyberpunk styles of books, please join the LitRPG Books Facebook group.

For another great Facebook group, visit LitRPG Rebels as well.

To learn more about LitRPG, talk to authors including myself, and just have an awesome time, please join the LitRPG Group.

If you would like to contact me with any questions, comments, or suggestions for future books you would like to see, you can reach me at jonathanbrooksauthor@gmail.com.

I will try to keep my blog updated on any new developments which you can find on my Author Page on Amazon.

To sign up for my mailing list, please visit:

http://eepurl.com/dl0bK5

Appendix – Attacks/Special Abilities

1. Localized Cold Spot (LCS):

Description: *Generates a perceived temperature drop in a specific area*

Magnitude: *Fills a sphere 500 cubic inches in volume (Approximately the size of a basketball)*

Duration: *5 minutes*

SF Cost: *50*

Target FEAR Requirement: *Level 1*

Max Generated FEAR: *5*

Unmodified Reward Upon Successful Attack: *50 SF*

1. Errant Breeze (EB):

Description: *Generates a brief room-temperature breeze in an otherwise calm environment*

Magnitude: *Variable – strength and size are dependent upon SF used*

Duration: *Variable – duration is dependent upon SF used, lasting from 1 to 3 seconds*

SF Cost: *Variable – depending upon strength/size/duration desired, starting from 20 up to 100*

Target FEAR Requirement: *Level 3*

Max Generated FEAR: *10*

Unmodified Reward Upon Successful Attack: *20 SF*

1. Piloerection Reflex (PR):

Description: *Generates a large spiritual field that affects all targets within its vicinity; causes target's hair to stand on end*

Magnitude: *Fills a large rectangular box about 60 cubic feet in size (Approximately the size of a telephone booth)*

Duration: *2 minutes*

SF Cost: *100*

Target FEAR Requirement: *Level 5*

Max Generated FEAR: *10*

Unmodified Reward Upon Successful Attack: *100 SF*

1. Depressive Miasma (DM):

Description: *Generates a field of negative spiritual energy that induces a depressive state for those that stay within it; depressive states can increase the effectiveness of FEAR-based attacks*

Magnitude: *1 entire room within your Area of Influence*

Duration: *Lasts for the remainder of the current attack period*

SF Cost: *200*

Target FEAR Requirement: *Level 7*

Max Generated FEAR: *0*

Unmodified Reward Upon Successful Attack: *0 SF*

1. Spectral Cobwebs (SC):

Description: *Creates an invisible, rectangular floating screen; a target passing through it is subjected to the feeling of cobwebs on their skin*

Magnitude: *4 square feet*

Duration: *Lasts for the remainder of the attack period or until contact is made, whichever comes first*

SF Cost: *250*

Target FEAR Requirement: *Level 9*

Max Generated FEAR: *25*

Unmodified Reward Upon Successful Attack: *250 SF*

2. Peripheral Anxiety (PA):

Description: *Causes the target to experience seeing indecipherable objects out of the corner of their eyes, prompting a heightened sense of stress*

Magnitude: *Single target*

Duration: *Single use*

SF Cost: *300*

Target FEAR Requirement: *Level 15*

Max Generated FEAR: *30*

Unmodified Reward Upon Successful Attack: *300 SF*

3. Spectral Touch (SpTo):

Description: *Ignoring all clothing or other physical defenses, cause the target to feel an invisible touch on any chosen part of their body; does no physical harm, though a slight pressure can be felt by the target; can be moved to different parts of the body if there is sufficient duration available*

Magnitude: *Single target, no larger than the size of an adult hand, though it can be reduced down in size depending upon need*

Duration: *Variable – 1 second to 1 minute, depending upon SF spent*

SF Cost: *Variable – 100 to 985, depending upon duration desired (100 for the first second, 15 for each additional second)*

Target FEAR Requirement: *Level 18*

Max Generated FEAR: *100*

Unmodified Reward Upon Successful Attack: *100 SF*

4. Auditory Hallucination – Footsteps (AHF):

Description: *Causes all targets within range to hear the sounds of heavy footsteps coming from a specified direction*

Magnitude: *1 entire room inside your Area of Influence*

Duration: *Variable – 1 to 12 footsteps, depending upon SF spent*

SF Cost: *Variable – 150 to 1250, depending upon footsteps desired (150 for the first footstep, 100 for each additional)*

Target FEAR Requirement: *Level 20*

Max Generated FEAR: *125*

Unmodified Reward Upon Successful Attack: *150 SF*

5. Wide-range Temperature Change (WTC):

Description: *Create a significant increase or decrease in a room's ambient temperature, lowers all targets' FEAR Resistance*

Magnitude: *1 entire room inside your Area of Influence, lowers FEAR Resistance by 25%*

Duration: *20 minutes*

SF Cost: *500*

Target FEAR Requirement: *Level 22*

Max Generated FEAR: *50*

Unmodified Reward Upon Successful Attack: *500 SF*

6. Electrical Manipulation (EM):

Description: *Distort, disrupt, suppress, or manipulate the flow of electricity in a single object*

Magnitude: *1 object powered by electricity, whether AC-powered or battery-powered*

Duration: *Variable – 1 second to 10 minutes, depending upon SF used*

SF Cost: *Variable – 200 to 3195, depending upon duration desired (200 for the first second, 5 for each additional second)*

Target FEAR Requirement: *Level 25*

Max Generated FEAR: *300*

Unmodified Reward Upon Successful Attack: *200 SF*

7. Auditory Hallucination – Whispers (AHW):

Description: *Causes a single target to hear the sound of faint, largely indistinguishable whispering, with the only distinguishable word they can understand being their name*

Magnitude: *1 single target*

Duration: *Variable – 5 seconds to 30 seconds, depending upon SF used*

SF Cost: *Variable – 500 to 3400, depending upon duration desired (500 for the first second, 100 for each additional)*

Target FEAR Requirement: *Level 30*

Max Generated FEAR: *340*

Unmodified Reward Upon Successful Attack: *500 SF*

8. Heavy Fog (HF):

Description: *Creates a thick, opaque room-temperature fog in an enclosed room for a limited amount of time; all doors and windows must be closed; may be cancelled at any time by user*

Magnitude: *1 entire enclosed room inside your Area of Influence*

Duration: *3 minutes*

SF Cost: *1000*

Target FEAR Requirement: *Level 35*

Max Generated FEAR: *100*

Unmodified Reward Upon Successful Attack: *1000 SF*

9. Auditory Hallucination – Giggling Children (AHGC):

Description: *Causes a single target to experience the sound of young, giggling children*

Magnitude: *Choice of 2 giggling girls, boys, or one of each*

Duration: *Variable – 1 to 30 seconds, depending upon SF spent*

SF Cost: *Variable – 750 to 3650, depending upon duration desired (750 for the first second, 100 for each additional)*

Target FEAR Requirement: *Level 40*

Max Generated FEAR: 360

Unmodified Reward Upon Successful Attack: *750 SF*

10. Shadow Form (SWF):

Description: *Creates a stationary shadow form of something vaguely human-shaped, an inky blackness that swallows all light around it; the form is completely opaque, blocking sight of everything beyond its shape; cannot intersect with targets – if one comes into contact with the shadow form, it will instantly disappear*

Magnitude: *1 shadow form that is visible to all targets*

Duration: *15 seconds, but may be dismissed before time limit*

SF Cost: *2000*

Target FEAR Requirement: *Level 50*

Max Generated FEAR: *200*

Unmodified Reward Upon Successful Attack: *2000 SF*

10.1 Special Ability – Spiritual Nullifier

Once every 6 days, 6 hours, and 6 minutes, you can destroy all spiritual constructs within your area of influence for 30 seconds. Spiritual constructs include protections as well as your own FEAR-based attacks.

Cost: 4500 SF

Duration: 30 seconds

Cooldown: 6 days, 5 hours, 33 minutes

11. Glowing Eyes (GE):

Description: *Creates a pair of incorporeal red glowing eyes that can hover in place or can teleport to a different place when the target is distracted; contact with the target will cause the glowing eyes to disappear*

Magnitude: *1 pair of eyes, the size of a human's, unlimited teleports (as long as the target is distracted)*

Duration: *1 minute, but may be dismissed before time limit*

SF Cost: *1500*

Target FEAR Requirement: *Level 55*

Max Generated FEAR: *150*

Unmodified Reward Upon Successful Attack: *1500 SF*

12. Object Manipulation – Open or Close Doors (OMOCD):

Description: *Allows for the opening or closing of unlocked doors at whatever reasonable speed chosen; locked doors must be opened with a different attack; doors may not physically impact your targets and cannot do any physical harm, otherwise the action will be cancelled*

Magnitude: *Close or open 1 unlocked door*

Duration: *Specified by user, speed of action dependent upon choice*

SF Cost: *1800*

Target FEAR Requirement: *Level 60*

Max Generated FEAR: *180*

Unmodified Reward Upon Successful Attack: *1800 SF*

13. Visual Hallucination – Mirror Entity (VHME):

Description: *Creates a visual hallucination in a single target that will see an entity of user's choice in the mirror; the Mirror Entity cannot attack or physically harm target; Mirror Entity will disappear if target takes their eyes off of the mirror or after 10 seconds*

Magnitude: *1 Entity of user's choice*

Duration: *10 seconds or if target takes eyes off of mirror*

SF Cost: *2000*

Target FEAR Requirement: *Level 65*

Max Generated FEAR: *200*

Unmodified Reward Upon Successful Attack: *2000 SF*

14. Object Manipulation – Throw Object (OMTO):

Description: *Allows the user to quickly move an object from one place to another; object cannot impact any target(s) or inadvertently intercept the path of any target(s); no physical harm can be produced from the initial attack*

Magnitude: *Move 1 object that weighs less than 2 lbs.*

Duration: *Instant use*

SF Cost: *2200*

Target FEAR Requirement: *Level 70*

Max Generated FEAR: *220*

Unmodified Reward Upon Successful Attack: *2200 SF*

15. Spiritual Telepathy (SpTe):

Description: *Allows the user to communicate a short message telepathically to a single target; user can choose what type of voice to use – either the user's voice or the target's internal voice*

Magnitude: *1 Telepathic Message*

Duration: *Short message no longer than 3 seconds*

SF Cost: *2500*

Target FEAR Requirement: *Level 75*

Max Generated FEAR: *250*

Unmodified Reward Upon Successful Attack: *2500 SF*

16. Object Manipulation – Move Furniture (OMMF):

Description: *Allows the user to move a piece of furniture from one place to another; object cannot impact any target(s) or inadvertently intercept the path of any target(s); no physical harm can be produced from the initial attack; no targets may be in physical contact with the piece of furniture*

Magnitude: *Move 1 piece of furniture that weighs less than 200 lbs.*

Duration: *Instant use*

SF Cost: *2400*

Target FEAR Requirement: *Level 80*

Max Generated FEAR: *240*

Unmodified Reward Upon Successful Attack: *2400 SF*

17. Object Manipulation – Light Fixture

18. Object Manipulation – Bedsheet Pull

20.1 Special Ability – Force Absorption

Once every 15 days, you can drain the batteries of all portable electronic devices with a charge within your area of influence; the amount drained from said devices will provide you with Spiritual Force; in addition, all Spiritual Force earned during the assault so far and for the rest of the night will be added immediately to your pool, with a result that you will not receive any for use the next attack period (starts without a cooldown)

Cost: 0 SF

Duration: Instant

SF Provided: Dependent upon number of drained devices

Cooldown: 0 days, 0 hours, 0 minutes, 0 seconds

21. Auditory Hallucination – Custom (AHC):

Description: *Causes a single target to hear a custom auditory hallucination for predetermined amount of time; the custom auditory hallucination can be whatever the user decides; does not block out other sounds and can be cancelled at any time*

Magnitude: *Single target*

Duration: Variable – from 1 to 30 seconds (depending upon SF spent)

SF Cost: *Variable – 375 to 4000 (375 for the first second, 125 for each additional second)*

Target FEAR Requirement: *Level 110*

Max Generated FEAR: *400*

Unmodified Reward Upon Successful Attack: *4000 SF*

22. Object Manipulation – Open All Cabinets and Drawers (OMOACD):

Description: *Use of this ability must be out of visual sight of any targets; one-by-one or all-at-once, open all of the cabinets and/or* drawers in a single room; generates FEAR, but does not provide any Spiritual Force; does not apply to appliances

Magnitude: *Open all drawers and cabinets in a single room*

SF Cost: *3000*

Target FEAR Requirement: *Level 120*

Max Generated FEAR: *300*

Unmodified Reward Upon Successful Attack: *0 SF*

28. Silent Void (SV):

Description: *Creates a bubble of silence around the head of a single target, preventing them from hearing anything outside of it; will move with them, though the more they move the shorter it will last; does not distort or prevent sounds they make from reaching outside sources; if another target physically touches the invisible bubble, it will immediately be canceled; may be cancelled at any time by user; generates no FEAR or SF*

Magnitude: *Single target*

Duration: 3 minutes

SF Cost: *2900*

Target FEAR Requirement: *Level 180*

Max Generated FEAR: *0*

Unmodified Reward Upon Successful Attack: *0 SF*

29. Object Manipulation – Unlock Door (OMUD):

Description: *Use of this ability must be out of visual sight of any targets; fully unlocks 1 door with manual locks; does not affect doors with electronic keypads or other technological defenses (use of*

Electrical Manipulation is needed to deactivate them before using this ability); does not generate FEAR or Spiritual Force

Magnitude: *Unlock 1 door that has manual locks*

SF Cost: *800*

Target FEAR Requirement: *Level 190*

Max Generated FEAR: *0*

Unmodified Reward Upon Successful Attack: *0 SF*

30.1 Special Ability – Power Surge

Once every 10 days, you can shut off all incoming electrical power to your Area of Influence for up to 1 minute, though you can end this before the time limit if you choose to; does not affect cordless or battery-operated electrical objects; generates no FEAR

Cost: 1000 SF

Duration: Up to 1 minute

Cooldown: 9 days, 13 hours, 34 minutes, 16 seconds

31. Sleep Paralysis (SP):

Description: *Must be initiated while target is still asleep; when the target wakes up, they are completely immobilized for up to 10 minutes, allowing for only the movement of their eyes; does not physically harm the target, and if any external harm is experienced, the target will regain all mobility*

Magnitude: *Full-body paralysis following a period of sleep, with only eye-movement permitted*

Duration: *Up to 10 minutes, can be cancelled at any time*

SF Cost: *2700*

Target FEAR Requirement: *Level 220*

Max Generated FEAR: *270*

Unmodified Reward Upon Successful Attack: *2700 SF*

32. Dream Control (DC):

Description: *Allows the user to slip into the dreams of a single target, inserting their own dream sequence of their choosing; cannot last for more than 10 minutes; only one use of Dream Control can be used on a single target per attack period; may be canceled at any time*

Magnitude: *1 Complete dream sequence*

Duration: *Variable – 1 second up to 10 minutes based upon user's choice*

SF Cost: *3500*

Target FEAR Requirement: *Level 240*

Max Generated FEAR: *350*

Unmodified Reward Upon Successful Attack: *3500 SF*

33. Visual Hallucination – Custom (VHC):

Description: *Creates a visual hallucination to a single target of whatever the user desires; the more believable and life-like the hallucination, the more effective it will be (rewarded SF dependent upon effectiveness); does not create auditory hallucinations (must use a different attack for sounds); if a target interacts with the hallucination, they will pass right through it; can be cancelled at any time*

Magnitude: *Single target*

Duration: 3 minutes

SF Cost: *5000*

Target FEAR Requirement: *Level 260*

Max Generated FEAR: *500*

Unmodified Reward Upon Successful Attack: *100 SF*

34. Short-term Amnesia (STA):

Description: *Destroys 99% of the memories of the last 2 minutes of a single target, eliminating most knowledge of any FEAR-based attacks that they may have suffered at your direction; eliminates all Lifetime FEAR gains and SF earned during those 2 minutes and provides no SF, but maintains the FEAR of the target; may cause a minor headache in the target when activated and increases their Fatigue; dream-like echoes of the attack will affect the target during times of stress*

Magnitude: *2 minutes of memories are erased*

Duration: *Permanent*

SF Cost: 8500

Target FEAR Requirement: *Level 280*

Max Generated FEAR: *0*

Unmodified Reward Upon Successful Attack: *0 SF*

Books by Jonathan Brooks

Glendaria Awakens Trilogy

Dungeon Player

Dungeon Crisis

Dungeon Guild

Glendaria Awakens Trilogy Compilation w/bonus material

Uniworld Online Trilogy

The Song Maiden

The Song Mistress

The Song Matron

Station Cores Series

The Station Core

The Quizard Mountains

The Guardian Guild (Feb 2019)

Core of Fear

.

Made in the USA
Middletown, DE
18 January 2023

22507672R00213